Crazy
Jane Feaver

corsair

CORSAIR

First published in the UK in 2021 by Corsair
This paperback edition published in 2022

1 3 5 7 9 10 8 6 4 2

Copyright © 2021 by Jane Feaver

The moral right of the author has been asserted.

A CIP catalogue record for this book is available from the British Library.

ISBN: 978-1-4721-5577-1

Typeset in Dante MT by Hewer Text UK Ltd, Edinburgh
Printed and bound in Great Britain by Clays Ltd, Elcograf S.p.A.

Papers used by Corsair are from well-managed forests
and other responsible sources.

Corsair
An imprint of
Little, Brown Book Group
Carmelite House
50 Victoria Embankment
London EC4Y 0DZ

An Hachette UK Company
www.hachette.co.uk

www.littlebrown.co.uk

We are, I am, you are
by cowardice or courage
the one who find our way
back to this scene

'Diving into the Wreck', Adrienne Rich

For Esther

1. *The General Synopsis (prologue)*

Sometimes it's a man, sometimes a woman, both from a school of unflappable pronunciation, soothing and sure, as if permanently stationed, permanently on the lookout. The Coastal Stations at 0500, regular as clockwork, a ritual against ill fortune: *falling more slowly, now rising. Falling more slowly. Rising slowly. Channel light vessel automatic.* I am curled up in bed, and the stopping places register down the curve of my spine – *Berwick upon Tweed to Whitby, Whitby to Gibraltar Point* – until the names recede in the lapping of oars: *Fog patches, occasionally poor later. Rain or showers. Good, occasionally poor at first. Rain or showers, perhaps thundery. Showers then occasional rain. Moderate or good.* There's never a panic in the voice, that *good*, a press of reassurance, the blessing of a hand on top of the head. *Loch Foil to Carlingford Loch, Mull of Galloway to Mull of Kintyre* – the places come into focus again with a quickening of the heart – *Mull of Kintyre to Ardnamurchan Point.* Stop: here in the throat. And as night follows day: *Ardnamurchan Point to Cape Wrath.*

Argyll, Easter, 2019

Portbeag is at the end of the road. The drop into the hamlet is steep and I have to stop twice to consult the instructions that will lead us to a Tupperware box on the doorstep where the

I

key to the bothy has been stowed. As I come back to the car, a man appears waving to show us where we can pull in to park. He's in long shorts and boots: just back from a walk, he says. 'I'll give you a hand with your bags, if you like?' There are no shops, and we have supplies for the week. 'Mother and daughter?' he asks, and it pleases me that he sees it.

'It's a bit of a way,' he says, cheerfully, taking the heavier suitcase from Shirin and a couple of bags of shopping from the boot. He has an Edinburgh accent: 'Across the stream,' he says, raising the hand with the bags to indicate, 'up through those trees, along the cliff path.'

As we set off after him, I tell him about the car hire: what a rip-off it was, how stupid I was to book online; that it turned out, with the insurance, to be three times the cost.

He listens patiently. 'It can be a minefield,' he agrees, clambering up around the rocks on the track. 'Have you been to these parts before?'

Shirin's granny, I explain, her paternal grandmother, lives around the corner at Sonnadh. But I haven't been back for years.

'I come up in the summer holidays,' Shirin tells him.

'You're on your holidays now?'

'Working holiday,' I say. 'I've got work, Shirin's got a dissertation to write.'

'Perfect place, I'd have thought,' he says. 'Plenty of peace and quiet.' He is friendly, guileless. 'I doubt you'll find much changed,' he says to me. 'My family have a house. We've been coming here since I was six years old.'

From the cliff path, we dip down through a gate and swing around the side of a low stone building built into the rocky cove. There's a plastic chain to ward off walkers, which he unlatches, and I wonder for an instant what a life would have been like with a steady man like this.

He stands back to let me turn the big key in the door and I push inside. 'Cosy,' he says, as he stoops. He's been curious to see how they've done the bothy up, heads straight for the window. 'Fantastic view you've got,' he says, peering out.

There's a sofa bed with a tartan rug, a kitchen sink, and a wood burner in the corner by the window.

'Well,' he says, straightening up. 'I'll leave you to your peace.'

'Wasn't he nice?' I say as soon as he's gone. I've never thought of the place as belonging to anyone but Ardu, which is why it's taken me so long to come back.

The big window frames a view across the sea to Rum, two hills turned by their proximity to water into mountains. The afternoon is extraordinarily clear. It's as if we're watching from the inside of an old television set. Everything outside is bigger and vaster and brighter than I remember.

'Which way are you going?' Ardu was bound to ask. He'd rung before we set off.

'Whichever way the satnav takes us,' I say.

'You don't want to bother with that.' He reels off the names: 'Stirling, Callander, Tyndrum.'

'Okay,' because it's easier to agree.

Soon there'll be no reason for us to speak at all: Shirin will be finished at university and off into her own life.

'Did I tell you, I won't be up there 'til you're gone?' he says.

3

The whole point of Shirin coming up with me is for her to see him. 'Why?'

'Things to do,' he says.

'Like what?'

The click of a vape against his teeth. 'Nothing to stop her staying with Mother,' he says, 'when you two fall out.'

'What *things*?' I ask. Though I'm cross on Shirin's account, I, too, had counted on his being there. It's fifteen years since I last clapped eyes on him, and though he doesn't know it, I'm writing about it, writing at last about him. *Seeing* him: this is how I imagined finding an end, picturing – what? – not reconciliation exactly, but some kind of undoing, an untying of the knot.

'There's no signal and no Wi-Fi,' Shirin says, holding out her phone.

'It'll be good for us,' I say, pulling the duvet from where it's been hung over a beam to air. 'I didn't realize there'd only be one bed,' I say. 'Sorry.'

She opens a door, peers inside. 'At least there's a shower,' she says. 'And a loo.' In the kitchen area she begins unloading shopping from the bags, cramming cartons of milk and yoghurt into the small box of the fridge.

'I can't believe we're both here,' I say, lying back to rest my eyes: *the last time, when I carried you in my belly, dragging myself from the sofa to the beach to breathe in the sea air, and you inside like Jonah, tapping your radar. How lovely it will be, I'd have told you, when you can run over the sand with your bucket and spade, your sandy knickers. I imagined this for you then, your growing-up, the matter of this place lacing your blood, your bones: yours in a way that it could never be mine.*

4

We sit with mugs of tea at the picnic table outside. If we smoked – or could admit to each other that we smoked – we'd have lit cigarettes, something to attach us to the landscape, which vibrates but is impervious.

'When was the last time you were here?' she asks.

'I was pregnant with you. It was our honeymoon.'

'*Honeymoon?*' she says, disbelieving. (And she's right: my word, not his.)

'What was it like?' she asks.

'I was always trying to make it romantic. We stopped at the lighthouse on the way, and when I climbed over the rocks to watch the sunset, he refused to get out of the car.' I catch her eye: she is the only one who can understand exactly how it goes. 'There was another time,' I say, remembering. 'It was a beautiful clear night: full moon, and we'd come out to the beach. The water was so still I took off my boots and my jeans and waded in up to my thighs— Don't you think anyone else might have followed me in?'

'Was it ever nice?' she asks, not expecting an answer. 'I don't know why you put up with it.' The water laps lazily in the bay, the air around us moving with the same currents.

'Do you think we'd have got on, if we'd met when you were my age?' she asks.

Even the way she sits, the extension of her neck, is far more poised and assured than I ever was. 'I wasn't very cool,' I say.

'But you knew Dad?'

'I was eighteen and knew nothing. He was in the third year. I didn't believe anything could happen.'

'Why not?'

It takes no effort to picture the way he was, the voice, the sheer bulk of him that made the rest of them look like little boys. 'He was far more glamorous and clever than I was—'

'It's weird to think that you came here,' she says, 'with him. And I've been here with him, and now we're here together.'

I raise my mug to hers. We sit as the few remaining clouds are swept to a heap over the islands and the sky becomes translucent, aquamarine, and then one cloud is gently released from the others, floating adrift, glowing like a Chinese lantern in the setting sun.

'You snore,' she says. 'It's horrible.'

'You talk in your sleep.'

'What do I say?'

'Oh, mutter, mutter – lovely mother – mutter.'

'Really what do I say?' she asks, as if, suddenly, I'm withholding vital information.

The visitor book is full of messages about wildlife. Seals, otters, pine martens. The signatures are all from couples, whose eyes have been eagerly pressed into the two pairs of binoculars kept on the window ledge. I suggest that one day Shirin might come back with someone else: it's made for a couple in love, we agree, the only morning warm enough to eat our porridge outside on the bench. 'We'll have to visit your granny,' I say, 'let her know you've arrived.'

The man was right, little has changed but the odd nip and tuck where a footpath has been tidied, a signpost that points the way to the beach. We take the coast path down from the bothy, over the stepping-stones of a stream and up through sparsely planted trees until the climb becomes so steep, I have to stop to catch my breath. From the top of the hill you can see round the coast to the half dozen cottages at Sonnadh scattered like toys. His mother's is the bungalow beyond the car park, above the incongruous red streak of the public phone box. The sea shifts below in emeralds and blues; it doesn't take long to get down to the beach, its pristine oyster-shell sand; ours, the only footsteps to disturb it.

The tide is out. We follow the rocks round into the next bay where there's a channel running between banks of sand. Shirin climbs up. 'Dad used to bring me here,' she says. 'We used to play *lifts*.' She demonstrates, jumping. 'Going down!' She lands and some of the bank crumples with her. 'We did it for hours.'

It's like watching a film in Super 8, playing over and over, flickering and spotted with sunlight: all the times I wasn't there.

On the dunes the marram grass is long and bleached to straw. '*Machair*, it's called,' I tell her. 'Your dad told me that.' It's harder going, the squelch of moss underfoot. We climb a stile, work our way between long-abandoned bothies, their gap-toothed windows and doors. It must be possible now to see us coming. I'm careful to keep abreast of her: I don't want it to look as if we're in any way disconnected.

As we approach the porch, there's movement from the dark window, a call, 'Hallooo.' Shirin pushes open the porch door; there's a buffer of coats as there always was, a radio, the singsong of a local wavelength. 'Hello, Granny!' she calls, and by the time I follow her inside, she is hugging the figure who is seated at a table by the window. The table is piled with papers; there's a vase of yellow chrysanthemums, a cigarette in a saucer smoking unattended. As Shirin moves aside, Pauline lifts her face to greet me. It's a shock, the time-lapse waterfall of all the years. She's an old lady, the starkness of her skull, big bleary eyes, hair loose about her head and white as dandelion fluff. 'Hallooo.' She reaches her arms like a child to be picked up from its cot. 'You're here,' she says.

'We arrived last night,' Shirin says.

'Nothing's secret,' Pauline says, cheerily. 'My carer works for the letting company.' She turns off the radio, puts her hands together decisively. 'Would you like a drink? Shirin, there's a bottle of gin on the side for you. Anything to eat?'

We've had our breakfast, we say, thank you.

'But have a drink?' she says. 'Whatever you like. There's wine? A cup of tea, Jane?'

'I'll make it, Granny.' Shirin goes off into the kitchen, part of a new extension built long after my time.

'Did you have a good journey?' Pauline asks.

Before I know it, I'm telling her about the car hire company, knowing it will only get back to Ardu, who'll tell her how typical it is of me to get ripped off.

'Your dad's been on the phone,' she says to Shirin as she comes back with the tea. 'He says to say *hello*, and to say that now I've the extra room, why don't you come and stay with me? Save you from getting on top of one another.'

I tell her we'll be fine. 'Won't we?' I ask Shirin.

'I know you've got exams, Shirin. If you want somewhere to work,' Pauline says, 'somewhere quiet?'

His control is like a high-pitched radio signal.

'When did you have the extension done?' I ask.

'That's right,' she says, 'you won't have seen it? Room for all the family.'

I am not family and yet I'm here, the raised ghost of the person I once was.

When she gets to her feet, she's bent double, in the same skinny black leggings she always wore. She shuffles towards a sideboard. 'Shirin, would you do me a favour?' she asks, producing a key from a dish and handing it over. 'Could you fetch me four bottles of white wine in from the shed?'

On the fridge there are print-outs of photographs stuck with Tam-o'-Shanter fridge magnets, among them a photo of Shirin and her dad. She must be about eleven years old, and they are standing side by side with the tan and white terrier at their feet.

Shirin is in the kitchen; she sets down a bag that clinks.

'Thank you, Shirin,' Pauline calls.

'I heard about Whisky,' Shirin says, coming through.

'Poor Whisky.'

'What happened?'

'She died last week, Jane. She was sixteen, old for a dog. I had the vet out three or four times.' She reaches for a card. 'I'm sat here waiting for the bill.' On the card: a puppy holding a love-heart, and inside, *in deepest sympathy*. 'It's from the vet,' Pauline says, her grouty laugh, 'buttering me up!'

I sip at the tea, which is dark from the teabag floating in it. 'How do you manage with your shopping?' I ask, abandoning the mug to the table.

'Donna, my carer, she's the driver round here. She takes me to shop in the week.' Pauline sips from a glass that is dark and cloudy, chuckles. 'She's a terrible driver,' she says. 'You have to close your eyes and hope for the best. You're going along, and Donna is saying, *fuckin' Japanese, fuckin' English—*' We laugh, but it gives me a jolt: she'd never have sworn out loud when Faether was alive.

'Ach,' she says to Shirin, 'it's a shame you'll miss your dad. He's up here next week to look after the place when I'm on my cruise.'

'Where are you going, Granny?'

'It's a Med-iter-ranean cruise,' she says, carefully, as if reading from a brochure. 'I'm looking forward to it.'

Pauline moved up to the bungalow when her husband died. It had something to do with probate originally, Ardu staying on in the family house. But he's been there years, and now his siblings want to sell up and have their share of the proceeds.

'Is the house on the market?' I ask.

'The house? Any moment, Jane. It's a slow business as you can imagine.'

'Shirin says Ardu's found a flat in Stirling?'

'That's right. Has he shown you the pictures, Shirin?'

Shirin hasn't seen pictures yet. She asks about walking boots because she's forgotten to bring anything but sandals, and Pauline sends her back to look in the shed. When she's gone, Pauline takes a drag from her cigarette, the room gauzy with smoke.

'What are you writing about now, Jane?' she asks, tapping the ashtray.

I hadn't anticipated this level of interest, or that she'd have remembered that I wrote at all. 'About where I live,' I say, faltering. 'Country things,' feeling the lie as if I've swallowed it.

'Ach, lovely,' she says.

How treacherous I am, stewing as we wait.

'Are you sure you wouldn't like a drink, Jane? There's wine in the fridge?'

Shirin returns with a pair of grubby trainers.

'Check for mouse droppings,' Pauline says, and I catch the dismay on Shirin's face.

'What time will you leave on Saturday?' she asks.

'Early,' I say, 'the car hire'll be wanting an excuse to charge me extra.'

'What about Friday, then? Jazmine's coming up for the weekend. I'm sure she'd like to see you. Will you come for a drink? Early evening? And remember,' she says to Shirin, 'there's plenty of room, there's always a bed for you here.'

The air when we get out is a shock, the light so violet and gold we have to squint. My head is jangling with the suggestion that Shirin will elect not to stay with me and prove them all right: it was me all along, there was never anything wrong with him.

We move until we're safely out of earshot and Shirin sits on the tarmac to change her shoes.

'I didn't know you drank gin?' I say.

She bashes the trainers upside-down on the ground. 'I don't,' she says.

Jazmine is Ardu's younger sister. The last time I was in touch with her – twenty years ago it must be – she'd refused to listen. 'You knew what he was like,' she'd said. 'You knew what you were taking on,' and put the phone down on me.

I follow Shirin, heavy with his propaganda which is everywhere – in the craggy outlines of rock, in the stubborn tussocks of long grass – thinking it was a stupid idea to have come.

She stops and waits for me to catch up. 'You all right?' she asks.

11

I'm no good at disguising it. 'I hate the way they assume we can't be in the same place together.' My chest hurts.

'I know,' she says, lightly, reaching to take the bag with her shoes from me. 'It's fine, Mum. We can.'

It's all it takes. A breeze carries the train of the sun, which flips and lifts. We stick to the narrow sheep path, straight into a bog. We are as bad as each other, helpless, cracking up; it's like walking in toffee. Shirin is out of it first, up on the rocks and laughing because I'm stuck fast, wobbling with my arms out like blind man's buff. When I catch up with her, she's already on her haunches, raking through the pearly-grain sand of the beach.

'I found one,' she says, gleefully, and holds it out in her hand. Her eyes are sharper than mine. They're not like other shells, smaller than I expect, but perfect little jewels, the serration of their lips curled in on themselves, and we will be here for hours, collecting, happy as we've ever been, the slow, sedimentary build-up of our pockets.

'Why's he moving to Stirling?' I ask. We're clambering over rocks towards Seal Point. 'I always thought he'd end up here.'

'The flat was cheap,' she shrugs, making a leap between two stacks that I have no courage for. 'It's above a Chinese takeaway,' she says.

I have climbed down and have to shout to reach her. 'Has he cleaned up the house yet?'

'How would I know?'

'They'll never sell it if it's as bad as you say.'

I catch her up only in time to see a dozen or so seals slide from the rocks and flump into the water. 'Look at them!' I say, and for a while the sea is bobbing with their heads until, almost simultaneously, they disappear and there are none.

'There's a military thing called SEAL training,' I tell her. 'I read about it. They're like the SAS – the Navy version. They train recruits by tying up their ankles and wrists and throwing them into a swimming pool. The trick is not to struggle. Remember that. Though all your instincts are to fight, if you let yourself sink, the air in your lungs will naturally lift you back up again. That's the theory.'

The surface of the water where the seals have disappeared is choppy with interference. She has her back to me, and I can't tell if she's listening.

'Perhaps these are the ones that got away,' I say. 'What d'you think?'

She doesn't turn around. 'Is that going in your book?' she says. I recognize the pressure in her voice. She sets off, climbing up, performing a tightrope along the rocks.

I let her go, take my time following her back. When I reach the bothy, there's no sign of her. I come out again thinking to collect wood for the stove, dipping down to the copse beyond the stream. It's not a serious expedition: the pickings are poor, mostly too damp and rotten to bother with.

'Mum!' The shouting comes from above and is urgent. 'Mum, where are you?'

'What?' I shout in the direction of the voice.

'Mum!' as if I've been lost, and she is lost too.

'I'm here,' I shout. She's zigzagging down the hill.

When we meet, she says, angrily, 'I don't want you to be angry.'

'I'm not angry,' I say.

'Where did you go, then?'

'Nowhere.'

Her face is set. 'You need to remember when you talk about him that you're talking about my dad.'

There is no give in her. 'I know, I'm sorry,' I say.

'I don't think you realize how ill he is,' she says. 'When he moves, he shakes.' She glares at the skinny stick in my hand. 'What are you doing?'

'Collecting wood.'

'I'm going to the beach,' she says, and though she doesn't wait for me, it's understood that I will follow. She stops for a moment at the top of the hill. 'Your book,' she says, as if she's thought about it long and hard. 'It's a way of carrying on being obsessed. I don't think you realize that.' There's a hopping energy in her as she takes up the path again, down the rocky bed of the old stream. I am more careful going down, far less adept than she is. On the beach, there's no one else. She stands holding her elbows, waiting, and what she has to say comes out in a stream:

'You're never going to understand him. You can't presume to understand him.' She scuffs at the sand, then flicks her eyes straight at me. 'You've got to be more self-aware. You can't use a book to get back at people. You're not a victim. It isn't about him, it's about you.'

The sand is pale gold. The sea is blue, the waves feathery. Across the way are the islands, Rum, Eigg, Muck. Do they wonder at the child sprung from my rib? Listen to her. She is your voice, yelling in the whale, except she is not inside you any more, she has broken loose.

Part One

Iced Ink

Part One

Red Ink

2. *Iced Ink*

It's getting worse not better. There's a mustiness to the room that I imagine is endemic to institutional buildings: books, rotting plants, fear. I've never been able to untangle the cords of the blinds, the slats hitched up to one side like a skirt tucked into knickers. Two years' worth of unfiled papers, plastic bottles, books, the latest iteration of university finance procedures. Every morning I head straight for the window, brace myself against the stiff aluminium frame and prise it open, heave until the window is wide enough, should the need arise – *who knows?* – to throw myself out.

Later, I'm in a seminar room where, not for the first time, the audio equipment isn't working. 'One of you must be good at IT?' I ask. Under the tables they've begun to consult their phones. I poke at the array of buttons, my heart in the roof of my mouth. I know the drill: the evaluation they will fill in is called MACE.

On a scale of one to five: how well was your tutor prepared?

How enthusiastic was your tutor?

This is how it goes.

After class I return like a piece of elastic to my office. Though the room is a mess, I spot at once that something's amiss, a piece of paper tucked between the rows of computer keys and written in capital letters:

UR ROOM SMEELS OF SIC
CLEAN OUT UR MUG

(Say it, Deborah Gorman says because we have only just moved to London and have yet to be bought the correct school uniform. I'm wearing purple knee-length socks.

Iced Ink, I say.

Say it again, she says; say it faster:

Iced ink, Iced ink Iced ink, Iced ink. Iced ink. Iced ink. I stink. I stink.)

I spot the mugs on top of the filing cabinet: the lumpen pottery one is empty, but the other wobbles with a caramel-coloured blancmange. I dart out into the corridor with it, but in my haste do the thing I absolutely can't afford to do. I trip, the contents fly. There's nothing around to soak up the mess, a pancake crust, half-flipped. In a panic I rush down the corridor to the Ladies, yank a wad of loo roll from the dispenser and return, drop to my knees. Immediately the paper begins to disintegrate; my teeth on edge, I pick at the little worms of tissue where they've become stuck.

When I was six or seven (six and seven) I used to pick my nose and wipe it on the wall – there! – the shame of being exposed was so unbearable that the telling of that tale was held over me for years. My mattress was on the floor, flush to the wall, and all along the skirting in neat vertical lines were the three-dimensional forms arranged like trophies – fox, stag, moose. Pick-a-nose! Although

I'd been caught and publicly shamed, although I'd been warned repeatedly, I couldn't stop. It was compulsive, a wonder at something produced out of myself; the thrill of prospecting, gold or oil, as if my body were a mine.

But one morning I woke and there was something horribly wrong: an acrid stench like tarmac, so pervasive that I thought the smell must be coming from inside me, something rotten, some long overdue punishment. It was dark and I reached for the lamp-switch, the lamp that was new and mine, its two white halves slotting together over the bulb to form a moon-like whole. The switch wasn't working. I fumbled out of bed towards the bunks where the babies slept. I wondered if the stench could be them, though it was far stronger than the smell of pee. Only when I pulled aside the curtains and turned around did I see that something terrible had happened. The lamp, which had been so perfect, had been grotesquely altered, a palsy down one side of melted plastic that exposed the ugly grey bulb in a kind of curse – a pox on your house.

'Gosh,' a voice says, affably. Anthony is clean-cut, wears a mauve jumper. He stands by the swing door and sniffs the air. 'It stinks of drains out here.'

I freeze. 'Does it?' I say.

'It really does smell as if someone has *vomited*,' he says, pronouncing the word with relish.

I am fifty-two, middle-aged by any definition, and these days sleep fitfully, in and out of recurring dreams: a huge public building, a museum or a concert house, with corridors and wide staircases. I need to pee. I'm directed far away from where eventually I'll need to be, not sure if I'll ever remember my way back; take a staircase that winds down and down until I reach a dank basement, L-shaped, the tinkling noise of water dripping from tiles. There's a row of ceramic toilet bowls. I walk the length of the floor, which is slick with water, and around the corner to try and find a cubicle: there are none. In some bowls the foul liquid threatens to overspill, others are blocked with wads of loo roll. I select the emptiest-looking, though there is piss all around the seat. And now because, thank goodness, I find that I'm alone, and because there may not be another opportunity for a while, I decide, fatally, to shit. It takes no effort, everything I've hoovered up into my body, out it comes in an earthy homogeneous mass, which, at first, I admit, is a huge relief. It's only when I get up and discover that the bowl isn't connected in any way to the sewer that I realize my mistake. It's a trap. Who else performs such degraded acts?

The next morning I'm on the campus by quarter to seven. I have yellow gloves and anti-bacterial spray. The smell is like dead rat, and because it hovers at my door, I am entirely impli-cated. On my knees I pump the spray, little bubbles fizzing into the carpet. With a green kitchen scourer I scrub, sneeze. At which point the door from the landing swings open: Anthony.

'Hello?' he says and performs a double-take. 'What are you up to?'

My face distorts. Anthony sets his hand on his chest and throws back his head. For a moment I'm out of my mind to be discovered. But then I hear laughter, unbridled, friendly, and recognize, in my comedy gloves, how bad I've let things get.

A week later, the smell is no more than a haunting: it might be ascribed to the sea-weedy ozone of the photocopier, the fustiness of the unventilated corridor. But in the spirit of truth and reconciliation, I decide to hunt out the cleaner. He's a small, wiry man of indeterminate age, and I find him in his grey overalls with a packet of crisps, sitting under the back stairs where he takes his breaks. I prostrate myself. 'I am so sorry,' I say. 'I can't believe how bad it was.'

'It is bad,' he says, refusing to acknowledge that it is over.

'I know. I'm sorry.'

'Very bad. It make me sick,' he says, taking another handful of crisps and turning them over elaborately in his mouth as if they are pieces of glass.

When Ardu rings on my mobile, his name comes up. I wonder sometimes whether he has a nose for my low ebbs.

'I can't get hold of Shirin,' he says.

'She's gone back to college.'

'What's she doing this term?'

'Tragedy.'

'Tragedy?' He glosses every word with irony. 'Okay,' he says, though I can tell by the pop of his fag that he isn't finished.

'You know your Shakespeare?' he asks, which can only be a prelude to showing that I don't.

'Not especially,' I say to head him off.

He huffs. 'And they let you teach?'

'I don't teach literature.'

'What do you teach, then?'

'Not formally.'

'What do they call it?'

If I say the words *creative writing*, he'll choke. 'I'm at work. Is it important?'

'How's the Professor?'

'I told you, he moved, he got another job.'

'Did you? Are you sad?' he mocks. Rarely does a conversation go by but that he'll tell me he's heard the Professor on some late-night art review. He takes another puff. 'Maieutic is a good word,' he says. 'You should look it up.'

'I know what it means.'

'What?'

'It's to do with being a midwife,' I say. 'A way of teaching. From Socrates.'

He hums a surprise, forgetting that it was he who introduced me to the word in the first place. I don't discourage him. He's five hundred miles away and yet he is right here, in my ear – deeper – in a corner of my head, sitting like a guard who, after a little nap, has woken up.

'It baffles me that anyone would employ you as a teacher,' he says.

'You've said that already.'

'You don't know anything; you've read nothing.'

'Have you been drinking?'

'What business is it of yours? Anyway,' he says, 'where were we? Shakespeare: people are stupid: they say that if Shakespeare were around today, he'd be writing for Netflix. But I say,' he draws on his fag again, 'I say, he'd be writing computer games. What do you think?'

He reminds me of the Professor is what I think, and, so unusual is it for Ardu to express admiration for anyone I might have a connection with, I am sensible enough not to have told him the whole story.

'Quiz the wallpaper,' the Professor used to exhort us, when, late in the day, I'd returned as a student to the university. 'Never write in the first person, never write in the present tense.' *How right he was*, is what, immediately, I thought. He'd sit in the Senior Common Room, Bunter-ish, with a bag of sweets. 'I never want to read again about girls getting their periods!'

Only a rare type of man could pull off such an act, a man of discernment, expert in literature, in music and in art, is what I thought. And my fortune was that I knew how to please such men, had been hard-wired for it, the Professor's chuckle reminding me of the pleasure of being on my toes, a testing in allegiance and taste that, at one time or other, had seemed the only way to be alive.

ii

I haven't got all their names yet and the animal exercise gives me a second go at trying to work them out. I ask them to think what sort of animal they'd choose to be, and, if it's different (it may well be different, I say), what sort of animal they think others might see them as.

'I'll start,' I say, and of course it's a cheat, something I've prepared earlier. I give the impression that I'm thinking hard. 'Ant-eater,' I say. They look askance. 'This is how you'll see me,' I say, 'thinking how pernickety I am. But,' I gaze at the big aluminium windows, 'what I see myself as: a hare.' I give them a second, open to laughter, aware of how I must appear to them, in the same bracket as their mothers. But no one bats an eye.

'I can clear a field at a hundred miles an hour,' I say. 'I box, I sing to the moon, I tremble.' This last I slip in slyly as a concession to truth: if I make myself vulnerable, I reason, so might they.

As we go around the room, I write the animals down next to their names on the register: a girl who sees herself as a puppy, whom her friends, too, see as a puppy: she is enthusiastic and she is bubbly; there's a cat/rabbit, a lion/puppy, a golden retriever/kitten. Next time I resolve to rule out puppies and kittens. It's easy to lose heart. When I reach the girl in the white sweatshirt, we stall. I am gentle with her because I think she may be one of the particularly anxious ones I'm obliged to look out for. 'We can come back to you,' I say.

'It's childish,' she says, and her gaze is direct.

'What's wrong with being childish?' I ask. She fixes me and in that moment I am gone, a trigger of heat that sweeps up from my thighs to my scalp, fiery and slippery as a salamander.

The boy next to her has dyed black hair which falls over his pale face. He has been doodling intently but stops, raises his chin.

'Adam?' I ask, steeling myself.

'A raven,' he mumbles. 'I like black.'

'Great,' I squawk. The girl in the sweatshirt makes a face at someone across the table, shifts perceptibly in her seat.

'And what creature would you *like* to be?' I ask.

He doesn't have to think. 'A kingfisher,' he says. He uses the biro as a crutch. 'I saw one at my nan's.' He shrugs, turns pink. 'That's all.'

'Brilliant,' I say, and look around, the heat dissipating.

I hand out a poem by Ted Hughes, 'Wodwo'. 'What am I?' the poem asks. I get them each to read a line of the poem, which they do, haltingly, stumbling on the unusual syntax and repetitions, and in the breather I've allowed myself a thought comes to my rescue:

'By the way,' I say when they've finished reading. 'Ted Hughes wrote wonderful letters. There's one to his son, Nicholas. About the importance, the necessity even, of being childish.' I have their attention, a washing line of faces. 'He talks about the creature that's in all of us that peers through the slits of armour we create as adults. It's the only real thing about us, he says.' *Should they be writing this down?* I see them thinking. 'Part of what I hope this class is about,' I say, 'is unlearning everything you've been taught, dis-arming yourselves.'

They shift like shale, the threat of un-learning, too much at this stage to take on.

The office doors along my corridor contain panels of frosted glass. I shut mine behind me, lean against the bordello-like curtain of flowers I've put up so that no one can see if I'm there or not. In the top drawer of my desk there are paraceta-mol, and I take the last two from the packet, swallow them down with what's left of a glass of water. I've learned to iden-tify the pain, which approaches and amplifies very gradually, from a long way off, a small orb with a built-in homing device. I can't work out if it's triggered by anything in particular, but over the last twelve months the episodes have become more frequent. Sometimes, sifting through the stories that pile my desk, I imagine that what these students need is an injection of pain, an electric shock, anything to break the circuit. I have to correct myself: there is pain, there must be; there is, of course, experience of sorts – if we've lived a childhood, Flannery O'Connor says, we've enough experience to last a lifetime – but how to recognize it, how to gain access?

The best drawings are by four-year-olds who haven't yet learned to be afraid of getting paint over their nice clean clothes. Somewhere in this so-called education, the fear enters in, as if from henceforth we must learn to disguise the unpalatable truth about ourselves. Everything must be mediated, a kind of police state where words, too, are neutered and deprived of agency. So that the stories can't be real, they're not allowed to be alive.

At our last department meeting we were asked what could be done about student anxiety, of which, apparently, there's an epidemic: what *we* might do about it. I'd raised my hand rashly at the back of the lecture theatre: 'But what if we have it, too?'

The monitor in front of me has gone to sleep, but safe to assume that the camera eye in the forehead of the computer is never inactive. I give nothing away. Behind a layer of microscopic dust lies the murky sludge of an ocean floor, where it's difficult but not impossible to make out a figure bound and gagged in her revolving chair. (*Cromarty, Forth, Tyne, Dogger.*)

iii

Black was my favourite colour, too. When we lived in Newcastle, I was going to be a nun. I'd seen nuns out in pairs gliding along the street by the railway line where we lived,

26

utterly self-contained, as if wherever they were going, they'd already arrived. In assembly Miss Trotter, who had a thick helmet of honey-coloured hair, got us to sing from *The Sound of Music*. *Raindrops on roses*, a kind of spell. *Bright copper kettles*: rewards for enduring, for being good. It was the same good that was in stories, in *Cinderella*, *Cap O'Rushes*, *The Little Princess*, the good that might drive you to run away, because, by definition, it wasn't a kind that could be valued at home. God recognized it, and that was a comfort, God who I came to see as the secret speaking voice of books. But I was so good, I began to worry that he'd end up choosing me for the next virgin birth. How would I get out of that?

'Bourgie' was our father's word, and all things bourgie we were primed to despise: Abba, new furniture, cleanliness, *lounge*, *settee*, perms, hot pants, dancing, God, sport of any kind, Renoir (the painter), *The Sound of Music* (all musicals), public schools, ITV, the Southern counties. We were trained to covet battered things, like Persian rugs, horsehair sofas, dry-stone walls; had a Geiger counter for aesthetics, sensitive to within a hair's breadth for what he liked and what he didn't.

Anne and Wendy lived next door to us. Our father called them 'the bourgie kids'. But it didn't stop us taking turns to ride their bikes or going back to their house to stuff plastic skittles up our jumpers like the nurses in *Carry On*. When she caught us, their mother brought us home, standing on the path beside the dusty hydrangeas to explain what we'd done wrong, cradling her beautiful bourgie hands. ('I beg your pardon, I never promised you a rose garden,' is what we heard from next door, the song their dad sang (so ours said) when he hit their mother with a frying pan.)

Granny's was the epitome of bourgie, though we went there often in the school holidays; Granny Georgie with her beds of perfect pink and yellow roses, her hostess trolley, her tubs of raspberry ripple ice cream. At Granny's we had clean clothes and bath-time every night; we had trips to the boating lake and expeditions in the Dormobile to the seaside. It mattered to her that we loved her. She gave us individual packs of Coco Pops and Frosties for breakfast. 'Which Granny do you like the best?' she'd ask, an easy enough question to answer.

Sometimes we were left so long that when they arrived to fetch us home, it was as if we had been brainwashed: we didn't want to go, we said, clinging to the bannisters, crying, all that careful anti-bourgeois training undone.

We moved to London when I was nine. In my non-uniform purple socks I was introduced to the whole class. I warmed to Mr Richards because he had a beard, and because he said I reminded him of the girl in *Carrie's War*, which is exactly how I saw myself. He sat me next to Deborah Gorman, whose job, he said, was to look after me, Deborah, who smiled and kicked my shins under the table, daring me to tell and die: *Jane Feaver, a Newcastle Geezer, caught her nose in a lemon squeezer*.

iv

This student comes in to see me: she's skinny, with lank dark hair, hooded eyes and a bad cold. She sniffs. She is buried in an oversized black coat made from curly woollen fur – an ape suit almost – and she doesn't take it off. She sits in the farther away of the two chairs, and I suggest she moves nearer. She produces a piece of paper from her bag and at the same time, from within, her phone rings. I take the paper from her as she deals with the phone. There are two or three typed paragraphs.

'It's the child's-eye exercise, is it?' I ask, buying myself time. *My bedroom has always been my safe place,* I read. Two goldfish are introduced. *They reside in a luxurious black bucket.* 'Reside? Luxurious?' I ask. 'How old is the child?' The girl shrugs as if, surely, it's up to me to tell her. 'Think about it,' I say.

We read on. *In my youthful ignorance I named them Target and Zero.*

'I like the names,' I say, trying to sound encouraging, 'but do you need to tell us she is ignorant or youthful?' My heart is sinking because we haven't got very far, and I can feel her turning to stone in front of me.

They are the saddest goldfish in the world, the story goes. Then Target dies.

'Why are they sad?' I ask. 'And how does she know which fish is which? How does she tell them apart?'

A mother appears in the next paragraph, making dinner. In another room, a younger sister is playing on her computer.

I want to ask what the point of the story is because *What is the point?* is a question I ask of myself again and again.

('You should write about it,' Ardu has said, because what else do I have to write about?

'Why would I want to do that?', the ground shifting under my feet, sensing the pulse of his satisfaction: my resistance, enough of a reaction for him to know he has me still, can feel the tug, his end of the line.)

The girl is waiting, her chin set.

'I wonder whether there is something missing?' I venture. I'm not sure how far I can push her. 'Or someone missing maybe?'

The girl is flint. 'My father died two years ago,' she says matter-of-fact. She is quite still, Estella-like, with her paper-pale skin, the pink end of her nose.

For a moment in that room we have fallen through the ice and our limbs are incoherent and flailing. 'I'm so sorry,' I say, drawing back into my chair. 'Maybe,' I say, tentatively, 'that's what's at the back of the story. It might be too difficult to write,' I say, putting it as a question. 'You'd only need a hint, but it would put a different slant on everything.'

She takes another sniff and folds her story into her bag. She gives a tight smile. I feel a surge of validation. This is what writing is about, I want to tell her, it is difficult and hard, and you just have to keep going until that moment when you prod and feel yourself come up against something real, something live.

3. Dut

We had it from our father: vanity was the deadliest of sins, the first thing we were taught, the three oldest of us, who were girls. There was no make-up for us, no shaved legs or armpits, no contact lenses, no plucked eyebrows. To be caught looking in a mirror would warrant instant exposure, trained as we were to police and inform on one another. There was one bathroom at the top of the house in Brixton, and you weren't allowed to lock the door. 'What are you doing in there?' A violent rattling. At so much as a glimpse in a mirror, or the reflection from a shop window, 'Vain cow!', as if by paying attention to yourself you had the nerve to imagine you could be anything other than the ugly sister.

I know precisely the moment when vanity stole in. I was fifteen and, over the space of one weekend, the small gang of girls at school to which I was attached had turned themselves into mods, each arriving into our form room on Monday morning with a sleekly cut bob.

Mum had always cut my hair, which was long and frizzy and which latterly I wore in two plaits fixed to the top of my head. I was sick of being the odd one out, four-eyes, fleabag, and, without telling anyone, set off with my birthday money for Pratt's in Streatham, where, on the top floor, sectioned off from rails of lingerie, there was a hairdresser.

The girl behind the desk appeared to be waiting for me: she scooped me up and sat me down across from the old lady asleep under a helmet. Here was a punitive expanse of mirror. Tina was her name, set in a gold chain that swung forwards as she leaned in towards me. She had flicks from her temples, a wedge of hair at her nape, and my heart sank: a full-blown soul girl. A style like hers? she suggested, lifting the ends of my hair dispassionately. 'Bob,' is what I'd primed myself to say, but couldn't bring myself to do anything but agree. When she'd finished cutting, she got out the rubber brush, spiked like a weapon, and pulled and ground, the engine of the blow-dryer. She took up one of the golden spray-cans and set the flat of her hand against my eyes, sprayed in loops as if she were killing flies.

You're so vain, the song filled my head, braced as I was like a cat whose nose is pushed into its own vomit. It was as if I were wearing a hat or a wig that could be lifted off, my eyes in the mirror all over the place.

When our father opened the front door, he started. 'Christ,' he said. 'You look like Princess Anne.'

Princess Anne, galloping all the way up the stairs to the top of the house, the bathroom where I turned the key in the lock. Above the sink my image popped, two cardboard wings of hair, a face I wanted to graffiti, to deface. I leaned over into the sink and splashed water in handfuls from the cold tap on hair that seemed waterproof, foreign and stiff as fur. I lifted my head, took up the bar of soap and worked it in to the fringe, the sides, but there was nothing to be done. 'Basil Brush,' the mirror said. 'Boom, boom!'

'You used to be pretty,' someone said in the changing rooms when I went back to school, and it sounded like a life sentence.

At that time, we were obsessed with the atomic bomb. The last thing any of us wanted was to die a nun. What would you do if you had five minutes' warning? The one piece of business to which we'd urgently attend would be to find a boy, any boy. How utterly tragic to have died before you'd had it off!

Have it off, how easily it tripped from the tongue, as if any of us had any idea what we were talking about. Sex was like a combination code, the mechanism by way of which we'd enter Love. Soft focus. It would make sense of everything we were turning into – the little marbles in our breasts, those embarrassing hairy purses we carried around as if they weren't yet ours, dressing up as our mothers. We couldn't imagine the mysterious union for which we yearned, but we knew that once we'd found it, we'd be complete, activated as our own true selves. And we'd be better at it, a hundred times better, for instance, than our parents.

At the top of Helen's house we lay in our sleeping bags taking slugs of Martini listening to 'You Really Got Me', aching to be got going, speculating on the year 2000 when people would be taking shuttles to the moon: we'd be thirty-six, married, no question, with children. 'She'll end up marrying a man with a beard,' they scoffed, rolling their eyes at me. Just like her dad, like George Harrison. *My Sweet Lord.*

ii

'You think I'm a fool?' Mum screeched. She'd found the photograph in his wallet, a photograph of a dark-haired woman with pencil-thin brows. 'You're having an affair! I know you are.'

He gave his constipated laugh.

She hurled the pot of coffee, which spattered the tartan painting on the wall behind his head. It was his prize painting, the canvas stretched in a frame that had been made to fit the whole wall.

Our father shook with rage; he stormed down the stairs.

'Oh God,' she said, 'what have I done?' She ran to the kitchen, filled the washing-up bowl with water and Ajax, found the scrubbing brush under the sink and came back, threw handfuls of water, scrubbed, watching the blue colour fade under the brush to clouds of pale denim. We were on the stairs. She'd done it now.

'She's mad,' he said, and we had to agree with him. She was the flirtatious one; he wasn't remotely the type to have an affair, impervious to the way anyone looked, let alone a woman with plucked eyebrows, or a woman, as he told us – *la-di-da-Gunner-Graham* – who'd been to a posh, private school.

He'd been abroad with this woman for work, and was at pains to explain that, yes, he had the picture in his wallet because he imagined he was bound at some point to run into her. Simple as that.

We were used to Mum's eruptions: mad because he never bought her flowers, mad because he never took her out, because he didn't wash up properly, because he never once commented on the way she looked. Vanitas vanitatum. How trivial it all was. And plenty of times we'd fallen foul of her ourselves. 'You stink,' she'd yell in certain moods for everyone to hear. 'Get yourself some bloody deodorant!'

He had loved her, he did love her, he just wasn't the kind to show it. *I'll love you till your thighs are wrinkled*, that's what he'd written before any of us arrived. And we'd seen it for ourselves,

34

the one or two times when on a day out he'd taken her hand and we'd moved off in a knot, embarrassed.

'She's impossible,' he said, conspiratorially, catching me on my way in from school. 'I'm beginning to think it would be better for everyone if I found my own place to live. Just for a while. What do you think?'

None of my friends had parents who were divorced; it was the girls from broken homes who got put on the pill, who, if they stayed on in the sixth form, took speed before assembly, smoked in the street. There was the trace of a thrill about the idea as I turned it over.

The landline doesn't ring very often. At this time of night – ten-thirty – the phone sounds blear, demanding, and I'm dragged downstairs, answering just in case it's something important, something to do with Shirin.

I know it will be him.

When I pick up, there's a hiatus in the connection, as if whatever phone system he's plugged into is from another era. (*Wait while I connect you.*)

A space opens up, cave-shaped. Eventually he'll say, 'Jane?' as if it's me that has called him.

I know the voice, it's as it ever was, a man selling honey from the Gorbals, talking in a way that is perfectly familiar yet, familiarly, puts me on my mettle, as if the twenty years between then and now have disappeared in a puff of smoke, and what I've done with those years means nothing, Zero, we're back to where we started.

'Hello,' I say.

'You heard from Shirin?'

'Not since we last spoke.'

'Tell her to ring me, if you speak to her.' And then he says, 'Your friend was on the radio.'

'What friend?'

'The Professor,' he says. 'On about punctuation.'

'He's not my friend,' I say.

'He was talking sense, I thought. Though if he's not your friend, I don't suppose you're bothered.' He sucks on his fag. 'What's the weather like down there?'

'Rain.'

'Same up here. Shite.' He exhales. 'As a matter of fact,' he says, 'I thought he sounded a bit of a twat, which – as he's not your friend – perhaps you'll allow me?'

'Anything else?' I ask, because this is the game, and sometimes it's good to have him on the back foot.

'It was only your friend, who, it turns out, is not your friend. That was all.'

'Okay.'

But the line is dead. He is gone, rolling over and under, the turn of his smooth whale skin.

iii

Two goldfish, Target and Zero, in a luxurious black bucket. Target. Zero. I am mesmerized by this flung-together pointless-ness, watching the two fish, one of them with a pale mange on its side like the map of an island, tightly circling each other. Should they have been in love this would indeed have been a luxurious bucket, five litres in capacity, and filled from the tap just short of the brim. But, on the contrary, there is little love lost between them: they are sick of the sight of one another, sick of the daily reminder of decay, of the wretched four-hourly haggle for fish flakes, the spurious promise of a green wine gum that has sunk to the bottom, on which their lips can make no purchase.

Target dies, floats to the surface; Zero will die in due course, not of love or of grief, but of apathy.

'Did you see that Sean Hughes died?' I ask; I have rung specially to tell him.

'Who's Sean Hughes?'

'You know who he is: that comic. He was on the *Buzzcocks*. Our age, early fifties. Dark hair. Irish.'

He thinks for a moment. 'Gangly bloke?'

'Not when he died: you can see from the photograph how bloated he'd got.'

'What did he die of?'

'Heart attack. Cirrhosis of the liver.' I let that sink in. 'Don't you ever worry about dying?' I ask.

'We're all dying. Can't say I give it much thought.' He tugs on his fag.

'A friend of his wrote a piece about him: people are complaining about it.'

'Why?'

'It talks about how cruel and vicious he could be. Especially to women.'

Ardu huffs.

'Why do people never use the word "alcoholic"?' I ask.

'You're repeating yourself.'

'Are you drinking?' I ask.

He draws on the fag, pushes out in a whistling stream. 'What's it to you?'

'He was fifty-one,' I say.

'*The fury of men's gullets and their groins* – where's that from?'

'No idea.'

'Come on, guess.'

'I can't.'

'Who does it sound like?'

'Alcoholics everywhere?'

He snorts. 'Your friend the Professor would know.'

iv

Over the last couple of years, Mum had been studying for a degree in English, determined to prove, perhaps, she wasn't as stupid as our father made out. On the eve of her final exams some cataclysmic impulse had driven her to ring for the taxi that would transport her to the flat where she'd discovered the other woman – the woman in the photograph – lived. She was prepared for it not to be true, but there, outside, unmistakeably, was our car, the Cortina with the coat hanger antenna, badly parked on the corner.

She pays the taxi and hops out, making straight for the heavy communal door, its ladder of printed names, and presses the bell, the woman's name, rings it several times. She bangs on the door: she won't go away until they let her in, she shouts up at random windows. People hurry past, others, out walking dogs, are watching from the corners of their eyes. The door gives out an impatient buzz, and she fumbles into it. He's waiting for her on the first floor at the top of the stairs, ready to usher her inside.

'You bastard,' as she climbs, following him into the flat, where the light is dim.

The door to the bedroom is wide open, dominated by a great bed on which the woman is in the process of strewing letters, hundreds of them, all, at a glance, written in the illegible scrawl that is his.

'How long's it been going on?' Mum demands.

'Two years,' the woman says, no hesitation.

Our father doesn't know what to do, these women who were never supposed to meet, so magnetically opposed to one another: it is appalling being the common denominator, it is petrifying; he is ashen, cowed, the stress plastering his hair to his scalp.

The woman is not shy. She is glad to spell things out, confident that she is about to get what she wants. Our father cannot speak, and she is furious, will not brook this show of indecision. She marches over, snatches the glasses from his face and, peremptorily, breaks them in two.

'She broke his glasses?' we say, aghast, when Mum tells us what has happened. How could she do that? It's like poking out his eyes, and inconceivable that any of us would have done such a thing or could have got away with it.

And so it turns out. After a few weeks, almost disappointingly, our father, who had packed his bags to be with her, returns home: it's like a wedding so short-lived the presents have to be sent back; or crying wolf, because at school, having made such an effort to be nice to me, they were going to feel conned of their sympathy.

Mum has had her results, and in spite of everything has got a First, the top First in her year – she has a medal for it – and to celebrate this and his prodigal return, we are going out to supper.

We've never been out together for a meal, all six of us. It's an Italian place our father knows on Charlotte Street. We drive through the spangly lights of Brixton, as subdued and well behaved as we've ever been, over the smeary trawl of the Thames: it's dark and it's raining. The street, when we arrive, glints silver. Two waiters in red waistcoats are ready to shed us from our coats, folding and patting them over their arms as if they are precious. We don't know what to do with ourselves, helped like little Fauntleroys into our seats.

Choose anything you like, our father says, within reason, he and she sitting at opposite ends. There's only one thing we decide we all want: lasagne. It's our favourite. The waiter with steely hair whisks away the menus.

'You can't all have the same,' our father mutters, though the deed is done.

Mum has to bite her tongue: this is supposed to be an end to arguments. She smiles her wan smile and her eyes waver, though he can't meet them.

We are inured to the telegraph that runs between them, here for the food, the novelty of the ride, diverted by where the napkins are supposed to go and who is drinking what.

They order a bottle of wine because, although our father doesn't like drink, that is what's expected. He raises his glass to her when it arrives but can't think of anything to say.

'You'll take the pattern off,' Amelia says to Jack, who is the first to finish and has begun furiously to lick his plate.

'Don't,' I elbow him, looking at Mum to confirm it.

'Let him do what he likes,' she says, irritably.

Jack is her favourite, though he was the one six months ago they were talking of sending away. He'd been raiding her purse, appeared after Christmas with a sledge from the school fete and a state-of-the-art digital wristwatch, both items he claimed he'd been given by friends. He was able to lie so blatantly I'd come to believe he didn't have a conscience. How can you deal with someone who has no moral compass?

Our father wanted to thrash him; they talked about sending him away, that it might be good for him. Though most often we are at war, if you prick one of us, we all bleed. We'd listened at the door to their conversation and burst into the room in unison: 'You can't send him away!'

'Pudding?' our father asks.

Pudding is the main event, and it seems impossible to choose from the delectable array that is on offer. The waiter makes a suggestion given that none of us, he ascertains, have ever had profiteroles. 'I insist,' he says. And when he returns, he makes a great show of presentation, the large silver cloche gleaming under the lights. With a flourish, he removes the lid. A gasp. Piled high, a pyramid of dark chocolate, fluffy white, sweet soft pastry melting; it's what we've been missing had we but known it, an instant craving as we grab our spoons, and set to work like vultures on a corpse.

v

I have an expanding list of arbitrary rules: if you introduce a pet in a story, I say, it either has to be incredibly ugly, or it has to die. The girl in the sweatshirt has been taking notes as if she's mounting a case against me. 'Why?' she asks.

Because happiness and being okay with your parents and having cuddly pets is boring, I say, and now – I can see by the gleam in her eye – I sound as if I have an axe to grind. I rummage for something to back me up, tell them the Chinese proverb about the lamp: how the light is meaningless without the dark and the shadows. 'Where's the contrast, the friction?' I ask, waving my lobster claws.

Mid-term, they queue up to see me one on one. They want to know if they are on the right track, and, again, what the marking criteria are. 'I hate to give you marks,' I say. 'But what do you want?' they ask, as if I'm intent on throwing obstacles in their way.

'It's not about what I want,' I say.

There's been a steady trail all morning, and the girl in the ape suit is the last. She appears to be over her cold, more cheerful and confident. I ask after the goldfish story. She dismisses it, shaking her head, and I say I'm sorry not to see it again.

'I've got another one,' she says, and seems pleased to present it.

This one is about a man, dark and good-looking. He wears designer suits. He is a psychopath.

I have seen the type so many times that I resolve to add him to my list of don'ts. But for the time being, I go with it. In this version he requires human scalps to make the paintbrushes he uses for his miniature paintings.

She waits for my reaction.

'Does he know what sort of hair he's after?' I ask. 'Presumably he has something in mind – fine, thick, fair, dark?'

She looks at me as if she can't believe what she's hearing. Either I am taking it far too seriously, or I, too, am some kind of psycho.

When he came back, we were better behaved, polite even, doing our best not to squabble, holding each other to account as if the slightest squall from us might rock the boat. Mum was tight-lipped, heaving baskets of sodden washing to hang out of the landing window on a line that had been set up on a loop, a pulley system, which, as she'd haul, would squeak in protest, sending the sheets out above the well of the back yard.

Why couldn't she be more happy? He'd come back, he'd chosen us: why couldn't she be more forgiving?

We did it in your bed, the other woman had told her, the brass bed that was theirs, its moveable golden orbs, the meshes of its underside, where, if you hid, your hair would get caught and painfully extracted. It was the bed where the babies had been brought home from hospital to sleep; where once or twice Mum was so ill she didn't get out of it for days; where in the mornings, because they loved that bed so much, we'd learned not to disturb them, getting ourselves ready for school and leaving the house before they were up.

We did it in your bed: the smell of it, the sweat like acid on her skin. How those sheets burned!

And meanwhile, 'I'll sleep with him!' the woman is threatening, meaning the man in the flat next door to hers, who, with his ear to the wall, is waiting, just gagging, now that our father appears to have vanished, to jump into his shoes. Our father, who sits in his usual place with an art catalogue open on his knees. He lets us watch anything we like on the telly, which should have raised our suspicions. Though it looks as if he's here, it's only the shell of him pretending to be reading, leafing through, his mind already given to the planet where the alien siren lives, and on the tip of his tongue to say it: *Beam me up.*

vii

'You can fucking tell her,' we hear Mum in the kitchen, because it seems that he who has written the rules and the laws of the house also has the power to change them.

Rose is called downstairs, Rose he calls Biddy Pumpkin, who's the one, she's told us, he's taken aside and promised he'll never leave again.

Amelia and I are ambushed in a union that is rare, sitting together upstairs outside the bathroom. We crane towards the bannisters to hear. There's a rumble and then an outburst, their voices a crossing of knives; nothing from Rose. (That painting, *And When Did You Last See Your Father?*: Rose, in blue silks, standing quite still and upright in the centre.) We are given no part in this drama but to listen, listening so hard we find that we are both holding our breath, and then, in a balloon of suppressed laughter, we lose it, knowing that laughing is the last thing we should be doing, like being tickled to death, laughing until it hurts and there are tears in our eyes and we think that if we carry on like this, we'll laugh ourselves to pieces.

I take the opportunity before he dares come back to remove his things, to raid his study. It's freezing in there. The gas fire

44

hasn't been on for a week. The room smells of typewriter ribbon and chlorophyll from all the plants that continue to grow without any attention in the several fish tanks along the windowsill. The metal handles to the drawers of his desk jangle. In the top right, straight away I find the mirror: a mirror? I can't work out what it can be doing there so close to hand, congenitally unable to believe that he'd have any use for it. It's old, envelope-sized, its bevelled glass held in place by a tin-metal frame, functional. Perhaps it was his father's, who was posted out in the desert in the War, the handy support at the back allowing him to keep up appearances, the foamy rotations of the badger-hair brush, his cut-throat razor?

But our father has a beard: what possible use could he have for a mirror?

I confiscate it, all the way upstairs under my jumper, and late at night when everyone's in bed, I prop it on my pillow and by the light of the lamp examine my face in detail, the pink indents either side of my nose where my glasses have been; the dilated pores around my nostrils; the furrow in my brow which will end up permanent if I don't watch out. This is how I'd look face-on if I were here with someone else in bed. How to smile: with or without showing my teeth?

What am I?

  What am I doing here in mid-air?

              what shape am I what

    shape am I?

45

Which bits of me are hers, which his? Will I go blind, I wonder, the hours I spend worrying?

viii

When Mum met our father, her parents began to attend the church where his father was vicar. It was the biggest church in town, full of pomp and circumstance, the Reverend Grandpa entering in a golden threaded chasuble, guarding the silver cup of blood as if it were his own.

None of the grandparents much liked each other. The Reverend Grandpa had married up into a family of clerics and intellectuals, and with his double First was well on the way to proving that no one could be more clerical or intellectual than him. Amen.

'He's no better than the rest of us,' Granny Georgie would say, seething at his frostiness towards her on the steps outside church.

When Mum got pregnant, she and our father were still at university and both sets of parents privately cursed the other for ruining their son's/daughter's prospects. His parents asked hers if our father really was the father. A vicar's son! There'd have to be a wedding, and, much as it pained him, who but the Reverend Grandpa to marry them. Mum wore a grey suit, a handful of relations turning up with handbags and hats.

'Jane's going to a psychiatrist!' I hear Mum down the phone as if proof were needed of the damage he has done.

'Ridiculous!': our father's mother, who regrets having been the one to pick up, Grandpa in his purple robes, gesticulating from an armchair vehemently: no, I don't want to speak to her.

There was no question but that our father's family were a mighty step above Mum's. Sometimes our father took her head in his hands and told her, feeling his way round, that he could tell by the odd lump, the shape at the back, that she was from peasant stock. When Grandpa was made a bishop, we could marvel at our inflected importance, ushered into a front pew in this soaring house of God – its towering arches, carpet-patterned ceilings – to witness a ritual that involved him knocking at the door and then appearing like one of the three kings. He wore a golden mitre, bore an ivory crook, swept up the aisle by a thundering introit to take up his golden throne.

Afterwards we were lined up for the group photograph outside. Jack is in our father's arms, and us three in our Railway Children dresses. Granny is holding a glove in her fist like a black narcissus, and in the other hand, tightly, Rose, because Rose, who was four, didn't understand that she had to keep still for the nice man taking photographs. He can't have said 'smile': there are no smiles on any of our faces. Amelia is defiantly casual, slumped on one leg, and I am up against Grandpa's vestments clutching my stomach in due deference.

Grandpa was important and he was busy, his purple dress, his silver cross, loping down the dark corridor of the Palace offices with his dog skittering behind. His manner was teasing and gruff. His were the albums of Giles cartoons left out in our bedrooms, which were supposed to be funny, but whose jokes we could never work out. He was appalled by our fingernails. Every visit he'd manhandle us to his knee and cut them to the quick; threaten to attach a thread from the door handle to a wobbly tooth, slam the door shut.

ix

Apart from school, I don't go out at all if I can help it. So sickened have I become by my body's leakages, the hairs on my legs – gorilla legs! – that I have wanted only to be a head, bodiless, transported like a cherub with wings behind my ears.

I don't tell her this, the woman to whom I have been sent. She wears a yellow gingham shirt, a badge with Dawn Hillman, Clinical Psychologist.

'First thing in the morning,' she asks, having sat me down on the plastic chair beside her, 'the alarm goes off, you wake up. On a scale of one to ten?'

'I don't have an alarm clock,' I say, apologetically.

'When you wake up in the morning?' She leans towards me with her clipboard and her pencil, eager to tick the box.

'Where one is nothing much,' she prompts, 'and ten is severe.' Her jaw is heavy, her hair square cut.

'Seven, maybe eight?'

'On a scale of one to ten?' she repeats, as if perhaps I've misunderstood.

The chair is sticking to my thighs. 'Seven,' I say.

She makes a mark. 'So, setting out from the house. On a scale of one to ten?'

I can see the long, dense list ahead of us. Is the trajectory supposed to get worse or better?

'Think about it,' she says, 'no hurry.'

'You arrive at school,' she says. 'How does that feel? On a scale of one to ten.'

'Eight,' I say.

'Eight?'

'Yes.'

'And does the feeling get any better, during the morning, once you've had a chance to settle? On a scale of one to ten?' she prompts.

When we are done, she puts aside the clipboard. 'Now,' she says. 'I'm going to show you some exercises.'

This gives me hope, it's what I've come for, some secret formula that will unshackle me from myself. She sets her hands on her knees. 'Let me show you. I'd like you to screw up your face as tightly as you can. Don't worry what you look like. No one can see.' She squeezes her eyes, her cheeks, her upper lip, her nostrils flaring, hideous, holding it. 'Un, oo, ee, ore, ive,' she counts, releasing her face with a puff. 'See? Easy as that. Let's do it together.'

x

Grey is the colour of our school uniform. In the sixth form I start wearing the charcoal-grey roll-neck sweater Mum knitted for our father when she first met him; I stop responding to invitations from friends. It's become a kind of joke among them, how I've turned into a hermit. I'm one of three taking extra classes with Miss Jones for Oxbridge entrance, which only goes to show how I've reverted to form, become the swot they always knew I was, and convenient enough to let them think so.

Miss Jones is small and dark. She wears a V-neck tank-top, sensible slip-on shoes, and I am hers. *Batter my heart*, she reads, delivering a crash course in the Metaphysicals, whose name alone gives entry to some higher esoteric.

Except you enthrall me, never shall be free,
Nor ever chaste, except you ravish me.

I'm dizzy on the magic of this trick, which feels to reflect my condition precisely: the problem of God (being good) and the conflicting promise of release (sex), held in electrifying proximity.

As a child I'd been an avid reader, but had stopped abruptly, when other, more pressing obsessions had taken over. The crushes I had on male teachers were legion – Mr Robinson the recorder teacher, Mr Porteous the school chaplain, Mr Grey. The passion I have for Miss Jones is of an entirely different order, tapping into that neglected love of reading, which, under her careful cultivation, begins to bloom again.

The night before the interview, I travel to Oxford by train, don't talk to anyone, keep, when I arrive, to the room that I've been given, high-ceilinged but gloomy, a hospital bed, a sink. It is the pocket of a dream, and I move around it with no weight as if I might wake up at any moment.

In the morning, though Miss Jones has expressly advised against it, unwashed and thinned at the elbows as it is, I pull on the charcoal-grey jumper. For once, I imagine, my gold-rimmed glasses might come into their own, lending the impression I've been at pains till now to shrug off, that I am bookish and studious.

I'm directed to a studded door at the side of the chapel. A man appears from behind it in a chequered three-piece suit, thick pasty shoes. He ushers me into a long, panelled room where, at the end, two others await, a man in a wheelchair, and a woman, jaundiced-looking, with straggly blond hair. I am on the alert. Miss Jones has been full of advice: they might set fire to a newspaper, she says, or throw a rugby ball to test my reactions. I accept the empty seat before them.

The only question I am able specifically to recall is about the ha-ha in *Mansfield Park*, a fluke of knowledge I have Miss Jones to thank for, that and my predilection for Fanny Price, 'creepmouse' that she is, insufferably good, but ready – from one who knows it – to burst.

All through the interview, behind me, out of sight there's been a sucking and wheezing noise, the sound of air bubbling in water, which, determinedly, I've attempted to ignore, thinking this must be the test, imagining that the man who shut the door as I came in has reattached himself to some medicinal machine. I've never met an academic before and can only admire how little store they set by bodies.

'Off you go, dear,' he says when they signal that this is the end, no more questions. He has the handle of the door, but otherwise to my surprise is standing quite unsupported, no sign of tubes or wires, waving me off with the smouldering heel of a pipe.

Across the wooden hallway Miss Jones, who was always smaller than I remembered, moved apace and drew me into the cupboard room where the duplication machine was kept. 'They rang this morning,' she said, her eyes black and glazed as olives. 'You got in!' moving towards me to hug me stiffly, something she has never done before. She is shorter than I am. 'Clever girl! You did it!' 'How?' I want to ask. 'How can that be?' gaping fatuously. Game for a Laugh, I am tempted to say. Yet wanting to extend the moment indefinitely, her telling me, her giving me a hug, telling me, giving me a hug: 'You got in!' This is the golden ticket. How can she be sure? A phone call? 'Unconditional offer,' she says. 'You can relax.'

Dawn is pleased for me, she says. In the final week of four, in an unguarded moment, she confides, 'I'm sure you'll feel much better when you get to Oxford,' confirming what has long been my own suspicion: *when I get away*. I slip from the room with a feeling of elation, like a snake preparing to slough off its skin.

I can summon at will the plangent oboes, which are the theme tune to the TV version of *Brideshead Revisited*, instantly transported from the beleaguered holding station where I wait, to the honeyed quads of Oxford, the plash of punts, rooms of young men reading poetry.

As time goes on, all this – at home, or as I walk down Brixton Hill – plays in a golden circle above my head. I choose to walk instead of getting the bus, savouring the grinding surge of traffic, the scraggy margins where dogs from the flats are brought to crouch or cock their legs. For seven years I've been up and down this hill, a drab ordinariness that has had no conceivable end, and yet now takes on the thrilling edge of the soon to be abandoned.

Would you look at yourself? I say, full of the Irish, because, in order to illustrate the distance I have come, I call to witness my eleven-year-old self, setting off for secondary school. And what a goody-goody I was. Remember the hat?

In the rule book, whose small print I'd devoured – marvelling for instance at the far-off year in the sixth form, when discreet eye shadow was allowed – it stated, you must wear your hat from the moment you step out of the front door. Like the blouses I had from the pre-school sale, yellow and stiff under the arms, the hat must have been second or third hand, the grey felt softened beyond feasible shape, the ribbon inside a dirty, mushroomy pink.

Next to us, in Fred's tiny grocery store, I bought a little rectangular packet, which, opened out, became the plastic head-cover the old ladies wore in case of rain. I tied it solemnly over the top of my crumpled hat, convinced that if not God, someone would be on the lookout. I wore this contraption all the way down Brixton Hill, on the tube from the station, the fifty-minute journey into school – Oh, Fanny! – what stroke of providence prevented me from being beaten up?

By day, Brixton is like any other high street, a blackmail letter cut from magazines, stuck down, unstuck, the faded grandeur of the Town Hall po-faced against McDonald's. I move among the jostle of people incognito, no one aware of the Ready Brek glow that singles me out as chosen, or my mission, which is to buy the kettle and procure the college photograph that are requirements of my passage out.

Beyond the tills in Woolworths are two long aisles of pick 'n' mix, a squabble where a child has over-filled his bag so that it has split and sent lime-green gobstoppers rolling across the floor. I'm glad of the distraction, making my way towards the back of the shop where the photo-booth is parked. I ignore the metal mirror attached to the outside of the machine, and dive straight in, pull the grey-blue curtain across. *Adjust the stool*, the instructions read: but to what and how? The coins are hot in my hand. I feed them into the slot, and they rattle somewhere inside. I sit, try to arrange my face. The ghostly semblance of my former self peers from the other side of the glass. Magnesium flash. Stars. And the after-flash, red and metallic. I gather my bag from the floor and emerge head-first to bump into the suede shoulder bag of a skinny woman applying lipstick, lips thrust to the mirror: no shame, I note with a degree of envy.

The photographs will take a while, seven or eight minutes, so I go in search of a kettle, the old-fashioned kind, metal with a proper spout. By the time I come back, the woman has emerged and is chewing, bored. I inveigle myself between her and the hatchway where the band of photos is due to appear. Just in time, it turns out: something drops. I reach in carefully between the bars of the slot to take the strip in my fingers, hold it to one side to dry. The woman flicks me a glance, and I smile as if to say for her, too, the wait will soon be over.

The queue for the buses up Brixton Hill is directly outside, swollen beyond the confines of the shelter. There's a restlessness in the crowd, some of whom have broken out into the road to crane their necks towards the railway bridge, so preoccupied with the late arrival of the bus that I risk a glance down at the strip:

Four portraits, identical. A head, an upper body. Two pendulous breasts.

At first I'm startled: the machine must have some sort of X-ray function, a camera that can see through clothes! I am completely naked, can't make sense of it. Those breasts! And the eyebrows, too (how my friends have longed to pluck my eyebrows!): two delicate half-moons. Is this what the future holds?

With a clunk, the penny drops; I lift my burning face. She will have to kill me for setting eyes on this. As if on cue, her foxy face appears from the plate-glass doors; she sniffs the air. I declare myself, separating from the queue. She moves towards me in her spiky boots.

'You got my photos?' she says, her mouth a slit.

I perform a dumbshow, gladly handing over the strip in my hand: we swap, she stuffs hers straight into her bag.

Three buses have pulled up one behind the other. The crowd swarms. For a moment she has me by the eyes and won't let go, dives into the pupal sac of me and comes up with a crooked smile on her face: *Oh, Baby, You Ain't Seen Nothing Yet!*

I pick up. 'Hello?'

'Crazy!'

'It's eleven o'clock!'

'Is it? Were you in bed?'

'Some of us have work in the morning.' And then, because I mistake him for a normal person who might feel some compunction, I tell him, 'I've got a stomach-ache.'

'Do you remember . . .?' he asks, not to be side-tracked.

Over the years we've had to stay in touch because of Shirin, but recently, it has become more than that. No one else knows how often we speak; I wouldn't dare tell them.

'Remember what?'

He huffs his laugh. 'Someone got out the wrong side of the bed.'

'It's the middle of the night!'

'Forget it,' he says, and, on the turn of a sixpence, hangs up.

xi

Years of teaching and I am none the wiser. What is fiction? Fiction is the past, the old life. Fiction is memory: memory is fiction. Fiction is what happens but no longer pertains; fiction is where we go in our heads when we don't go anywhere. It is a pastoral landscape, a pastoral refrain. It is the bit in the middle of *The Winter's Tale* where bears exit, where babies are found. Can fiction be real?

In the end-of-term class, I know it's not them I'm trying to convince. I hear myself regaling them with a quotation. 'They say,' I say, 'that everyone has a novel in them. Here is Coleridge, writing to his friend Mr Poole: *My dear Poole,*' I read, '*I could inform the dullest author how he might write an interesting book. Let him relate the events of his own life with honesty, not disguising the feelings that accompanied them.*'

'Have you written a book?' It's an innocent question from a girl called Hannah, who has turned out to be one of the more engaged of the group. Hannah Waters. And for a vain and fleeting moment, I wonder if it's because she imagines I can.

I deflect her. 'Whether you've written anything before, or not, everything you write,' I say, 'you start from scratch. It doesn't have to be perfect; it doesn't have to be clever, but it has to be meant; you have to mean it.'

I hope they might be encouraged. 'Everything should feel new,' I say, 'and everything for a time will feel like failure, but perhaps a different kind of failure than before.'

There's a look among them turning their expressions like milk, as if to say: but what, then, are we doing here? What the hell is your job?

xii

Sometimes on the days I'm not in work, I'll seek out my bed, even on a bright sunny afternoon, disappear, horizontal. I'll doze or I'll sleep, nudged by currents of water, the only certainty: this is how the cradle was rocked; this, I imagine, is how the coffin might feel, lowering on its ropes.

When we lived in Newcastle, I used to pretend to sleepwalk so that I could come downstairs after the others had been put to bed. I'd sit in a trance, eyes glazed in front of the TV. The IRA with their black masks and guns, London buses, Piccadilly Circus and bombs; there were no cartoons at that time of night, no *Banana Splits*. There was one programme our father particularly liked, which I came to recognize by its music, dreamy and hypnotic, and which, having heard, I longed to hear again. There it was, emanating, it seemed, from a bottle that drifted across moonlit water towards the front of the screen until you could make out a word inside in pink fluorescent letters: *Arena*. I had a glimpse then of the leap in time when to know the meaning of that word would be to understand the jumble of impenetrable conversation and image that it ushered in; the ten-league boots that would one day convert me to a grown-up.

'Old duts' was our father's description for women like Granny, like Margaret Thatcher, who went to church with their hand-bags. It was the handbag that was the 'dut'. 'Look in your dut!' he'd yell when Mum complained that she'd lost the keys, her comb, her pills, as if the dut were a bottomless pit, filled with the paraphernalia and junk of womankind.

Until recently, in the way I don't think about the insides of computers or cars or the endlessness of the universe, I've preferred to remain ignorant about what goes on in my own insides. At a push I could give you a cross-section: flesh divided by a core, the blackness of two pips, which might be lungs, or kidneys, or ovaries. Stuff happens in there – I'm used to the revolutions, the cramps and effluences – and generally, left alone, they've sorted themselves out. But this pain, a relatively recent development, is more persistent and focused. I've googled, as anyone might, 'stomach-ache', 'pain left side', and found no end of matches: kidney disease, bowel cancer, IBS. I pride myself on how rational I can be about it, my overriding suspicion that it is probably my fault, that – old bag! – I can't help but be in the grip of some peculiarly female affliction.

The general synopsis at midnight: low fifty miles west of Shannon, 1015, moving rapidly east northeast and losing its identity: I'm awake and split in two, poked in the shoulder. *You need to get up.*

I don't ask questions but let myself be led out of the bedroom and up the stairs – *move in an orderly fashion, don't rush* – towards the bathroom.

There's a spasm in my stomach. I clench my jaw as if inside I have a spider to release, steady, rounding the corner, and over, expertly clasping my hair to the back of my neck as I release the catch and puke. Gah.

Good girl.

I balance against the wall and press my other hand to my side, that hole.

Is that better?

Hang on, wait. There's more. Here it comes. Retch. The shiny sinkhole. Yellowish-green bile. Bleurgh.

Good girl. Now, clean yourself up.

I pull some loo roll to wipe my mouth, spit, drop it into the lavatory pan, pull the chain. At the sink I run the tap and cup a handful of cold water, run it around my mouth, spit. All this, very matter-of-fact. I am shaky, but, yes, I do feel better, thank you. I pad back down the stairs to bed, climb up, and pull the sheets around me, though they are cold now, and the life has gone out of the water bottle.

Schmerz: the word is breathed into my ear. I have O-level German, remember? A far more descriptive word than pain, that squeezebox of consonants: *Schmerz*. I hug my knees.

What is wrong with you?

a) Mid-life crisis
b) Menopause
c) Stress
d) Loneliness

Each, more shameful than the last.

4. Drownproofing

Having bound your hands behind your back, tied up your feet, the cadres will deliver you to the edge of the pool. In the 'drownproofing' test, they'll explain, it helps not to be positively buoyant. The aim is to bob up and down to the bottom: nine feet, twenty times.

As you wait on the edge, there's the chance to appreciate your heart, how hard it works, hearing its drumbeat in your ears. And then – an extra drum-roll – someone will call out, Aye! And on his say-so, jump – jump now, without another thought – the soles of your feet smacking water, straight through a paper-covered hoop, a manhole cover closing above your head.

Don't fight it. The water is a plastic chute. Let yourself plummet, flying with your feet, and, before you know it, a little toe-tap at the bottom is all it will take to send you soaring in reverse. Trust the twin balloons of your lungs. That frosted pane of glass when you break the surface, a cap of shell from the top of an egg: this is how it must feel to be born, and how it must feel to be born all over again.

October, 1983

He isn't going to cross the threshold, hunched outside in the desert-coloured Cortina. I've lugged my stuff down the three flights of stairs from my half of the bedroom, piled it in the narrow hallway so that, when he arrives, it will be a simple and speedy matter of ferrying things into the back of the car. There isn't a great deal: the brown trunk, a box of books, the record player, and King Kong (mostly because, after *Brideshead*, a bear, I imagine, is de rigueur).

The others are at school. Mum's upstairs in the kitchen, will have nothing to do with the packing or disembarking; the white Formica of the table, permanent altar to her grief, where her head is cradled, overflowing as it's done the year since he's been gone like a leaky cistern.

I can't disguise the bounce in my step, far too easy for me to break away, make off. What will she do about the dry rot, the crack down the middle of the house, both of which have become apparent since he left?

'I'm going,' I shout when the hallway is clear. 'Mum?' I call up from the stairwell.

It's like the pull of a stopper and she appears, leaning furiously over the bannisters: 'Go with him! Do what you fucking like! You're just like him, him and his fucking father.'

Something has happened: I am immune. A lacquer of selfishness, Teflon. It has begun, this last push. I take the rope and cast it off.

He's poised outside, revving the engine. I let myself in at her side of the car. He doesn't want a scene, he says, and, before I'm strapped in, takes off so urgently that everything on the back seat lurches towards us. He glances in the rear-view mirror, adjusts his shoulders. It suits him fine, this final explosion, as if we can agree on how impossible she is.

Janus.

It's unusual to have the seat next to his, and not be banged up with the others in the back, where, in the old days, we'd be swung at randomly – *Belt up, you bleeders!* – that if we carried on like this, the car would crash. No more of that.

As soon as we're beyond reach, he's chipper, turns on the radio, which crackles because of the clothes hanger that has replaced the aerial Mum snapped off.

Peep, peep, peep: 'Let's have the news,' he says, turning up the volume. The headlines are from the Labour Party conference, where Neil Kinnock has been elected leader.

'Old windbag,' he says.

I'm not going to argue with him, he who's always right. But he's become, in politics as in everything, more mealy-mouthed. I'm pleased to note that I can note it, the sense that, though I might not be equal to him, I can be separate. The radio dispenses any need to talk, and I set up house in the frame of the wing mirror.

'You awake?' he asks, because we're almost there, turning his head to check.

He takes a proprietorial pleasure in navigating his way through town, pointing out landmarks, sure he knows just the place at the back end of the college to park. In the porter's lodge he's at my elbow, while the porter in a bowler hat sorts out a key, emerging from his cubby hole. 'New block,' he says, making a snake of his hand to show us. Our father has wandered off into the vast expanse of the main quad, its towering jacquard brickwork.

Grandpa sent me a postcard of himself, sepia-tinted, in his Oxford bags, taken exactly here, this corner, an expression on his face of smug assurance. Don't know what they're doing letting women in, he'd written on the back, intended, I suppose, to show how pleased he was.

'You must go and see the Holman Hunt,' our father says, waving at the chapel. *All right, all right, come on!* He's moved into the cavernous mouth of a stairway, turning as he climbs to look about. 'Dining hall up here,' he says, his voice too loud.

I don't want to bump into anyone until I can be safely unattached, keen to get to my room, to be rid of him.

The modern block is behind the spaceship construction that turns out to be the bar, down some steps into a sunken concrete tunnel. My room is off the penultimate staircase, two flights up.

'Sweetie,' he commiserates, peering through the oatmeal slats of the blinds. The room is drably bright, functional, nothing like the rooms in his time, he says.

'Can we get the rest of the stuff?' I say, my pulse hopping.

It takes us two runs, the trunk last of all, which we carry between us, him hauling upwards while I push.

'I think that's the lot,' he says, as we set it on the floor. 'Phew,' wiping his brow, and before he has a chance to ask for tea, for me to put the kettle on, I say, 'Thanks. No need to stick around.' The groundswell of wanting to get on with it on my own. Perhaps I am too abrupt. He blinks as if he's forgotten that the purpose of this expedition was to leave me behind. He checks himself, holds out his arms, and when I shuffle to meet him, closes them awkwardly about my shoulders, makes a grinding noise in his throat.

So astonished to be on my own at last, and in a place that I've fixed on for so long but have fixed at a distance in both time and space, I struggle to believe I'm here. The room revolves as I make a concerted effort to inhabit it, sitting on the orange hessian of the bench, the padded roll against my shoulder blades, passing my fingerprints along and over it. For the moment I'm a blank, but the terror that there's nothing to keep me from falling apart is balanced by the fluttering of liberation that gathers and mounts inside me like a wave. On my feet, I move from bed to desk, from the bench under the window to the opposite side, a row of built-in white cupboards, one of which contains a sink. I take to the practical task of unpacking my things, soap, toothpaste, deodorant, flannel, towels.

And here are my books: three small editions of Hardy; essays by Orwell and Virginia Woolf; a one-volume Shakespeare – my leaving prize, embossed with the watering can of the school crest – and the Larkin anthology of modern verse. I recognize the weight and exact appearance of each one, reassuringly familiar as I set them up in their accustomed line.

And last, in the tray of the trunk, there's the baton-sized roll that is the print Mum gave me. I slip the elastic band and counter-roll the card to get it flat. It's a painting, close-up, of a magnolia tree. Stanley Spencer. My skin flares.

When was he interested in anything you've done? I hear the recrimination loud and clear, because, in spite of everything, it was me who let him be the one to bring me here.

I have been found out, fumble for the long Perspex wand which turns the slats of the blind. The room becomes a tent. Above the small triangular sink, there's a mirror fixed with button bolts: *Look at you, your hippy hair, your John Lennon specs, exactly as you ever were.*

I will not listen to the voice, *la-la-la*, fetch the kettle, the kettle from Woolworths, the first domestic appliance I've ever bought. *Look*, I say, eyeballing her: *This is new and it is mine and this is where my life begins*. I turn the tap to let in oxygen.

ii

In the beginning, three of us gravitate: Lauren is from Huddersfield, tall and curvy with long crimped hair. She wears Indian smocks, her legs in tight jeans, a face (as Ardu will later point out) reminiscent of Henry Fielding. I bump into her that first evening in the queue for the payphone. We're hugging ourselves against the cold.

'Have you got a boyfriend?' she asks.

She has both a boyfriend and a room in Pusey quad, one of the proper old rooms with a wooden dresser and a separate bedroom. I envy her it, I say.

'What A-levels did you get?' she asks with the confidence of knowing mine can't better hers. The wind is shooting from one end of the quad to the other. Someone backs out of the booth, which is tucked in under a staircase, ducks their head sheepishly and lets Lauren in.

Freya has a Nordic face, so smooth and pale it looks as if it's been cast from a mould. She's in the new block, too, though a different staircase from mine. Sometimes you'll hear a whale song in the tunnel that connects us: Freya singing with her big black earphones on to 'Wuthering Heights'.

I pick her up on the way to Lauren's rooms, where Lauren lights a joss stick and we sit on the floor drinking wine, listening to tapes: Rickie Lee Jones is Lauren's favourite, and she mimics her faultlessly in a whispery voice, sashaying barefoot with one of six pink glass goblets. The three of us have gravitated, though Freya is the one Lauren has set her sights on, far cooler than I am, more self-possessed. Acting is what she does, Freya says. She has long blond hair, a melancholic mouth.

Lauren is at the mantelpiece. She takes down a small aerosol from one end, holds it for us to inspect: the girl on the can has Lauren-like hair. Limara, the all-over body spray we've seen in advertisements. She claws the air and purrs.

'What type of deodorant do you use?' she asks. 'No, wait,' she says, 'let me guess: Freya—?' She narrows her eyes. 'Sure?'

Freya smiles.

'And Jane, let's see.' It doesn't take her long. 'Mum!' she says, beaming at us both. 'Tell me I'm wrong!' (Miss Innocent. Miss Square.)

Soon we are accustomed to the privilege of institutional life, gathering in our short black gowns to climb the cavernous staircase to the dining hall. We stand when High Table enters, there's a Latin grace, a cacophony of taking to our seats, formalities we speedily learn to treat with the disdain of the habituated.

Of the seven of us doing English that year, Kim and Sally would swiftly buckle down and within a month secure the wide-eyed chemists they'd later marry in the chapel (a perk for alumni); Miranda, with a ready-made network from boarding school, would be swiftly extracted from the social doldrums in which the rest of us laboured. And then there was Neil Wotton. Do you remember Neil, who barely opened his mouth, who'd stumbled in, burly as an Anglo-Saxon with his raggedy beard and builder's crack? Sometime after we left, he'd been discovered in a bedsit in Bournemouth. The rumours, though grim, were never specific.

But this is the first Friday of our first week, and the job of the English students in the years above us, to be friendly and turn out: the Blind, so-called because the object is to get us blind drunk. We are breathless with anticipation, making our way up to a room that belongs to one of the second years, up to the very top of the stairs in the far corner of Liddon quad. We follow the thrum of music – 'Tainted Love'! – and the din of voices. It's a surprise to find our tutor up there with his pipe, standing sentinel, casting a benign eye through quizmaster glasses. Siobhan, whose room it is, hands out drinks in plastic beakers so flimsy they have to be doubled up. There's a stand-ard lamp with a green shade that casts a hooded light on bodies already bunched and sprawled on the floor, smoke rising like fog, the metallic stench of lotions, of damp, overheated jumpers.

We are snagged by a trio of boys in trainers, one with TV glasses and shoulder-length hair. Second years: Gordon, Dean and Mike – *Hello!* – Dean ending a story about what Gordon gets up to with a sock at night. Joke. Chit-chat. Siobhan, who has pink and black triangles painted around her eyes, has taken it upon herself to keep the drink flowing, weaving through the gathering bodies with a bottle under each arm.

Soon the room is so overcrowded that it's impossible to hear the mixtape playing. At some point a wiry boy appears on the periphery. The second years give him elbow room as he stands rolling a cigarette, using his pointy tongue to seal it.

'All right, Skunk?' one says.

'Shall we sit?' the boy asks, and I realize he's talking to me, indicating a small space between the bookcase and the base of the bed. Lauren pulls a face but is no help. As soon as I sit down, he has me cornered. A third year, he says. He's poking tobacco from a blue pouch into a cigarette paper. 'Skunk,' he says.

Having a nickname I take to be a sign of esteem and affection. How unthinkable a third year is; how clever he must be, books and ideas like radiation in his veins.

'How're you finding it?' he shouts.

'Good!'

'Where are you?'

'I'm in the new block.'

'Nice!' His knee is pushing against mine. 'Where're you from, Jane?' – a shock to hear him say my name, as if already he has a claim on me.

'Brixton,' I say. 'London.'

'Brixton riots,' he says. 'Was that you?' His jade-coloured eyes are slits. 'Have you got a boyfriend, Jane?'

I'm embarrassed not to be able to say yes, feeling squashed-in, straining for the possibility of an exit. On the bed above there's movement, a sort of rollicking in the springs as someone hauls themselves into the far corner. It's a man in an old-man suit, and immediately there is an aura of difference about him: he's swarthy, exotic-looking. He reaches for a fag that someone offers, and lights it in the big cup of his hands.

Skunk is watching, too. 'Ardu,' he says, flicking his head in that direction. 'Ar-du,' he says again, louder, a name that sounds like an Indian sweet. 'He's in my year.'

There's a flash of dishevelled shirt that picks out the whites of the man's eyes. Already Miranda has clocked him, and is perched on the side of the bed, tinkling laughter at something he's said. The empty beaker in my hand splits. 'I need another drink,' I say, levering myself up.

'Come back,' Skunk says in a panic, 'won't you?'

I fill a beaker with the remains of a can of lager and steer towards the top end of the bed.

The voice is measured, sonorous.

Miranda puffs her cashmere chest. 'Ardashield?' she says.

'Ar-da-shir,' he pronounces for her. 'You can call me Ardu. People do.'

'Ardu, cool,' she says. 'Nice to meet you, Ardu,' offering him her hand.

He leans his head to where I've come to sit behind her; Miranda turns. 'Oh, Jane,' she says, 'hi.'

'Ardu,' he repeats, and my face burns.

'It's Persian,' Miranda explains.

He has black, curly hair, a sculptural head and under his steady eye I am emptied of all matter. He blinks slow as a panda. 'Who's your favourite writer?' he asks.

My brain is in spasm. 'Edward Thomas?' I say – is that a name?

He takes a drag. 'Edwardians,' he pronounces, dismissively. 'Have you read Hardy's poetry?' (The way he pronounces 'poetry', as if it's a region to which he has special access.)

'A bit,' I say, fumbling.

'Do you know, "The Convergence of the Twain?" ' he asks.

'It's about the *Titanic*,' Miranda pipes up; she has read everything.

He starts to quote, looking straight at me: 'Alien they seemed to be;/No mortal eye could see/The intimate *welding* of their later history.'

'Wedding?' I say, as if he's tapped a reflex, redden, buckle.

He has a smile that slices me open. He's of a different species, all the stuff I've hoarded from novels, from *Breathless*, *Jules et Jim* . . .

'Are you Scottish?' Miranda asks, determined to wrest the conversation back.

'From Glasgow,' he says. 'Mother's Scottish.'

I can't imagine a human provenance, as if he must have come out of a furnace, fully formed, a tongue of molten iron. Heathcliff. Richard Burton. He takes a long swig of beer from the can in his hand, crushes it to an hourglass, pulls a smile, Jack Nicholson. His limbs begin a landslide on the bed. 'I'm off,' he says – we're not enough to keep him – swinging his legs, lifting a hand in salutation. He saunters out through the open door – to what palaces, what opium dens . . .

Skunk has sidled up to me on the bed. 'I see you've met,' he says. 'We're sharing a house. Diana's,' he says, looking around. 'She was here a minute ago. Did she interview you? Daft as a brush.'

Siobhan is tottering, picking up crushed beakers and cans, exhorting herself quietly. The room has thinned out, the ghetto blaster thrilling with a song I recognize, the familiar throb of drum and bass guitar, 'Love,' the man intones, 'Love will tear us apart.'

'Look,' Skunk says, 'things are breaking up. Shall we go to your room?'

I dart around for Lauren, for Freya. Dean's jumper is down

to his knees, his head level with Lauren's breasts, hands glued into her back pockets as they rotate in the middle of the floor; Freya, nowhere to be seen.

The cold is sobering. He follows where I lead. I fumble with the key and let him in, turn on the light, which flickers to life. 'Shall I make tea?' which makes me sound ridiculous, I realize, like an old granny.

Already he's made himself at home, his arm stretched along the tubular back rest of the orange seat. He shakes his head. 'Come and sit,' he says, patting.

'Where do you live?' I ask, concentrating.

'Osney Island.'

'I don't know Oxford yet,' I say.

'Down the Botley Road, beyond the station.'

'With Ardu?'

'Diana's. We left it too late to find anywhere else. Anyway, tell me about you?'

'What?' I say.

He laughs. 'You're sweet.'

I blow like a whale.

'You are,' he says, and now he's leaning over the leg he's hitched up next to me, leaning forwards into the lamplight, his fishy mouth.

Oh God, Oh God, what was I supposed to do? The room heaves, his cold lizard eyes. I duck for the firm handle of the kettle, get to my feet and cross the room uncertainly. In the sink, the clatter's so loud I worry I've broken something; I turn the tap and water shoots out down my skirt. He'll tell them that I've no idea what I'm doing.

It's a task to keep a steady line as I make my way back to the socket, the kettle, impossibly heavy. I can't get the holes at the end of the lead to fit.

'Put that down,' he says, taking it from me.

'Actually, I'm not feeling great.'

He narrows his eyes. 'Okay,' he says. 'Okay.' He sets his hands on his thighs. 'Not to worry,' he says. 'I tell you what, I'll pop round in the morning, shall I?' He pulls a pair of leather gloves from his pocket and presses them home by interlocking his fingers. At the doorway, he hovers an inch or so from my nose. 'Night, night,' he says, 'sleep tight.'

As soon as I push the door to, listening for the descending thrum of his shoes, I grab my shoulders, and in the brace position, ahhhhhhhhhhh, plunge towards the bed.

iii

I bump into Anthony in the corridor.

'How are your *stones* today?' he asks, finding it amusing that I refer to my Wednesday class as 'stones'. He is far more relaxed about teaching than I am. 'You have to remember,' he says, 'that all they're thinking about as they're sitting there is who they're going to get off with next. It's all about sex, that age, don't you remember?'

I am older by a mile than my peers, having come into teaching late and by a curious, non-academic route. 'It seems such a long way off,' I say, to which, archly, gallantly, he replies, 'Not so long ago as all *that*.'

Though he cannot know it, he is right. Perhaps it is the university itself that has sent me back on this loop? Or that

Shirin is the age I was (as these students are, year after year)? I remember, after a gap of twenty years or so, first setting foot into a university library again, the familiar leaf-mulch promise of printed paper, a dive that took me back to before I was a mother, before I ever had a proper job, when everything lay ahead and could have gone in any direction.

These, too, are the days that Ardu likes to recall, reverting to what we talked about then – the books I should have read, the films I should have seen – as if we've agreed to put aside our differences and everything that has happened since. It's an easy illusion to sustain, sending our voices, which are ageless, out into the no-man's-land of the telephone ('I am the enemy you killed, my friend').

'Tell me,' Ardu says. 'How would you pronounce this word? I'll spell it for you: H.O.M.A.G.E.'

'Homidge,' I say, deliberately. 'As in garidge, as in Faridge.'

'*Farage.*' He huffs a laugh. 'Okay. And this one: J.E.J.U.N.E. Try that?'

'You should have been a teacher,' I say, batting him off with sarcasm, though it is true, he'd have made a far more natural teacher than I am.

'Do you know what it means?' he asks, alight at the possibility of my not-knowing.

'I do,' I say, hunting my brain to prove it.

'What?'

I stare at the hexagonal shapes on the carpet. 'Young, stupidly innocent?'

'Look up the etymology. You'll find you've made a classic mistake.'

'Which is?'

'*Jeune* is the French for—?'

'Young?'

'But it has nothing to do with the word *jejune*,' he says, triumphantly. 'You'll find it comes from the Latin "to fast": *jejunus*. It means starved in some way, dull, insipid. *Attenuated*: do you know that word?'

'What do you actually do all day?'

'What do I do?' He takes a drag of a cigarette. 'Oh, nothing, sit on my arse.'

'Don't you get bored?'

He exhales. 'I read. Do you ever read?'

'How do you live?'

'Does it always come down to money with you?'

'You need to live,' I say. I'd once tried to find him in Tulse Hill. We'd had an argument. He'd stormed off. I was frantic, chasing after him through the multicoloured ribbons of three different betting shops.

'You'd be surprised,' he says. 'You don't need as much as you think.'

iv

Skunk and Ardu live with Diana, a junior Fellow in college not much older than they are. It must have been Diana who interviewed me. I remember the hair, the blue eyes, the sallowness of her skin, which kept her from being attractive.

'Does anyone recognize the poem?' she asks in our first session, a round of practical criticism.

Miranda does. 'Thomas Hardy,' she says. 'It's about his wife.'

74

'Would you like to read it for us, Miranda?'

It's a long poem, and Miranda delivers it with the sort of dramatic emphases that, if we'd been at school, she'd have been strung up for. Finally, she reaches the end:

I am just the same as when
Our days were a joy, and our paths through flowers.

'Nicely read, Miranda, thank you.'

Miranda sits back, the afterglow of performance. 'Well,' Diana asks. 'Immediate reactions?'

We duck our heads, staring into the photocopies on our laps.

Miranda raises her hand to say something, but, at a signal from Diana, holds back. Lauren can't resist. 'It's sexual,' she says.

'What makes you say that?' Diana asks.

'Ejaculates?' Lauren says, pleased to demonstrate how utterly at ease with the word she is.

Diana casts her eyes back over the poem. 'Oh,' she says. *'Unseen waters' ejaculations.'* She surveys the room. 'What do we think?'

We're like worms on the end of a rod.

'Well?' She gives a little puff. 'I wonder – Lauren, is it? – if you're being a little anachronistic in your reading?' She pauses. 'What is Hardy describing here?'

We make a show of beavering to the page.

'Spurtings?' someone suggests. 'Is spurtings a word?' We take the opportunity to laugh.

'Spume?' Miranda says.

Lauren raises her hand.

'There's no need to put your hand up,' Diana says. 'We're not at school.'

'Can I ask, then,' Lauren says, 'how that isn't sexual?'

'Okay,' Diana says, giving herself a moment. 'Okay. Perhaps it is, but not, I don't think, in the literal way you're suggesting?'

'I'm not being literal,' Lauren says.

'Ejaculates?' Diana says again.

'You're being literal,' Lauren says. The room draws breath.

Diana quivers. 'I think we're getting tied up unnecessarily. Shall we move on?'

'*You are leading me on,*' Miranda pipes, '*to the spots we knew when we haunted here together.*'

'And what can you tell us about the language here?' Diana asks.

'*You're leading me on?*' Miranda suggests, trying to be helpful.

'*Haunted,*' Diana says. 'What can you tell us about the use of that word "haunted"?' She casts around, brightly. 'Let's discuss haunting in the poem. Who is being referred to here, for instance? You tell me. How does that word open up for us the concept of time in the poem?'

There's an odd noise from the end of the row where Neil is sitting, curled up into himself, quivering, as if he has a little hog pressed under his jumper.

Diana watches him for a moment, to no avail. Everyone turns to watch him. 'Are you all right over there? Water?' she suggests.

His head is swallowed by his beard as he lumbers from the room.

'Anyone else in need of water?' Diana asks, tersely. 'Before we carry on?'

Skunk in the context of *boyfriend* sounded, I thought, too weird: we agreed, though no one else but his mother did, that I would call him Aidan.

The heavy clang of his bike chain as it rings out from the stands near the porter's lodge:

'You don't have to go out with him,' one of the chemists says, shyly, though by now I suspect them all of ulterior motives. It's too late, in any case. He has taken me to Debenhams, where he's paid half towards a black silk petti-coat, a tiny black bra and suspenders. Both Freya and Lauren have high-heeled shoes, he points out. And all I want to be now is like everyone else, to learn to drink Pils and roll cigarettes, to pronounce *ejaculates* without blushing, to learn how not to be a virgin.

He soon gets into the habit of staying over in my room. 'No one cares,' he says when I squirm at leaving the DO NOT DISTURB note on the door. He has the spottiest back, pustular, cratered, which, tactfully, I never mention. In fact, I see it as a blessing, because it means he'll never leave me. His eyes, too, are on my side, pale and reptilian, not the eyes I'd ever have considered gazing into – blue like Steve McQueen's, brown like Bogart's or, for that matter, Ardu's: in his case, almond-shaped, which is why, more or less instantly, I had to rule him out.

But here is a man lying in my bed, parallel, looking at me as if to say, *What are you going to do about it?* He fumbles for my hand and brings it firmly down, wrapping my fingers around with his. I feel a pulse as if we have a bird or a tiny field creature nestled between us, amazed at the way this little pet, flexing, appears to have a life of its own. He presses my fingers, moving them in increments, up, down. How much pressure, I wonder, is too much? I am inept, cack-handed, but nonetheless appear to be doing something right.

Don't think, I'm thinking. Because when I do, I picture udders. He sighs, pulls back his head, his eyes closing as if he can leave me to it. *Don't leave!* There's too much going on, too much for me to be in charge, like being handed the controls of a plane as if I have any idea at all how to land; I don't have a clue, a sort of shuddering in the thin frame of the machine. How am I supposed to bring us home?

Did I let go too soon?

I pull my hand from the mess and hide it around my back. His eyes are screwed shut as if whatever has gone on is not his affair, not his job in any way to clear up. If there's embarrassment, it's mine, the cold patch on the side of my thigh, and on my belly, a thin gruel, crusting. It would be easier, I think, so much easier, he says, if I were on the pill.

vi

Aidan grew up in Oxford and hangs out with the same gang he's known from school, who've been drinking in the Royal Oak since they were sixteen: it's one of the things I like about him, a ready-made routine. This is what *real* life is, I think: rounds of drink and pool, both of which, I note with a frisson of independent thought, would be anathema to our father. Being a girlfriend, I have gained a certain immunity: I'm not available generally to be chatted up; and being Aidan's girl-friend brings me into Ardu's orbit.

When Ardu rocks up, he's the humming centre of a room. At the pool table, he circles, takes his time. Under the gleaming eyes of assembled onlookers, he leans across, hitching up on one corner to pour like tar, the balls kissing, gliding home to their various holes.

'How do you like being a pool widow?' he asks, sauntering over to my corner after his game. Even the way he moves is an enchantment, the way the room's abstract patterns fall in a kaleidoscope around him.

He stretches his legs. 'Crazy', he's begun to call me. 'You've read your Yeats? Look it up,' he says, 'Crazy Jane and the Bishop.'

'My grandfather was a bishop,' I tell him.

'Ha! Why doesn't that surprise me?'

'He introduced me to the Bishop of Rochester once,' I say. 'He said, "Jane, meet Rochester." I was mortified; I thought it meant I'd have to marry him.'

'Crazy Jane,' he says.

'Shitface', I call him, to prove that I understand his ironies, that I'm not susceptible to how handsome he is, resorting to a Krankie *och aye the noo*, a banter that shows how unlike other girls I am, the girls he calls *Bakies*.

'What's all this?' Aidan says.

'Skunk! I was telling Crazy she should be reading Gramsci,' he says, winking, which is his way of winding him up.

Sometimes I wonder if Aidan resents how animated I can be in his absence. 'Shall we head off?' he asks, though it's unheard of for him to disappear before Last Orders. I catch another heavy wink.

'Did you tell anyone?' I ask when we get outside, unlock our bikes.

'What?'

On the blister pack of pills the days are numbered: fourteen to be safe, the doctor has said.

'Why would I do that?' he asks. 'Our little secret, Froglet. Come on,' he says, and his bicycle quivers as it takes to the road.

Every male teacher in the school I'd had a crush on at one time or another, the good, the bad, the ugly.

On Thursday, I was wandering around the school looking for Mr Robinson for a recorder lesson when I was met in the hall by Mr Grey and Mr Robinson. Mr Grey said that Mr Robinson had put on Brut specially to see me and squashed my hand into Mr Robinson's, then grilled his hands on my face and sang, 'Here comes the bride'.

Very few of us had had the opportunity to actually meet a boy. Though it was X-rated, we'd managed when we were fifteen to get ourselves into *Quadrophenia*, which we saw four times in a row, watching Leslie Ash pushed up against a wall in an alleyway by Phil Daniels. Would that ever happen to us? Her lollipop, dreamy face as he pressed her home?

It must have been a brewery, a distillery of hormone, all those girls in the building. 'I'm on,' we'd say grimly. The squelch of the towel as you got up from your seat at the end of class. I was anxious not to be found to be the last using sanitary towels, a humiliation that would put me in the same bracket as Wendy Winterbottom. Tampons were a sign of sophistication, of being at ease with your body and ready to move on. At Granny's I'd spotted a box of Tampax, tucked at the back of the wardrobe. The box was from the 1960s. Inserting a tampon, according to the instructions, was as easy as applying lipstick. There were maps, a cross-section of a woman showing 'rectum', 'bladder', 'uterus', 'vagina'. It was important to get the angle right, to aim the tampon towards the small of the back. Fig. 4. Try sitting, try standing, try putting your foot up on a chair. I unwrapped the tubes from their sleeve and held them as shown. Tentatively I drew back the strange lips of my 'vagina', pushed, aiming approximately, hoping for the best. Though I could picture my insides as a cave, I met a wall of resistance. I tried everything: I stood, I sat, I leaned towards the bed with my forehead against the mattress, jiggled, pushed, shoved, shoved harder. And then, like a sheet of black ice, I slipped. Was it a second or two that I was gone? Or half the night? I woke up with my face squashed against the pillow, could feel the foreign body stuck between my legs, which hastily I removed and wrapped in loo roll to hide in the inside pocket of the suitcase so that Granny would never find out.

As he rises on his forearm and begins to lower his free hand to direct himself towards me, aware of how life-changing this will be, it is the night of the Tampax that fills my head: what if there's some obstruction, some peculiar arrangement of my insides that forbids entry? I grit my teeth, expecting pain, rupture. He adjusts himself like the upper part of an extending ladder, moving downwards on his elbows. He prods, glassy-eyed, intent, steering with his hand. (—.) And then his eyes swivel – 'Ah!' he says – 'Ah!' I say – he is inside! He hovers, fixed above me like a dragonfly, and for a terrible moment I think, *we're stuck!* Like conjoined twins. We'll be forced to give in and call for help. Jean, the scout, her face as tanned and lined as a brown paper bag, will wonder how long a DO NOT DISTURB means do not disturb. His mouth is a thin line, he's up on his elbows again, and shifts, lifts, presses; the movement is a wooden bung, tap, tap, tapping home. I'm braced, stiff as a barrel, no feeling but the possibility of splintering along the grain of wood. I wonder how long this will go on. With no warning he sinks on top of me, a heavy sigh of deflation, bearing down on my ribcage so that it's hard to breathe, his heart thumping against mine. He makes a noise, *'Phwoof!'* and lifts himself up on the jack of his arms, pulls away. There's a farting sound of air released, a trickle of something cold in the crack of my buttocks. 'Did it hurt?' he asks.

I wonder if it should have hurt more, if somehow, the seal on the box had already been broken. The white magnolias above my head are shot through with cherry-pink, each one a little outburst.

'Was it nice?' he asks.

We'd done it, and there was no reason in future not to repeat the exercise. This, after all, was what people did, as much as possible, whenever they could. Like rabbits. On the record player, last thing at night, I take to putting on Jacqueline du Pré. The cello helps bring some gravity to proceedings, a sense that what we're doing has what I imagined it should have, some deeper purpose.

And it's a novelty to wake up in the morning naked with someone in bed. Like being on a raft, I say. Aidan is using his razor at the sink, taking careful swipes from under his chin, upwards, the skin raw and purplish. He pats himself down with one of my towels, wounded-looking, his mouth like an ostrich's.

'Damn, blast,' he says, suddenly.

'What?'

'I've forgotten the Medi-Swabs.'

'Does it matter?'

'Yes, it does. It does matter.' He passes his hand around his chin, pacing the room.

It's Ardu who's put him onto Medi-Swabs. His father's a GP and can get hold of them in bulk.

'Where are they?'

'Ardu has them,' he says, irritably.

'I'll go,' I offer.

'It's a total waste of bloody time,' he says.

'I don't mind.'

He's furious, flings himself onto the orange bench.

The more difficult and irascible a man is, the cleverer, and the cleverer, the better: that was the logic we imbibed. The world revolves and jumps around such clever men, and it's a kind of thrill to come up against it, to be able to prove, if I'm good at anything, how good I am at appeasing them. It's in my blood. And I'd been able to watch Mum all those years, to listen and learn from her mistakes, who tried her best but didn't seem particularly good at it.

'You think I'm a doormat?' she'd shrill.

'Take your pills,' our father would say.

And she'd lock herself in the bathroom, threaten to take them all.

Outside the wind is bitter and, up on my bike, raw as the Arctic. I know my way around Oxford now, which is another kind of thrill, the way to Osney Island, mostly downhill.

At Diana's I set my bike against the wall, let myself in. There's a Sunday morning suspension in the air. I climb the stairs, carefully; Diana sleeps at the front of the house, and I don't want to disturb her. Ardu's in the box room at the top of the stairs. His door is shut. I listen, knock tentatively, knock again. There's a grunt from the other side. 'Hello,' I say, a stage whisper. 'Can I come in?' Another grunt. I push the door. There's barely room for the double bed, the door stopped against it. His head, poking from the sheets, in disarray. There's a splutter of giggling from somewhere, and then another head pops up, a cap of elfin hair, which takes one look at me and twists on its shoulder, vanishes.

'Sorry,' I say. 'He forgot the Medi-Swabs.'

'What?' Ardu grunts, his eyes sticky. He humphs, nods towards the floor. 'Help yourself,' he says. 'In the plastic bag, there.' He rolls away.

On my hands and knees, the bag hisses as I pull it open. I take a strip from the concertinas of sealed packets and fold it into my pocket. 'Sorry,' I say again, backing out of the door. As I creep down the stairs, there's a clap of girly laughter.

'She couldn't believe what you were like,' he tells me later. 'She said you looked as if you'd walked straight out of a Victorian novel.'

5. Whatever Love Is

Halfway through term, Adam, the kingfisher boy, has appeared with emerald blue hair. I know enough not to pass personal comment, but it's such a startling transformation that it would seem odd not to acknowledge it. He takes the compliment in good part. He has a piercing through his nose, which is also new – the nostril angry and yellow – but which I manage to refrain from mentioning.

At this point we have a routine: the students have been split into pairs and take it in turns week by week to present the story they've written. The uncooperative girl, whose turn it is to share her work today, has failed to show up. We spend the first half of the class discussing this week's focus, point of view, looking at a story by Lucia Berlin. In the break, I take off Adam's work to make copies for the others. I make one for myself first and begin to read it as multiple copies reel through the machine. I see immediately that it isn't his usual thing: not fantasy, not gothic horror.

We've been discussing clothing associated with people, how expressive a piece of clothing can be, and I'd asked them to write a story with three different scenes connected by a piece of clothing. Adam has chosen to set his story at the seaside, but he manages to avoid the usual clichés – fluffy clouds, splashing waves, dropped ice creams – his seaside is inhabited and experienced through the eyes of a little boy. We have first-hand access, for instance, to his fascination with sand-hoppers, the way the sea seeps into whatever he digs out, even this far away from the water. It's about a small boy and his grandmother, who keeps a tissue stuffed in the cuff of her cardigan.

'Excuse me, have you finished there?' The wiry French lecturer has been waiting so quietly I haven't noticed him. He waves a sheaf of papers at me. 'I could go upstairs?'

'No, no. Sorry,' I say. 'I won't be a minute.' I collect the copies from the delivery tray. 'I was dreaming, sorry.'

His smile is pained and, under it, I can hear his pounding heart.

They are all on their phones when I come back into the room. When the copies are distributed, I ask Adam if he would mind reading his story for us. 'Read in a loud voice,' this is what I always tell them, 'as if I am deaf.'

He begins reading in a way that confirms to me immediately that he is the boy in the story, his voice – in a way I rarely hear – so at ease with the writing. I let him go on right to the end. He describes the boy's awareness of his grandmother's watchful eye, her need to keep him within eyeshot, the strain on her, which we hear in her voice, her anxious 'not too far' as he moves closer to the sea. The story goes over the page and the scene has changed. It is some years later, and we are in a conservatory tacked onto a house, where the grandmother sits shredding a tissue and the boy, who is a teenager, is cross that he has been left in sole charge, not knowing what to say. The last scene, he is older again, and she is in a hospice. He has brought her something he made at college in woodwork, an

86

owl. She doesn't recognize him, but she won't let go of the owl. All the anxiety she once showed him, he now shows her. The tissue has dropped to the floor. Something like that, it goes.

When he finishes reading there is the usual silence, because no one wants to be first to begin, and, usually, it is up to me. But I am afraid that if I speak, I will betray myself. I swallow. It's a sentimental story, on one hand, but more than that: told with such clarity and emotional restraint, so deftly put together that I find it overwhelming. My eyes are heavy, and blinking will only release the weight they carry. I try to breathe from my stomach.

'Well,' I say, and they can tell something's up because there's a catch which I squash with a cough. 'What do we think?'

They are watching me for their cue.

'Good?' a girl suggests.

'Why do you think so?' I ask.

'Good description of the seaside?' she suggests.

'What's good about it?'

She looks at the typescript.

'Is it something about the voice?' I say.

She looks up, blankly.

'What's the point of view?'

Another girl puts up her hand.

'Yes?' I say.

'It's the boy's point of view.'

'Good. Yes. And how does a point of view manifest itself?'

'In the words?' she asks, shakily.

'In particular words?' I prompt her.

'In the way the words are used,' someone else says.

'Yes, yes. Give us an example.'

After the class, I catch Adam up on the steps of the building, because I'm not sure that I've conveyed to him how good I think his story is. 'It was excellent,' I say (and saying so, in danger of setting myself off again).

'Thanks,' he says. I can't tell if he's embarrassed to be seen with me or pleased at what I've said.

'It felt very real,' I say. 'Do you see the difference? Whether it's real or not, that's the important thing: that it feels real?'

He's keen to be off. 'Thanks,' he says again and speeds away from me up the hill.

ii

There's a pattern to evenings at Diana's. If Ardu and Aidan decide to stay in, it means there's sport on the TV. Diana will appear downstairs in a kimono loosely tied, balance flirtatiously where the ashtray has been, her arm draped along the chair behind Ardu's head. But she has a boyfriend now: Hoover, Ardu has taken to calling him, on account of his asthma. He is Diana's first boyfriend, Ardu claims, which is why, without consulting them, she's been so keen to move him in. As soon as the key rattles in the door, she gives a little shriek, and skips off to the hallway. *Wabbit!*: her special voice, chasing him up the stairs – he can hardly have got his coat undone – along the landing, thud, thud, thud, and into the far bedroom.

'Carnage.' Ardu rolls his eyes to the ceiling. We've all been up there to take a peek: *The Joy of Sex* is marked up on a bedside table, the ape-man and the woman in boots. Aidan has told me what Ardu's told him about the girl I'd caught that time in his bed. 'She'll do anything,' he says, enviously, 'any position.'

There were plenty of stories about Ardu and girls: *Bakies*, Ardu calls them, which Aidan is pleased to tell me is Glaswegian slang: *Bakewell Tart*. Safe to say, women found Ardu irresistible. There was the girl whose boyfriend, a posh boy from Radley, had rolled him down the slope of the quad, a tumble of arms and legs that ended in a broken nose; the pretty nurse in the Royal Oak who, Ardu claimed, had made all the running before he found himself cornered by a pot-bellied man with a pool cue in the Gents and 'Hands off, Paki!'

But it wasn't the whole story. Aidan was eager to demonstrate that he knew Ardu better than most, and that it wasn't all one-way. In their first year, he told me, Ardu had had a girlfriend and, however he might dismiss it now, it had clearly meant something to him. Clare was her name. When they broke up, he had sat outside on the bench at the foot of her stairwell, sat there all through the night, not caring who saw him. In the morning, his overcoat was stiff with frost, he wouldn't speak; he was like a bear, who'd bite off your hand just to look at him.

To Aidan there was only weakness in the story, because it showed, in spite of appearances, how susceptible Ardu could be. In telling me the tale, he had no conception of the seeds he planted in my head: that bench, the frozen vigil, the suffering heart.

Clare Montgomery was in the third year and lived out of college. It was a while before I met her in the flesh, but I'd already conjured her as a creature of beauty and sophistication. The first time I saw her was at someone's birthday party. She wore classic slightly old-fashioned clothes – a circle skirt, hand-knitted cardigan – that conferred on her a certain grace and aloofness. She wasn't afraid to dance, but danced on her own, a fluid kind of shuffle, her arms playing about her middle, before, behind. Unlike the others she didn't need to drink or smoke or disappear off into the room at the back, where people went to flake out on the floor.

'Mon,' Ardu called her, fondly, 'Mad Mon. She's got a good chin,' he'd say, exhaling. 'Good teeth: you can tell a winning horse by its teeth.'

It was sometime in the Easter break that Aidan invited me to stay over. Diana and Hoover were going to be away, he said, and it wasn't often they had the house to themselves.

I was flummoxed when I turned up and Clare answered the door – her almond eyes, her handsome chin.

'Oh,' she says. 'They're in the pub. You can come in if you like.'

She doesn't wait for me to make up my mind. Awkwardly I follow her, not sure if that's what she means me to do, into the kitchen. On the table there's an industrial-sized aluminium tray of cooked mince and carrots onto which she begins to smooth and primp spoonfuls of mashed potato.

'They'll be back soon,' she says. 'Plenty here, if you want?'

She opens the oven, which churns as if it's chewing heat, and bears the tray down to the shelf, slides it in.

'Can I do anything?' I ask.

She shuts the oven door, adjusts the temperature. 'It's done,' she says, unhitching herself from the apron.

'Shall I lay the table?'

She gives a shrug. The cutlery is in a drawer in the table and I have to squeeze past her to reach it.

'How many of us?' I ask.

She calculates. 'Seven with you,' she says. The table is four-square and there's no way of making it look anything but cramped. I don't separate the knives and forks but spread them in their pairs approximately; find four wine glasses and three plastic beakers in the cupboard and set them down together on the tabletop. She has her back to me at the sink, indifferent to my efforts, and I mutter my excuses, taking my stuff up to Aidan's room.

The curtains are drawn. When I switch on the light Aidan's rat begins to hurl itself against the bars of its cage (a birthday present from his parents, so how could I object?). The smell of sawdust prickles in my nose. I sit on the bed as far away as it's possible to be. At the end of the bed there's a big black and white poster of Patti Smith, a jacket slung over one shoulder. He fancies her like mad, he's told me. I don't suppose I'm anything like her, though someone at school once said I looked like Joey from The Ramones.

I hear them bundling in at the front door.

'There you are,' Aidan says when I appear. He's with the two Kevins, Blackpool Kevin and Oxford Kevin.

'All right, Crazy?' they say.

'Where's Ardu?'

Aidan looks shiftily to where Clare is peering through the window of the oven door. 'Being a dick,' he says.

'Where is he?'

'In the pub.'

Clare is unflinching.

'I'll go and fetch him,' I say, wanting to prove that I'm on her side.

'You'll be wasting your breath,' Aidan says.

I discover Ardu sitting with Will in their usual corner by the fruit machine. Will doesn't speak much, but has a jovial demeanour, happy enough to sit and sup and observe.

'Supper's ready,' I say. 'It's on the table.'

Will looks sheepish, glances sideways at Ardu, who's flipping a beer mat between his fingers and refusing to look at me.

'Ardu?' I say.

His eyes show how dreary I am.

'Come on,' I say. 'Don't be mean.'

The juke box is playing 'Reach Out I'll Be There'.

'Will you come when the song's finished?' I ask, the kind of technique that works on children.

Ardu blinks but doesn't look up. He bunches his lips, staring down his nose. Sand runs through me.

'Will?' I say, appealing to him and his public-school manners. He shrugs: what can he do?

The more I stand there, the tighter the knot. It's painfully evident that I have no sway. I swallow. 'I think you should come. She's made all that effort.'

Though I've witnessed the occasional spat at the end of an evening, this is the first time I've come up against Ardu myself. It's a shock to find how out of my depth I am. The rules are not as I understood them. He sits impassive, and all I can do is surrender. I turn, and feel an icy chill, though outside my eyes burn for what I'll have to tell them.

'Told you, Froglet,' Aidan says, which only adds to the humiliation. They're squashed round the table, platefuls of steaming food before them.

'Sit down, flower,' Blackpool Kevin says, cheerfully. 'All the more for us.'

Clare looks unsurprised, vindicated even. She elicits in the others a kind of doe-eyed attention, as if some unspecified wrong has been done for which they feel obliged to atone. She adjusts her chair to let me have a corner of the table, five of us elbow to elbow. They pass the ketchup between them, squeezing it out like paint.

There is no question but that Clare and I will clear up. The TV's on so loud we can hear it in the kitchen, *Please adore me, Now I'm no longer alone*, one of those old crooning songs, whose irony is not lost on me. Clare's tidied the tin tray back into the oven. I scrape the plates into the bin, run the tap which fires the boiler, and for a while we hear nothing but its roar.

The only light in the sitting room glimmers from the TV screen, splashing their faces where they sit in a row, all three in the same attitude, jaws slack. They've seen the film before. Clare takes the arm of the big chair, where Ardu usually sits, and I drop down to the foot of the sofa. Every now and again they pass an anticipatory comment, which makes it even harder to sustain interest. It's a kind of purgatory where all I can do is pick at my failure.

A fumbling outside the window gives me a start, sends a flicker through the room: someone incompetent, searching for the lock. The front door gives way heavily. No one calls out, as if we've each made a pact to ignore him, eyes fixed to

93

the TV, where Van Morrison has struck up, double bass, sax, a loping smooth-talking beat, to which Ardu enters – *a marvellous time for a Moondance* – giving a sardonic huff.

On the screen the girl is kissing her boyfriend in the shower, his hands running over her soapy back. Ardu collapses into the seat of the chair, where Clare, on the arm, stiffens.

Legs adjust and tense in the row alongside me: this is the scene they've been waiting for, the girl, who I recognize now as Jenny Agutter, is biting the man's shoulder. The next minute, they're in bed, naked, he's all over her, her face, that immaculate, soft focus face. I made the mistake of telling Aidan once that I was Jenny Agutter in *The Railway Children* and panic that he'll choose this moment to reveal it.

The man on screen is writhing around on the floor, sprouting hair, a muzzle, he's turning into a beast.

You're a beast, I'm thinking, *an utter beast*.

'I love you,' Jenny says in her madly posh voice, when in the end they corner the werewolf-boyfriend, and he's shot, and turns from frenzied beast back to naked man.

In the morning, I meet Clare at the top of the stairs in a long white nightie. I've brought up two mugs of tea. She stands aside to let me pass.

'Morning,' I say.

Aidan is waiting for me, propped up on pillows, his unwholesome torso.

We speak in whispers. 'I don't know why she lets him get away with it,' I say.

'You know what he's like: because he's *Ardu*,' he says, 'and he can.' He blows across his tea.

The rat is awake, rattling the cage as it has done all through the night. 'Does it have to be in here?' I moan.

'Otto? He's telling us he's here.'

'He's a rat!'

'Perhaps you should bring ear plugs?'

A drop of tea flips into my windpipe: I choke, my eyes fill with water.

'Put the mug down,' he says as if it's a weapon.

He hits me on my back.

I splutter, 'I'm fine.'

'Breathe,' he says.

My eyes are rinsing themselves out. 'I don't. Want. Ear plugs,' I say.

'Okay, okay, don't talk.'

I hold my neck.

'What's the matter?' he asks.

My worst dreams are about chewing gum, chewing gum that I can't get rid of, the texture obscene, a clammy paste that sticks to the roof of my mouth, between my teeth. The smell of masticated chewing gum is the smell of his skin.

'Let's get up,' he says, decisively. 'Get something to eat. Come on, you'll feel better.' He throws off the bedclothes. 'All this mooching about. Cheer up.' He lunges for my sides.

The bathroom at Osney is downstairs off the kitchen and several degrees colder than the rest of the house. You could keep ice cubes in here. I whistle to pee, and it comes in fits and starts. I splash my armpits inside his fusty dressing gown, handfuls of tepid water, take my toothbrush from the pocket, pulling fluff from the bristles. By the time I'm out, Ardu's downstairs, supporting himself in the kitchen doorway, eyes half-closed. He pulls his joker smile.

'How's Crazy this morning?' he asks, drags out a chair, winces at the noise, and hangs his head to one side then the other. 'Got any Alka-Seltzer?'

'Try the cupboard,' Aidan says, nodding over.

Ardu feels his way to the cupboard door. 'Yep,' he says, pulling out the box. 'Just what the doctor ordered.'

He fills a beaker of water and drops in two of the white discs, watches as they bubble and hiss.

'Clare not coming down?' Aidan asks.

'She's gone.'

'You two back together, then?' Aidan says.

Ardu circles his shoulders to stretch.

'She cooked,' I say, accusingly.

'No one asked her to.' He arches his back, yawns. 'No-one-asked-her-to,' he says in a singsong, squeezing shut his eyes, blinking them open. 'So,' cracks his jaw, 'what did you think of the film?'

'I wasn't watching it,' I say.

'Not arty enough for you?'

'It was nice of her to cook,' I say.

'Nice?' he says. 'You'd be surprised—'

At that moment the front door opens. *The front door.* I'm still in Aidan's dressing gown. I grab the back of the chair.

'Hello-o? Anyone in?' A second later she's among us, Diana, glowing. 'Oh, amazing,' she says. 'You're all here. Hello! John?' she calls. 'This is perfect!'

Hoover appears, drops the two bags. She claps her hands, popping eyes, hardly able to contain herself. 'You'll never guess? Don't get up, Jane,' she says. 'I'm so glad you're here.'

'Never guess what?' Ardu says.

'Well,' she turns to Hoover, grabs his hand. 'John and I,' she gulps, 'are going to get – MARRIED!' She lets out a little shriek.

'Commiserations,' Ardu says.

'Congratulations,' Aidan says, emphatically.

She's squeezing Hoover so hard it shows in his face. 'We were dying to tell,' she says, 'weren't we.'

'Well done,' I say, because I have to say something.

'It's only going to be a small do. Registry office. In a few weeks, hopefully,' she squeezes Hoover again, 'soon as we can.'

'You got a dress?' Ardu asks, as if suddenly he's an expert on weddings.

She blossoms. 'There's a lovely green dress in Marks. It's velvet. It's got sort of long, pointy sleeves.'

'Very Lady of Shalott,' Ardu says.

'Exactly,' she says, and I see how he has her in thrall. 'And don't you think green's unusual?'

'If you say so,' he says.

She appeals to him, anxiously.

'You'd look good in a bin bag,' he says.

'I can never tell if you're joking,' she says, pulling Hoover's hand around the base of her spine.

'Good for you,' Aidan says.

Hoover coughs. 'Right then,' he says, retrieving his hand from hers, 'I'm off. Things to do.'

'Is it secret?' she asks, her baby voice.

'No secrets,' he says.

'Just a sec, darling. I'll follow you up.'

She dips into the bathroom. Through the door we hear the trundle of her pee, the tug of the loo roll. Ardu has sought me out, and his eyes glint. He winds a finger at the side of his head, slits a hand across his throat.

How easily I'm restored by his attention. As if I can be clever enough to understand that this is all part of his elaborate game to sort people out.

Diana is beaming as she comes back through. 'Tell me, truthfully, what you think?' she asks, looking at Ardu.

'You're a dark horse,' Ardu says.

'I'm not,' Diana protests. 'I'm really not. I'm an open book.'

'If you say so.'

'I do!' she laughs. 'I do, I do, I do.' She takes a breath. 'We just didn't see the point in hanging around. Once you know you sort of – don't you?' She flicks her eyes to the ceiling, lowering her voice. 'My only worry is Daddy,' she says. 'I'll need all my courage. It's a bit *Lear* in our house. He can be funny; I'm the youngest. Keep your fingers crossed, won't you?'

iii

You'd think – I thought – that I'd recognize Love, the years I'd been in gestation. 'Mouth it,' we'd say at school: *co-lour-ful*, exactly the same choreography of lip and tongue that got the unsuspecting to say, *I love you*, as if saying so was a trap impossible to wriggle out of.

Love was everywhere, fed to us intravenously by books and films, in the songs that we played incessantly. But how to get our hands on it, lumbering about with our butterfly nets? All we could do, like disciples of the Second Coming, was pray that it might be imminent.

Wednesday, 29th July, 1981, was the morning of the Royal Wedding, the beginning of the summer holidays. I was sixteen and one of the few people out and about – not at work or glued to a TV – travelling north from Brixton on the tube to see my friend, Jane (there were four Janes in our class). We were determined to boycott proceedings. This publicly condoned, fancy-dress kind of love was not what we were after.

Jane had acquired the 12" version of 'Love Will Tear Us Apart' and we listened to it on repeat, lying flat out on her bedroom floor like the angel on the sleeve. We could feel the pressure and the seriousness pumping in our veins, a dense and oily propellant which the song both fed and divined in us.

It thrilled us to imagine that in another bedroom in perhaps another part of the country altogether there could be a boy, as yet unknown to us, but by whom one day – Alleluia! – we'd be intimately known. The conjunction of stars that would bring us together to wake up in the same bed to 'Here Comes the Sun' must already be in motion. It would be an attic flat with a record player, a black cat, clothes strewn over a velvet armchair, the mod clothes we bought from jumble sales – taken-in skirts, pointy shoes, berets – which we swore to wear for ever until we were old ladies.

It was sunny as the seaside outside Jane's house, yet eerily quiet, saturated with the story we thought we were above: a princess, a carriage, an enormous dress. She was welcome to it, we said, shuddering at what an old fogey Prince Charles was.

'Can you find the words to sum up how you feel?' the interviewer had asked on the day they got engaged.

'Difficult to find the right sort of word, isn't it really . . .?' Charles had puzzled.

'Mhm,' Diana agrees, taking her lead from him (she's only a few years older than us).

'Just delighted and happy. I-I'm amazed,' scratching his nose, 'that she's been brave enough to take me on.'

'And I suppose,' the interviewer prompts, 'in love?'

Charles leaves that to her. 'Of course,' she says, a sharp intake of breath, those rangy, teenage eyes.

And then he comes out with it, a line we repeat to each other in a *one-step-for-mankind* kind of way: 'Whatever love means?' he says.

Whatever Love Means: poor cow, a cavil that must have entered her like a dart. He hasn't listened to the right records or read the right books or seen the right films. And all she can do is surmise because he's older and wiser, he's got Love – that romantic, yearning obliteration, *whatever* – out of his system.

iv

I couldn't afford at this point to upset Aidan: he had finals coming up and was determined to do well. In the six weeks beforehand, he went home so that his mother could look after him. Towards the end of the month an invitation came to join them all for Sunday lunch, and there seemed no way to avoid it.

His father is a Medievalist, an expert on hermits. They live up the Banbury Road, where many of the professors live, the house, detached, a house where in the children's books every proper family lives (I am still susceptible to how inferior this makes me): a mummy who dusts, a daddy with a briefcase and an office.

The porch is thick with hydrangea bushes, the door, heavy oak with a frosted glass porthole. His mother has short dark hair and a toothy smile. 'Valerie,' she says, holding out her hand. 'So pleased to meet you. We're almost ready to eat.' There's a floury gravy smell that reminds me of meals at Granny's.

In the smallish dining room where she leads me, his father is busy reading the Sunday paper. He's pulled back from the table to give himself room to stretch, the table laid with rectangular placemats of watercolours of the various colleges.

'Nigel?' Valerie says. 'Here's Jane.'

He nods cursorily over the top of the paper.

'Hello,' I say.

'If you'll excuse me a moment, I'll go and serve up,' Valerie says.

'Can I do anything?' I ask. *Where is he?*

'No, no. You take a seat. Everything's in hand,' Valerie says.

Nigel continues reading, shaking out the paper when he turns a page. 'Lunch is ready, darling,' a singsong up the stairs.

I recognize the footfall. 'Why didn't you say?' Aidan's voice in the kitchen. He comes through with a willow pattern gravy boat. 'No one told me you were here,' he says. 'You've introduced yourself to Dad?'

Nigel grunts, folds the paper in half, smooths it out, and sets it on the floor at his feet.

'Find us all right?' Aidan asks.

We're oddly formal, though I can read the delight in his face.

Valerie comes through with two plates, making a little humming noise as she goes. She sets one before me – Yorkshire puddings, slabs of beef, runner beans – and the other, a far meaner version, in front of Nigel.

'Don't worry,' Aidan says, seeing my hesitation. 'Dad hardly eats.'

'Help yourselves to gravy,' Valerie says.

Nigel pulls his plate towards him with a look of distaste.

'It's an experiment,' Valerie explains.

'Tell her, Dad,' Aidan says.

'You tell Jane, and I'll pop up with Andrew's,' Valerie says. (Aidan has told me about his brother: he has a stutter and terrible acne; rarely comes out of his room.)

'Dad?' Aidan says.

Nigel coughs into his napkin. 'Not sure why anyone else would be interested,' he says. He remains half-turned from the table, one tan trouser leg set over the other.

Aidan says, 'They've tried it out on rats. If you starve a rat, apparently, they live longer. You have to get it right, of course. Otherwise you can starve them to death.'

'Everyone got everything they want?' Valerie says, brightly, hurrying back into the room, laying a napkin over her knee.

'Apparently,' she says, 'if you starve rats, they do much better, live longer.'

'We've told her that,' Aidan says.

'Fascinating, don't you think?' she says. 'Though I'm far too much of a piggy to try it myself. Do tuck in.'

With a fork Nigel separates the beans on his plate from the scrap of meat.

'Bon appétit,' Valerie says, raising her glass of rosé.

'Thank you.' I lift my glass and taste the sweet metal of the wine.

'Everything all right, Nigel?' she asks.

'Humph,' Nigel says.

'Have you got exams, Jane?' Valerie asks.

'Mods.'

'Of course. Mods. How's it going? You're in college, aren't you? Have you a nice room?'

'I'm in the new block. It wasn't really how I imagined Oxford to be.'

'I bet it's warmer, though?' she says.

'Jane thinks it's too corporate,' Aidan says. 'She doesn't approve of central heating.'

'I know what she means,' Valerie says. 'There's not much sense of history, is there? Ade was in Pusey, weren't you, darling? Rather spartan as I remember, but plenty of history.'

Aidan burps. 'Pardon,' he says. 'Isn't he joining us?' he asks.

'Stop it, darling,' Valerie says. 'He's quite all right upstairs.'

'Jane might like to have met him,' he says, smirking.

'There'll be plenty of opportunity for that, I hope,' she says, giving me a full beam. 'Have you got brothers and sisters, Jane?'

'Two sisters and a brother.'

'A big family. How lovely! And where are you in the pecking order?'

'The oldest. My brother's the youngest.'

'Mum,' Aidan says, 'I was going to take Jane up to my room. There's some books she's after.'

'Fine, sweetheart. Whatever you like. Is everyone finished?'

'Stuffed,' Aidan says, pushing away his plate, looking at me brazenly as if the others won't notice.

Nigel has barely touched his food.

Valerie begins to gather up the plates. 'We don't have pudding; I hope that's all right? There's some cream crackers, if anyone would like?'

'Can we have coffee later?' Aidan says.

'Oh? Whatever you like,' Valerie says. 'Daddy will want to finish his paper.'

'Can I help?' I ask, not wanting to appear party to undue haste.

'No, no. Much more important for you to see what books you need. It'll all go in the dishwasher. Off you go, you two.'

I catch Nigel's eye. For a moment I detect disgust. Then vacancy. He reaches down for his paper.

At the top of the stairs against the wall of the long landing there's a wooden ladder on a steep slant. Aidan goes up first and I follow. There's a trap door on a hinge and as soon as he's pulled me through, he unhooks it from its post and sets it down in place. 'There,' he says. 'You're trapped.'

There are bookcases built into the eaves with books in alphabetical order and a deep shelf for records; there's a double divan under the apex of the ceiling. He throws himself on the bed, turns onto his side. 'Leave that,' he says. 'Come over here.'

He takes my wrist and draws me down, pushes me out straight.

'Couldn't wait to get my hands on you,' he says.

'Won't they hear?'

'Not if we're quiet.'

He plucks at the belt around the waist of my dress. 'How does this work?'

'I'll do it.' I sit up and undo it.

'Take it off,' he says.

'My dress?'

'Yes.'

'What if they come up?'

'They won't.'

'Are you sure?'

'They never come up.'

Before I have the dress over my head, he's spread me back. 'It's a bit cold,' I say, drawing my arms around me.

He moves over to lie up against me. 'Better?'

He's undone his jeans and shoves them down around his thighs, his whole body swollen and pulsing, beef on his breath. He makes a whistling noise to let off steam, fumbles for my knickers, yanks at them.

I flatten myself to the mattress. He finds me out in no time, he is expert, holds himself, pushes. 'God,' he says. 'God. Ah.' His eyes gleaming. 'Oh. That's good. Oh.' He pulls back his head; there are toothmarks where he's bitten the skin under his lip. It's over before I know it. 'Argh!' He collapses, flumps down on me, and I turn my head quickly to avoid his ear.

He blows out. 'Sorry,' he says. 'Phew. Been too long. Sorry.'

Where he's slunk out of me, there's a hole and I'm filled with an urgent need to fill it, to staunch the wound. There's a tingling like poison ivy. I wrap my legs around his thigh and press, pressing as if to rub something out, as if the only solution is to press, to suffocate. Once I start, I can't stop, I want to erase and be erased, using him as if he were the trunk of a tree, ignoring him, though I can sense him perking up, paying a sort of baffled attention. I cling without looking, as if to a log in a river, little explosions of breath, blood radiating from my face and from the notches of my spine.

'Froglet!' he says, when finally I let go and roll up into myself. 'Wow!' As if what has happened has had anything to do with him. 'What was that?' he says. He prods me. 'Best get dressed,' he says.

The thought of going downstairs: 'I can't,' I say.

'Don't be silly.'

My hair is all over the place, I'm sticky and hot.

'Here,' he says, passing over a patterned hand towel. 'Use this.'

I press the towel between my legs.

'You're fine,' he says, pushing hair behind my ears.

I climb into the tunnel of my dress, fix the belt around it. He tucks himself back into his jeans.

'Better find you a book,' he says.

When we get downstairs, Valerie's in the hallway, as if she's on the point of coming up to find us. 'There you are,' she says. 'You've a visitor,' nodding towards the living room.

'Who?' Aidan asks.

'I'm making coffee. I'll bring it in.'

He pulls a face at me and then heads on through the door.

'Skunk!' I hear, and I recognize the voice immediately.

'*Arduuuu!*' Aidan says. 'What are *you* doing here?'

I can't bear it, as if I've been irradiated with a tell-tale dye. Ardu is settled in one of the armchairs, his broad face lifts. He

106

plants his hands on his knees and grins. 'Didn't expect to find Crazy here.'

'We've been upstairs,' Aidan says, 'checking out books.'

'Is that what they call it?'

I'm stiff as a doll, though aware of the marshiness between my legs.

'Go on, show him,' Aidan says, enjoying the joke.

I hold out the book. *Thomas Hardy: Distance and Desire*.

'Bit old hat, isn't it?' Ardu says, an effortless putdown.

'Here we are,' Valerie says, butting the tray into the door to let herself through. 'Sit down, make yourselves comfortable. It's lovely to see you again, Ardu. It seems such a long time.'

'You're looking well, Valerie,' Ardu says.

I sit on the edge of the chair, worrying that I'll leak on the velvet plush.

'This the first time you've met Jane?' Ardu asks.

'We've been so looking forward to it,' Valerie says. 'If you'll excuse me a moment, I'll just pop Nigel a cup. Got everything you need?'

'Hope I wasn't interrupting anything?' Ardu asks, slow blink, as she shuts the door behind her. There's a terrible clarity in the room. Aidan is back on side; he asks about the cricket, picky and prosaic, and, though I'm tarred all over by his brush, I am no one, and needn't worry that anyone will notice. I re-cross my legs. If I had a knife, I'd use it, cut out the offending piece of flesh and throw it to the lions.

6. Typecast

Oxford, 1984

Ardu is gone. The life of pubs and pool with the third years is over, broken off like a bit of tooth, leaving a jagged hole for me to ponder. I am living at the top of the staircase where we had the Blind in the first year, high up and diagonally across from the porter's lodge. Freya is in the room next door and in the evenings I listen out for her return. We sit and drink ginger wine together while she decompresses – she is in two plays at once this term.

'I don't know what I was doing,' I say, because, after a year, it seems I was doing nothing. Aidan is living at home, and though he's finished has not given up coming into college. I recognize the ricochet of his bike chain and from the vantage of my window watch him dart around the skirting of the quad. He's written to Mum to tell her what a mistake he thinks I'm making, and can she do something about it, please? I lock the door. He has left a small edition of Betjeman in my pigeonhole, an unwearable pair of screw-on earrings.

'I know you're in there,' he pleads. 'I'm not going anywhere.'

The first half of the spring term is bitterly cold. There's been snow on the ground for a week, frozen to icy yellow troughs. Two people in college have broken bones and are hopping around on crutches.

The address I have is somewhere the other side of Folly Bridge, and I ride over, using the tyre-tracks of the traffic. The house looks unpromising, dingy net curtains tacked up inside the windows. It seems, suddenly, a ridiculous idea – Freya will think I'm a copy-cat – but I don't want to be seen to be running away, and, anyway, the door opens and a man in a blue blazer appears at the top of the steps. 'Hi,' he says, reaching out. 'Here for the audition, right?' He's albino and American. He shuts the front door behind me. 'Come on through.'

In the living room there are two armchairs with old curtains thrown over them and a buzzing electric fire. A man separates from one of them. The top of his head glances the light fitting; he hunches forwards to take my hand.

'Stephen Critchley,' he says. He has a toothbrush moustache. 'And you are?'

'Jane,' I say.

'Okay, Jane,' he says. He folds back into the chair behind him, cracks his knuckles. 'Tell us a bit about yourself.'

'I haven't been to an audition before,' I say.

'Don't worry.' He folds back into the chair. 'Relax. We're not here to eat you. What year are you in?'

'Second year. English.'

He nods to the window. 'Brownie points for coming out in this. Why don't you slip off your coat?' His eyes are searching. 'So. Let's tell you how this goes: you do your bit,' he pulls at his moustache, which lifts as he smiles, 'then we – you and me – we nip upstairs for some wild sex – ha!'

'I'm the producer,' the albino says, reassuringly. He's wearing a blazer with gold buttons, keeps his hands behind his back.

'Okay,' I say, holding onto my coat.

Stephen sits back in his chair, brushes himself off. 'Joking aside,' he says, 'have you prepared something for us?'

My stomach pulses. I reach into my coat pocket for the copy of *The Prime of Miss Jean Brodie*, let my coat drop to the floor at my feet and open the book at the place I've marked.

He sweeps one leg over the other. 'No need to be nervous.'

I wet my lips, clear my throat. I have a version of the Scottish accent I've honed on Ardu; it takes a moment to hit my stride.

'Nice choice,' Stephen says, and he sounds surprised. He smooths his moustache. 'Are those real?' indicating my glasses. 'Perfect,' he says. 'Okay. Thanks, Jane. You're free to go. We'll get back to you.'

Freya has never heard of ODL. 'Oxford what?' she asks, irritated. 'Why didn't you ask me?' I described the man who looked like John Cleese, and we agree that it sounds like a cowboy outfit, a cover for something else.

'You had a lucky escape,' she says.

Except that I get the part. Rehearsals, the note says, start on Monday.

Stephen was older than the rest of us, studying medicine. He wanted to be a gynaecologist, which explained, I supposed, his cavalier attitude to women. He cast two Sloaney-looking girls as Gwendolen and Cecily, and was sleeping, it transpired, with the dark-haired Lady Bracknell.

'You were our first choice for Miss Prism,' he told me.

'The glasses?'

'That swung it,' he said.

It was only the second week of rehearsals when the butler, Merriman, a blond, good-looking boy straight out of *Brideshead*, didn't turn up.

Where's Merriman?

It didn't particularly matter, he was a small part, but it was an absolute pain when people didn't turn up for rehearsals, Stephen said.

The snow was turning to slush.

The next time we met, Stephen gathered us together, he and the producer shoulder to shoulder as if they were going to give us another dressing down.

'We've got some rather dreadful news, I'm afraid,' tugging at his moustache. 'It's Merriman. We heard today. He's been involved in a car crash.'

'Oh My God?' the two girls cried.

'It's bad, I'm afraid. An awful thing to have to pass on.'

The sound in the room went up like water off a hot plate.

'Did anyone know him?'

We didn't.

'What college is he from?' Gwendolen asked.

'*Was*,' Cecily said.

'Oh My God.'

We plunged into ourselves, trying to summon a picture – tall, blond hair – but where was his face? We turned to one another for corroboration, but none of us knew each other well enough to be able to tell: was this real or was it acting? Was she acting, or was I? As if we'd lost any sense of the difference.

Someone has died! Do you know what that means?

'I'm suggesting,' Stephen said, 'that we put off rehearsals for this evening. Sign of respect.' He glanced around, cagily.

'But I'd like you all here, on the dot of six on Monday, please. Okay?'

Perhaps it was because it had been snowing, and now the snow had thawed it seemed somehow explicable that Merriman, like the boy in *The Snow Queen*, had disappeared. People must be dying all the time and we shut our eyes to it. The death of relative strangers, the death of pop stars: these deaths are like an inoculation, a small dose to boost our immunity, the sense that somewhere else death has been satisfied. But there must have been a funeral, a broken-hearted mother; and later, on the table in the JCR, an edition of the *Cherwell* with a photograph on page two, blurry from magnification: Merriman grinning like a loon from the back row of the hockey team, all the confidence of having arrived somewhere – not the North Pole, not Mount Everest, but a place that for the time being took the pressure off being anywhere else.

ii

The week of our five performances, the wisteria in the quad in Oriel was in full bloom, long festoons of it, and, apart from one long day of rain when we performed double-time under umbrellas to a crowd of three, the weather was kind to us.

'I don't like novels that end happily,' Cecily says for the fifth time. 'They depress me so much.'

'The good ended happily, and the bad unhappily,' I tell her. 'That is what *fecktion* means.'

By the last performance, I'm enjoying the laughs. Stephen, too, is pleased, and suggests that if I get contact lenses, maybe I'll have more of a chance with other roles. 'You don't want to be type-cast,' he says. We're sitting in the back room of the pub. Lady

Bracknell has given him the boot and, for that reason, none of us can risk being the last to be left alone with him. 'You're so old-fashioned,' he says. 'Have you never heard of sexual liberation?'

When I hear the drag of ascending footsteps, the rap-rap-rap at my door, I'm convinced it will be him, Stephen, in a skin-coloured set of gynaecological gloves.

I fortify myself, pull open the door by a crack.

'Crazy!'

Boof! He's wearing an old raincoat, his hair and beard straggly like a stranger from an antique land.

'Aren't you going to invite me in?' he asks.

iii

I maintained to Ardu that I was an eighth Scottish. Our father had a cousin once removed who lived in a castle in Scotland and had a miniature of Mary Queen of Scots in a cabinet drawer to verify that this was one of the countless castles where Mary spent the night. When we lived in Newcastle, we used to stay up there for odd weekends. The place was run as a religious guest house; there were gongs for meals and prayers. We slept in a round tower with thick cold walls and a wardrobe made from a space behind a velvet curtain for someone to hide in.

The castle was so big, we had no idea where our parents were or how to get to them. We knew how to climb the spiral stone steps down; we knew how to leave by the armoured front door and make our way towards the river, where, just before the rope bridge – as far as we were allowed to go – was the summer house.

I was out on my own one time in the grounds and it began to rain, a hammering rain that turned the river, the summer house, the bridge into places I no longer recognized. I knew about Noah's Flood, and every time the rain fell heavily, I thought, *this is it*, the raindrops so heavy I could barely open my eyes. I was lost, I decided, following an entirely different path back to the castle, to a different door, my hair slimy in the neck of my jumper.

'Poor wee lamb,' the lady said, who opened up for me and brought me inside, sat me down on a little padded stool next to the fire, fetched a towel to rub me dry. 'You're soaked through!' she said, rubbing. There was a TV on in the corner of the room. At home we weren't allowed to watch TV during the day. 'You sit and get warm and I'll fetch you something nice and hot to drink.'

I wasn't feeling lost, I was feeling found, the room welcoming as a nest. I sat with my feet on a cushion, a tartan cloak around my shoulders, the black and white flicker of the TV. It wasn't long before I was drawn into what was happening, the music full of passion and agitation. I recognized the story from school: the man whose strength was in his hair, and of Delilah who cuts it off wickedly while he's sleeping. But I didn't know until I saw it with my own eyes that the story was real. Samson wore hardly any clothes. They'd blinded him, his chest streaked with blood, his arms bulging. He stood at the temple between two stone pillars and pushed them apart like curtains. He'd got back his strength! The gateway collapsed, great chunks of stone bobbing down the steps.

'We've split up,' I told Ardu, watching his face.

'That's a pity,' he said. 'I thought you two were well suited.'

'You didn't!'

'Darby and Joan,' he said.

'You did not.'

'Miss Prism, eh,' he'd tapped my forehead. 'Not worried you'll be typecast?'

We hadn't agreed on a time, only that he needed a haircut. I cut everyone's hair at home, I told him, any reason I could think of to see him again. All morning, I'd waited in, had arranged a patchwork of newspaper under the chair in the middle of the room; borrowed scissors from Freya.

'Crazy,' he says, when I pull back the door. 'All set?' He shrugs out of his coat. I hand him the small towel to put round his neck. 'You'll need to hold it in place,' I say. He steps forwards towards the newspaper, plonks himself down on the chair. His head at my chest is as big as one of the heads outside the Sheldonian.

'Problem?' he asks.

Where do I start? I take a chunk of his silky hair between my fingers, bring the scissors towards it and snip across, the sound of slicing apples. A chunk of hair falls into his lap. Any moment, I think, he'll tell me to stop, enough. But his big head hangs forwards.

'How short do you want it?' I ask.

'Whatever you think,' he says.

'I'll take off an inch, then, shall I?'

'Get on with it,' he says.

When Mum used to cut our hair, she worked round from ear to ear. I start at the back, use the comb as I've seen hairdressers do, setting the flange of the scissors against its teeth.

'Bakies are envious of my hair,' he says. 'They tell me how fine and soft it is.'

I use the top of my thumb as a rule of measure: as long as I'm consistent, I think.

'Aren't you going to ask me about my holidays?' he says.

'Where are you going for your holidays?'

'Have a guess.'

At the crown his hair is a whirlpool. I part off a section and comb it up straight, bring the scissors level, slice. *Give me the head of John the Baptist on a plate!* I'm radiating heat.

'Go on,' he says.

'Skegness? Brighton?'

'Ardnamurchan,' he says, rolling the word out because I'd never have guessed.

'Where's that?'

'West coast of Scotland,' he says. 'As far west as you can go. Mother's bought a place out there.'

'I want to go to Scotland,' I say. I'm at his front and I stop, the scissors and the comb separated.

'Don't look at me,' he says, and he flicks a lock of hair from his thigh. 'The girl I take home will be the girl I marry.' His breath stirs the tiny fibres of my jumper.

'You done, Crazy?' he asks, suddenly impatient. 'My head's stiff.'

'Hang on.' I comb a fringe over his thick brows.

'Oi,' he says. 'Watch my eyes!'

'Have you got a parting?' I ask.

'What d'you mean?'

'Does it fall in a particular direction?'

'I thought you knew what you were doing?'

'It's a perfectly valid hairdressing question.' I make a show of casting an appraising eye; stall by taking a finishing snip or two from the hair above his ears, which are damson at the tips.

'That'll do,' he says. He pulls away the towel, shakes it, gets to his feet and, tetchily, starts brushing himself off, reaching under his collar to the back of his neck. On the mantelpiece my father's mirror is propped. He walks over, crouches down to find himself in it, turns his head, one side, the other: 'You get what you pay for, I suppose,' he says.

iv

Our father didn't approve of taking photographs of us and they are few and far between. There's one of me taken from behind on a swing over the river to show how big my bum was; another that documents one winter at the cottage, our yellow piss-holes in the snow (we were encouraged to pee in the garden so that the bucket in the outhouse didn't fill up too quickly). Amelia sends me a copy of one of the rare ones that shows our faces, the original of which she keeps on her mantelpiece.

I remember the moment exactly: it was taken at the castle, the last time we were ever there. I am eight or nine, and it's of the three of us, three sisters, lined up outside the dented leaded windows of the summer house. The photo is black and white, but I see the colours quite clearly: Rose in the lemon and green Cinderella dress that was the first dress I remember; Amelia in one of the Railway Children dresses Mum made us, looking wistful as Phyllis (the goofy-looking sister, which was her part); and me in the orange polo-neck jumper bought with birthday money that year.

We'd not been primed, as children are now, to pose for the camera. My sisters are looking, seriously, elsewhere when our father clicks the shutter. I'm the only one who catches his eye, looking at him in exactly the way I might look at myself, a secret sharer, smile half-breaking.

What a strange thing now to be standing in his shoes. Not for the first time, that shiver of recognition (*you're just like him!*), except that he is gone, nowhere to be seen, and here I am in his place, alone, and it's as if she's been waiting all this time for me to turn up.

There you are, she says.

I recognize her hands, the fingers and thumb formed into two beaks that seek each other out. *I recognize your hands*, I tell her.

Tell me what's happened? she asks. *Do you live in a house? Do you have children? What are they like?*

I could show her all the stuff, trawled and gathered from the seabed, dripping, stinking of salt and sweat, but it seems unkind when everything is ahead of her, and she has the luxury of not knowing how it might turn out.

I remember the summer house, I say. *It was the opposite of summer inside, stuffed with old autumn leaves.*

Tell me something I don't know, she says.

7. Casual Fruition

December, 2017

It is the end of term, and my third visit to the surgery in five months. I've tried everything: drunk cider vinegar, bicarbonate of soda; bought pills on the advice of the boy in Holland & Barrett, Black Cohosh, Agnus Castus, Oil of Evening Primrose. I look up improbable yoga solutions on *YouTube*, have to stop and start the machine, stop and start while I try to get the position right. By the time I go to bed it's impossible to put myself into any shape that the pain, like a trickle of water, won't find out. I lie on my back, on my side, I pull up my knees, get up under the duvet on all fours, curl around the hot-water bottle. It builds in the day from almost nothing. I've learned to put my ear to the track; hear it coming, a distant nagging down the line, knowing by now that whatever I do to try and head it off – feet up, paracetamol – it's the night train and doesn't stop.

'What does it feel like?' the first doctor had asked, and I make a point the next time it comes along to pay attention. Here it is, at its worst: like a gunshot, a hole through my left side, wide enough to pass a small hand through.

Is it really that bad? I ask myself, once it's gone. The trouble is that I am too good at forgetting, and by the time I get an appointment the pain is only an after-image, a report.

With a noncommittal smile the receptionist acknowledges that she's remembered me, her dark fringe and heavy black eye-make-up. I sign myself in at the gadget on the wall. Birth date, name. There's an old man with a conspicuous hearing aid, propped forwards on his walking stick, staring into space. In the corner, by a box of toys, a toddler looks up for a second, his face glazed with snot, oblivious to the indignity of the nappies which sag from under his belly. He's trying to pass a wooden bead along a plastic-coated wire, whining because the toy appears designed to thwart him. I take a seat along from his mother, opposite a woman in leggings and a sleeveless top, a tattoo of a swallow above the strap of her sandal. When I catch her eye, there's a flash across her face: *none of your fucking business*. The toddler's mum is flicking through one of the dog-eared magazines, takes up another, thicker one, and passes through it like a fan. I hold onto my elbows. Our names come up in red lights on a running dashboard above the reception area. I keep a hawkish eye, thinking, if I miss my name, I miss my chance. *Ms Feaver for Dr Kearns.*

At the end of the corridor she holds the door open and follows me in. She's a locum I haven't seen before, young and brusque. 'I feel silly,' I say, sitting down, 'but it's happened twice in the past month.'

'How long does the pain last?' she asks.

'A couple of days.'

When she asks me to characterize it, I'm ready. I tell her it's like the worst kind of period pain; I tell her about the hole in my side.

'When was your last period?'

I have to admit I can't remember.

'Three months? Six months?'

'Maybe six.'

'Ah,' she says. She is fresh-faced, wears a wedding band below a row of tiny diamonds. I imagine that she's newly married, that her young husband is a comfort when she returns home from work.

'How are your bowels?' she asks.

'I wondered if it could be IBS?' I say. I'm talking too much. She pulls a laminated chart from her top drawer. 'It would be odd to develop IBS in middle age,' she says. 'Have you ever seen this?'

Bristol Stool Chart. I haven't.

'Looking at this chart, could you indicate the usual shape of your stool?' she asks.

It takes a moment to translate that word, stool. *Have you done a poo? Have you wiped your bottom?* I understand that we are grown-ups but point like a child towards the top of the chart, where words are printed next to pictures: one is 'sausage', one is 'snake'.

'Constipated?' she suggests.

I'm wondering if she thinks I'm making it up or making a fuss because there is nothing else in my life to make a fuss about.

'I see you were given something for anxiety last year?' she says. 'Did it help?'

I am apologetic. 'I didn't end up taking anything,' I say.

'So, you're not feeling so anxious?' she says, smiling positively.

'I think I feel anxious all the time,' I say, and laugh.

'Would you mind if I had a feel?' she asks. 'If you could pop up on the couch?'

I sit up on the paper sheet, pull my legs round and up, making sure that my shoes hang clear of the edge. She holds her hands over me for a moment. 'Would you mind lifting your top?'

I pull up my jumper and the shirt from my skirt band.

Her hands when they touch me are cool and gentle. She presses one on top of the other. It's both a shock and a comfort, and a shock that it is such a comfort. I clench my stomach.

'Feel anything?' she asks, working her way round below my ribs. 'Try to relax,' she says, the peculiar tin-warmth of contact, skin on skin. If I relax, I think, I will cry, and she will regret it.

'Any discomfort?' she asks.

'No,' I say, and bite the inside of my lip.

She gives a final pat. 'You can tuck yourself in now,' she says.

I sit up and involve myself in pushing the shirt ends back into my skirt, pulling my jumper straight.

'Well, I don't feel anything that would give us cause for concern.' She is back at her desk and typing as she speaks. 'But as it's been going on several months—'

'A year,' I say.

'I'll refer you to the hospital. They can take a proper look.'

'Thank you.' My eyes fill, and for a moment I am the man who loves her, full of radiant adoration, ready to slip the heels from her tired feet.

ii

Lisa was in the year below. By the time I got to know her properly I was in my third year and she'd gravitated to the small group of us who weren't rowers or hockey players or

Christians, identified by our refusal to join in. We shared a big ramshackle house up the Kingston Road, Freya and me, Freya's boyfriend and two of his friends. Ardu, they'd learned to regard with deep suspicion. *You were ga-ga*, Freya told me once it seemed Ardu was safely off the scene. And I had to admit that I was, *had been*.

But Lisa was a new and willing confidante. The boys were only jealous, we could agree. Someone like Ardu, someone cleverer, older, more sophisticated in the world, who was never going to give them the time of day. Lisa was no stranger it turned out to unrequited love, and, though she'd never met Ardu, from what she'd heard, she said, she could understand the attraction.

It was Aidan who let it slip that Ardu was back, Aidan, who was full of bitterness because, without even trying, Ardu had got a First, and secured himself a place to do the MPhil that, by rights, should have been his. He'll never stick it, Aidan predicted.

Lisa couldn't contain her delight when she came to find me. 'I'm sure it was him,' she said. She'd seen him in the porter's lodge. 'Scottish accent? Dark, curly hair?'

I grabbed her arm. We knew by looking at each other that it was fate.

We took a torpedo-sized bottle of cider with us when we went to find him. He was living in the new block, on the staircase where they put graduates. It was only nine o'clock, though it was black outside and felt like midnight. Rain hammered the Perspex of the tunnel. We bundled through the heavy fire door. The stairwell smelt of pine disinfectant. There were shower units on each half-landing as we climbed. On the third floor, in the metal holder outside the door, his name was typed. My stomach lurched to see it in print. Lisa took charge and tapped the door. Rat-a-tat. If it had opened, the ocean might have fallen through, the bottle of cider would be a lifebuoy that I clung to.

But there was no response.

'Let's wait,' she said, convinced she was speaking for us both: we could just as easily talk on the stairs. We took turns to take swigs from the bottle, whose heavy liquid occasionally misfired down our chins. It was past eleven when eventually below we heard a shouldering-in. Lisa gripped my leg; we held our breaths, aching in our guts from suppressed laughter.

A fumbling progress, slow, addled. The silky top of his head reared from the half-landing. I can never quite believe it when he's here, climbed out of the trap door of my head.

'Hello!' we said in a kind of terror.

His head hinged backwards. 'Crazy! What are you doing here?' He was good-natured, climbing up, barrelling against the door.

'Waiting for you,' I said as if it had been only days since we'd last met.

He sniggered, patted himself for a key, lifted a finger: 'Ah,' felt around to his back pocket, broke into a smile. 'Here,' he said. 'Here it is.' He drove the key towards the keyhole, chasing it with his stooped head. It took a couple of attempts before he had it, and we could follow him inside. 'Come in,' he said, 'why don't you?' throwing up his hands and flumping down on the bed, lying back. 'No,' he said, thinking better of it, rising onto an elbow.

'Where've you been?' I asked, showing off.

'Where've I been? Out,' he said.

'You've been drinking.'

'Drinking? Well spotted. Drinking.' He moved his head as if he were looking for something but had little hope of finding it. 'Who's this, then?' He held steady.

'Lisa,' Lisa said.

'Pleased to meet you. Lisa.' He bent a little from the waist, held out a hand semi-seriously. I'd never seen him acting drunk before. It was comical, made me feel proprietorial, as if, for once, I was more grown up than he was.

'Don't know what you want to do,' he said. 'But I'm ready for my bed.'

Was he suggesting we could stay?

'Well,' he said, 'make your minds up. In or out.'

Lisa was grinning conspiratorially. All the things I'd ever said. The blinds made vertical stripes of the window, pitch black outside and raining still, handfuls of pebble-dash against the glass. It was me who had the long ride home.

'We'll stay,' I said, because it occurred to me that there was nothing to stop Lisa staying on her own.

'Well,' he gestured vaguely. 'You two have the bed.' He lumbered over to the seat and pulled at the two rectangular cushions, pushing one to the top of the other to form a mattress on the floor. Sitting forwards, he unlaced his boots, threw them under the desk, shrugged out of the big coat, which he shook out and spread over the upper part of him. 'Night, night,' he said, hunkering down.

Lisa was full of the adventure, the two of us together. She set to getting undressed, slipping off her shoes, pulled down her black ski pants, her skin so pale it shone, her hard, flat stomach, bony hips. There was nothing for it but to follow, unzipping my skirt.

She wriggled over towards the wall; I climbed in and lay parallel, tucking the duvet around my back. We shivered. It was a single bed and difficult not to touch, our breathing out of sync. I couldn't imagine ever being able to sleep like this. Perhaps she'd realize what a silly idea it was, decide to head back to her room? But I couldn't be the one to suggest it. The darkness crackled with rain, the wind a foghorn in the tunnel below. The night was slow as a ferry crossing, getting wider, longer. If I slept, I'd fall from my perch; I couldn't afford to be off guard. I was alert, too, for the slightest movement from the floor. At any moment he might decide to insert himself and it would be a game of *roll over*.

When light eventually arrived, it came through a sieve. It must have been seven-ish, Lisa's breathing more alert than it had been.

'You awake?' I whispered.

Ardu was bunged up, snoring in his throat, the coat pulled from him like a net.

'What time is it do you think?'

'Must be seven, eight?'

Lisa twisted round. 'What are we doing?'

The paper-and-comb of my breath.

'I'm getting up,' she said.

'Okay.'

She sat on the edge of the bed, reached for the pile of clothes, put on her T-shirt, the black polo-neck.

'Did you sleep?' I asked.

'A bit,' she said. 'You?'

'Not much.'

She was standing, pulling up her ski pants. 'You coming?'

'In a bit. I'm going to try and get more sleep.'

'Good luck with that,' she said, making a line with her eyes from the floor to the bed, smirking. 'Okay, I'll see you later, shall I?' stuffing her bare feet into her shoes.

The door shut behind her with a sharp click. I opened out in the bed, stretched my legs under the duvet, man alive, the peach-coloured sheets, soft and crackling with static. My lips stuck to my teeth. There was too much to take in. Yesterday, I'd never expected to see him again, and now here I was in his bed, in his room.

On the stairs outside there was a clatter of buckets, the scout.

'Ardu?'

I pushed off the duvet. 'Ardu,' I hissed.

I knelt next to him on the floor, put my hand on his shoulder. 'Ardu.'

He made a growling noise.

'Shall I lock the door?'

'Do what you like,' he mumbled.

I turned the key in the lock, attempting to do so with as little noise as possible, slunk back to the bed.

'Are you awake?' I asked.

I could feel him listening. And then like an earthquake he shifted, the boulder of his back, his head, his shoulders, and before I knew it, he was up, staggered over to the sink in the cupboard, unzipped his jeans. In no time the splash and protracted hiss of pee; he ran the tap, and when he was finished, shunted out of his jeans, came to sit on the edge of the bed. The planks creaked. He moved with his eyes closed as if in sleep, pulling the shirt and jumper over his head, peeling off his socks. I backed against the wall to make room. He humphed and yanked at the duvet as he worked his way in, his great smooth back rearing towards me. I eased from the wall, let gravity take me down towards him, his pores exhaling hops and pheromone, until, in a fug of warmth, I lay fitted around him like a mould, my clapper heart, the bagpipes of our joint breathing.

I lay as still as I could, until the light in the room turned harsh and insistent, shouts from the tunnel and from stairwells, the knocks and whooshes of plumbing.

Eventually he stirred, turned over on his back, opened his elbows in a stretch I dodged. He groaned, did a double-take. 'What the fuck are you doing here?' yawning. Then, 'Lisa,' he said, as if remembering, tasting.

He slid his feet to the floor, pushed himself up and leaned out over his lap cradling his forehead. 'You took advantage.'

'I'll get up,' I said, 'if you move.' I set my hand on his shoulder and climbed over him like a stile.

'Ah, that's better,' he said, and for a split second I glanced the purple squash of his balls, his flaccid penis. He pulled up his knees and lay back into the bed, shook out the duvet. 'Lisa,' he said, as if he was dreaming. 'She got a boyfriend?'

'No.' My body tightened.

'Perhaps I'll ask her out sometime?' he said. His eyes were shut, the fixed smile of an effigy. It was a game of snakes and ladders. I clenched my jaw against the hundred-mile racing of my brain. How stupid I was. Of course he'd fall for Lisa. How could he not? I couldn't bear the torture of it: why had he come back?

I reversed the film: that dive into water, sucked up, flown to the apex of the pebble's mouth: the sitting out on the stairs that now seemed a hundred years ago, a time when everything had been going forwards instead of back, back to the hilt of the small black pebble before it had ever suggested itself as an object fit to be flung.

'*Lisa Grimshaw?!*' the Professor had asked. We discovered we'd missed each other by a year at Oxford, and that Lisa, who'd been a good friend of mine, was now a good friend of his.

'Ask her if she remembers Ardu,' I'd said.

The Professor, in his usual spot in the big armchair by the window, has a bag of jelly babies on his lap. 'Who's Ardu?'

'He was at college with us. He's my daughter's father.'

'Ardu? Where's that from?' He pops two jelly babies in at once.

'Persian. His father's Iranian, mother from Glasgow.'

The Professor stops chewing, purses his lips. 'Oo,' he says, tossing his head, 'he sounds *peng.*'

The warmth of his interest. 'Ask Lisa,' I say. 'She'll remember. He was like a bear.'

'A *bear?!*' he says, excitedly. 'Where does he live?'

'Outside Glasgow.'

He pops another sweet. 'What does he do?'

'Nothing,' I shrug, 'as far as I know.'

'How does he live, then?'

'He used to gamble. But anyone who ever met him thought he'd be a writer.'

'Why?'

'He talks about books. And he *looked* like a writer, I suppose.'

'Does he write?'

'Who knows?'

Though the Professor and Ardu were unlikely to meet, I felt as if I'd brokered a meeting; they consorted in my head, and it seemed by the association that I was marginally more interesting to each.

'What's Lisa up to?' I'd asked.

'She's a lawyer; plays football.'

'She was in a team at Oxford,' I said. I told him the story about the three of us and the bed.

'And you were terrified she'd run off with your boyfriend,' he said, sneering.

'He wasn't my boyfriend then.'

'You had no idea about Lisa?' he said, disbelieving.

'It didn't occur to me.'

'Queen Victoria,' he said. 'Poor Lisa.'

'We were friends!'

He'd finished the jelly babies, scrunched up the packet and took careful aim at the bin.

'Do you think Ardu might be gay?' Lisa had asked, quite seriously.

It was the last thing I would have thought. 'You mean,' I said, laughing, 'because he doesn't like me?'

'I think you make a good match,' she said.

'Do you? Really?'

'His loss,' she said.

In any case, he'd disappeared, and his disappearing seemed the best thing that could happen.

But it was only a week or so later that, again, he reappeared.

'Crazy!'

I was outside Blackwell's, unlocking my bike. My heart ballooned.

'How are you? Where's your sidekick today?'

'She's in the library,' I said. 'Sorry to disappoint you.'

He burst with laughter, watching my face, his whole frame shaking. 'You're far too easy to wind up. Come on, Crazy, I'll buy you a drink. You look as if you could do with one.'

iii

The bungalow was half an hour's bike ride out of town, just before Iffley village, set at the end of a cul-de-sac, the middle in a group of three. Ardu had moved out of college, couldn't stand the students. The doorbell was a suburban ding-dong. A figure gathered behind the pitted glass, and in a moment, he was standing there in his bare feet. He looked puzzled.

'I've brought my Milton,' I said. 'You said you'd look at it with me.'

He weighed this up, peering out into the road as if someone might be following me. 'I'm cooking,' he said. 'Take your shoes off,' turning to go inside.

The other rooms radiated from this hall, which, apart from the square of glass in the front door, was windowless. I left my shoes where I found his, under a small table with a telephone, and followed him into the kitchen, sat down in one of the stiff yellow chairs.

'How did you find me?' he asked.

'Aidan,' I said. 'He gave me directions.'

He huffed, turning to his task. It was a novelty to watch him doing something, the careful way he stripped bacon from its rind, his knack of cracking an egg against the bowl with one hand. '*Carbonara*,' he said, pronouncing the word with Italian flourish. The pan sizzled and spat as he added the pasta he'd drained at the sink, prodded and stirred. When it was done, he shoved me a fork. We sat at the Formica table. 'Delicious,' I said, sucking up a length of spaghetti, a joy to be cooked for by him, a kind of miracle that we were eating this food together. Yet it allowed me to imagine how ordinary and possible a life with him could be.

In the hallway outside, there was movement, a coughing and spluttering. A moment later a skinny old man appeared, wiping his hand against the ribs of his polo shirt.

'All right, Fred?' Ardu had raised his voice. 'This is a friend of mine. We'll be out in a minute from under your feet.'

The old man had a fuzz of unshaven hair on his chin. He didn't acknowledge me, muttered something indecipherable.

We ate quickly, and as soon as we were finished Ardu gathered the plates, ran them under the tap. 'All yours, Fred,' he shouted, the old man wandering in circles from the cupboard to the kettle.

'Shall I put the kettle on for you, Fred?' he asked.

There was a single bed in Ardu's room, a table at the window, with the Art Deco lamp I recognized from his room at Osney. The army bag was on the floor, clothes spilled from its opening. On top of the bookshelf by the door, there was a small collection of library books, a Collins Dictionary, a dimpled beer mug. There were no chairs.

'So,' he said, dropping down to the bed, 'what are you reading?' I brought out my copy of *Paradise Lost*.

'Let's see.' He took the book from me. 'I bet you've not looked at Book Four?' he said, flicking through. 'Here we are. How about this bit?' he said.

I was tipping towards him to take a closer look.

'Read it out,' he said, pointing.

I read:

'Here Love his golden shafts imploies, here lights
His constant Lamp, and waves his purple wings,
Reigns here and revels; not in the bought smile
Of Harlots, loveless, joyless, unindeard,
Casual fruition—'

'Stop,' he said. 'Casual fruition? What can you say about that?'

I'd been concentrating so hard on reading, 'harlots' was the only word I'd taken in. Casual fruition: 'Sex?' I said.

'Okay. What about that word "casual": where does it come from?'

I floundered.

'Cado, cadere, cecidi, casum,' he said. 'You did Latin, didn't you?'

'To fall?'

'Good. To fall. So?'

'I got a D for Latin.'

He ignored me. 'Notice how the Fall, although it hasn't yet

happened, is here in the language, and how it's connected with fruit, "fruition": there's no getting away from it.'

Sometimes when he told me things, I felt I didn't know anything. *Annihilating all that's made*. I wanted to take the lid off my head and let him fill me up.

'That's enough,' he said, slapping the book on the bed. 'Let's get out. You owe me a drink.'

When I was with him, any thought of consequence flew out of the window. I was perfectly happy to let Milton go. All I could think was how to extend the moment, my brain wired like a cat, a feral cat who had no idea when next she'd get a chance to eat.

The pub was lit with little red lampshades and bulbs in the shape of candle flames. We moved through to a back room where there was a fire, and next to it an elderly but handsome man sitting alone at a table. He was in a dark overcoat, looked Arabic, I thought, or Indian.

There was a settle on the far side of the fireplace which Ardu made for while I went to fetch us drinks. At the bar, a wait and a pecking order. By the time I came back, the settle was empty. For a moment I thought that Ardu had played a trick and vanished. But where the old man had been sitting there was now a small group, and Ardu ensconced among them. I stood with the drinks in either hand, hoping he might come away. There were two women, an older woman in shapeless dark clothes, and a younger, more beautiful: black eyes and long black hair.

'Jane,' Ardu said, though he made no sign of moving. The others nodded and smiled in my direction. Ardu held out a hand for his pint. 'Bring over a stool,' he said. I put my glass on the table and brought the low stool from the fire, which I set up by the old woman's knees. She touched my shoulder as I sat down and smiled at me emphatically in a way that made me think she didn't speak English.

Fatima was the name of the beautiful woman. She had two small children and was having trouble with immigration. The old man's face was beady with intelligence. He had taken to Ardu, whose surname identified him as Zoroastrian and Parsi. They were all from Iran. What a lucky meeting it was, he said, setting a hand to Ardu's shoulder. He asked him about his father.

'He came over here to study,' Ardu said. 'Before the Revolution. He worked on the buses to pay the fees, enrolled in a college in Wales. He met my mother on his first job.'

'Met a girl,' the man said, flicking his eyes to the ceiling. 'And he never went back?'

'They tried; drove all the way there in two cars with me and my younger brother, who was a baby then. They were hoping to sell the cars. Stayed six months. But it was difficult for him to get set up as a doctor. And Mother missed Scotland. So they came back to where her family was, had my sister. And then—', opening his hands to acknowledge what they all knew, 'it was too late.'

When the old man spoke, everyone listened, his tone mellifluous, his English considered. He talked about the importance of living in the now, not in the yesterday, not in the tomorrow. The younger woman was glossy-eyed. And I'd never seen Ardu so earnest and respectful. The old man, it seemed, had tapped into the roots of him; I'd been afforded a private and secret glimpse of a history that ran deep between them. Their two voices were a rumble that began to wash through and over me. I was drinking whisky macs and the fire and the warmth of ginger and whisky melted me so that, although they conversed in English, I felt suspended from the conversation, happy as the old woman was too, flashing her gold back teeth. It was like being allowed as a child to stay up late at an adult party, this moving image of a future world, and imagining the unimaginable, yourself alive and in it.

'The pink house, the colour of pomegranates,' the old man was saying. They were agreeing something, taking alternate hands and drawing together, patting each other's shoulders. Now the old man set his hand on the top of my head, a seal of approval I felt long after we'd set off into the night.

The lights are off in the bungalow. 'We'll have to be quiet,' Ardu says.

By the time I get back from the bathroom, he's undressed and is in bed. It's cold in the room. I remove my clothes quickly in the dark, down to my knickers, and climb in behind him.

'Fuck's sake, you're cold,' he says. I snake an arm across his hips and pull myself into the radiators of his thighs.

'I liked those people,' I whisper, my breathing shallow. I want to savour every moment, amazed that I am here again, his skin against mine, part whale, part tattooed Indian.

'They've asked me over,' he says.

'Did they ask me?'

'Did they ask you? I don't think so.' I can hear his brain. 'What did you think of the widow? Fa-ti-ma,' he pronounces dreamily.

'She seems too young to be a widow,' I say, defensively. 'I liked the old man. I liked what he said.'

He snorts, dismissively. 'She's living with them until she can sort out her status.'

'Will she stay?'

'That's the idea. They've asked me round. To the pomegranate house.' He shifts, belches. 'Anyway, it's late. Stop talking. Go to sleep.'

How can I sleep? We're on the high sea again, the waves of his breathing. I dip in and out where air and water meet. The blackness is vast and there is no land in sight, no knowing where or how we will fetch up.

And then I can't pretend to be asleep any longer; I am wide awake, the dead silence that is born of two or three in the morning. He is stirring and I can't tell whether he's asleep or not. I give his arm a shy kiss, and jump when he speaks, tutting, turning himself as if on a hinge. 'Prostitutes don't kiss,' he says.

Prostitutes? Is that what he said?

He doesn't say another word, but his movements are sure, purposeful. He pulls me over to the middle of the bed and he's up above me, but I can't see his face properly. I need him to speak, otherwise I don't know who or what he is. He takes my arm firmly and pulls it up above my head, there's a plucking at my side, the elastic of my knickers. His chin is a drawbridge and it is raised.

'What are you doing?' I whisper, and it sounds ridiculous. He ignores me. My heart is thumping. I have come off the pill, that is one thought, but it isn't the main one. He remains above me tensed through all his limbs and I have no idea what's in his head. I freeze, and then, as if he has thought better of it, something gives: his arm collapses and he falls back against the wall. I manoeuvre myself to the edge of the bed, stiff as a post.

'You didn't think I was serious?' he says, shifting onto the flat of his back. 'My God, if I wanted sex, you'd be the last person—'

He turns again, throws out his bottom and pulls at the duvet so that I hang out over the side. I am delirious with sleeplessness, hardly daring to touch him but needing to hear his human voice. 'Can I ask?'

He grunts.

I wait, shiver.

'Spit it out,' he says.

'It's like being at the dentist—'

'What the fuck are you talking about?'

'What is *this*?' I say, breathing into the space between us, willing him to capitulate, to swallow me up.

Suddenly, he rears, and in a vicious whisper he says, 'I've had enough. Whatever it is you've got going on in your head: forget it.'

My heart shrieks.

He yanks at the duvet. 'I don't know what it is you think you're doing, but it's not going to happen,' he says. 'End of story.'

Part Two

The Rose Garden

Part Two

The Rose Garden

8. The Rose Garden

At the age of fourteen, Valerie Fletcher, a schoolgirl from Leeds, heard John Gielgud over the wireless reading 'Journey of the Magi'. At once she was in thrall and decided then that she must somehow get to meet the poem's author, declaring by the time she left school that she intended to apply to the publishing house where he worked to become his secretary.

In 1949, at twenty-three, she stood outside his office waiting for him to call her in by name: 'Miss Fletcher?'

He was sixty-one, scrawny in his three-piece suits, a long hawkish face, pursing his lips around a cigarette. He looked to the others by then to be beyond love, a dry old stick. And yet. Perhaps it's the hair, a little thinner, but slicked and flattened in much the same way it had been as a boy on the terrace in Gloucester, ears exposed and cupped to the world, to the sound of the sea, the gypsy moths batting at the glass of a lantern.

Outside the heavy door to his office she is content to bide her time, her fifty-five words a minute; will come when required to stand at the corner of his desk, her comfortable flesh, her pale powdered face and sharp, bright eyes, the swish of something going on under her skirt, the lining of her skirt, which makes a sound, he begins to notice, like the sea at Gloucester, reassuring, a sound, in spite of himself, he begins to yearn for, calling her into his office more than strictly necessary, watching her approach, or looking askance, and, better, *hearing* her approach. Powder and swish, and dense flesh hugged by a skirt, by a blouse with two points that are like the rocks he's hunted down in a small sailing boat, breaking the ocean's surface off Cape Ann, the Dry Salvages. Sweet garden roses. The powdery smell is rose, those soft white thighs, a pillow from a metaphysical painting, in which to bury your head, to soften the blow, to cease.

It takes nearly ten years to pluck up the courage to ask her, though from the minute she'd set foot in his office, she tells him, she would have said, *yes*.

London, Autumn, 1989

Every morning we rise en masse on the escalators at Holborn Tube, office workers, lawyers, nurses, chamber maids, heads-down along Southampton Row, where those of us who work in Queen Square turn off at the brolly and souvenir shop, into the narrow alley of Cosmo Place, ignoring the church on the right where Ted Hughes and Sylvia Plath got married, turning left, past the weathered tables of the Queen's Larder, along the railings of a handsome Georgian house to purpose-built offices of concrete and plate glass – a place where in the War a bomb must have dropped. I climb the steps, push through heavy glass doors, past the diagonal display of recently published books, two black leather sofas, towards Betty from Harlow, who sits in front of the switch-board with the po-face of one whose job it is to arrive here first.

'Morning, Betty!' I can't believe my luck: Betty acknowl-edges me as one of the girls.

I press for the lift and enter in, let the doors slide shut upon me. Through the wardrobe, through the looking glass, I am born again, everything ahead of me, and *going up*.

The office on the fourth floor looks out on a latticework of fire escapes and funnels. Although there's no air conditioning, we keep the windows shut against the effluence of curry and cabbage steaming from the backs of hotel and restaurant kitchens.

The room is open plan. There are five desks, each of us boxed in behind piles of books and manuscripts, wire filing trays, big electric typewriters. Mary has bagged the best position, by the window, and she has the only computer, a monitor which takes up most of her desk. She swivels in her chair in an oversized white shirt, black leggings.

'Have you got a boyfriend?' is the first thing she asks, and I have to admit I don't. I don't have a boyfriend, and, worse (it will become apparent), I don't have a life, living again at the bottom of Mum's house in the room with the cat-flap and the nocturnal ins and outs of at least three cats.

Mary is engaged to be married; she has a large wedding to organize and the social lives of a dozen dear friends. The personal call is a new concept to me and will quickly find me out. 'Good laugh,' she says regularly as a way of signing off. She works for the editorial director, Richard, who stands tall and thunderous in the doorway until Mary rings off. 'Speak to you later, Smell,' she says, calmly, as he stalks over.

'Have you sent that bike?' he barks. 'Have you sent off that fax?' But he can never catch her out – *never apologize, never explain* – her desktop is immaculate.

Polly, who sits between us, is rarely at her desk. It's she who's taught me how to use the tape machine, ears plugged in, feet on the pedals to send the tape forwards, back. *Letter to, fax to.* She's skinny as a rake in her polka-dot dress, darting about with nervous energy, a gash of red lipstick.

In the far corner, a girl who keeps her back turned from the rest of us, works away assiduously. She brings back baked potatoes for lunch to eat at her desk, so that when we return in the afternoon the room smells of rabbit hutch. 'Rabbit' is her name. Sometimes she will disappear altogether, caught once in the basement loos crying with frustration because she appears to be the only one to take this job remotely seriously.

'Frigid,' Neve snorts. Neve has a carrot-coloured bob. She gives the impression of being half-asleep, slouching like Christine Keeler over the back of her chair. It's her job to catalogue and oversee 'the basket', the wicker pram on trundle wheels into which the daily sack of unsolicited manuscripts is stowed. Once a week she escorts the basket up in the lift to the Boardroom, where, summarily, the five of us will sit around and, on little more than a sniff at the typescript – stale cigarette, Parma Violet – scrawl a deliberately illegible signature on a rejection slip, refill the basket for Neve to transport back down to the post-room.

Neve's swagger is loaded, so weighed down with sex that sometimes she tells us she has to go to the Ladies to relieve herself. As soon as she's gone from the room, Mary and Polly down tools.

'Urgh!' Mary says. 'How did she get his address? I'd bloody kill her. Does she know you know?'

'I wouldn't mind,' Polly says, 'but they were the tackiest kind of knickers.'

'What did Freddie say?'

'He says she's pathetic.'

'Totally.'

Freddie is Polly's boyfriend. He plays in a band and is said to look like Jimi Hendrix.

I feel their eyes on my back.

'Do you smoke?' Mary asks.

I turn to look over my shoulder. 'Sometimes,' I say, knowing how important it is to distinguish myself from Rabbit.

ii

Once upon a time Mrs Eliot had been one of us, sending a postcard to the other girls in the office from her secret honeymoon with the boss: 'I have so much to tell you on Monday so prepare to do no work!' Several times a year she'll come into the office for Board Meetings and we'll discover her in the Ladies on the fourth floor. Her dresses appear to be made from silken flags; she has a candy-floss puff of blond hair, rosebud lips. We communicate through the mirror above the sinks. She calls us 'dear' and talks in the present tense of Tom and Wystan in the South of France as if they're flat out on sun-loungers, waiting for her to return with cocktails and hats.

Prepare to do no work!

Most of the time the work is a kind of serfdom, shackled to our typewriters, to the tapes that run instructions into our ears, a battery from our fingertips of electronic fire.

But every now and again there's a party upstairs and we inveigle our way in as waitresses, drinking as we work our way round, pinching bottoms, plunging our arms into the icy water in the Chairman's bath for more Sauvignon Blanc. Five floors up, it's like being on an ocean liner, rollicking, roaring, ducking out to grab some air on the thin strip of the balcony, where the firework lights of the city in all directions tell us there is nowhere else to be but here. None of us married, none of us with children: we are footloose, and – though it doesn't do to admit it too openly – this is family.

The Chairman, he's the Daddy. Though he looks like Milan Kundera, whose photograph hangs outside his office, he professes not to read books. He featured once in an ad for Martini – a fast car, a white suit; loves an impresario, a film director; to be recognized by a certain generation of pop star. Every now and again he takes a select group of us out for a treat. We go to the Groucho Club, or the Ivy, places we'd never have gained entrance to on our own. The gaggle of us out on his arm, we can't believe our good fortune. He orders far more wine than we can drink. 'Don't look round,' he'll say, raising a hand to the corner where Salman Rushdie is taking lunch. We eat posh fish and chips, and he grills us on our so-called love lives.

'You're such a puritan,' he says because I have no boyfriend to speak of. I remind him, he says, of his strait-laced sister. And when I walk, he says, I walk like an ape, like a lesbian.

At four o'clock, he packs us into a taxi to send us back to Queen Square, where, in the foyer, Betty greets us purse-lipped. We can barely walk, hold ourselves upright against the wall, collapse hysterically at her unforgiving face into the open arms of the lift.

Down in the basement, where every morning we go to collect our post, there's a stationery cupboard and two windowless loos reserved for emotional crises. On Valentine's Day the place is awash with disappointment or envy. Betty says she feels like a florist.

Nothing has arrived for Mary all morning, because he has forgotten, because he is a thoughtless bastard, because, *That's It! Wedding's Off!* Mary has locked herself in the loo downstairs.

But the biggest and the best of the bunch is saved till last, delivered just before Betty closes shop. 'He loves you!' Polly calls, wrestling with the bouquet out of the lift. 'You know he does.'

The caretaker lurks down there, small and bald-headed, in case he can be of assistance. He has contacts in the SAS and knows a man, he says, who can take a man out, or can mark a man for life with a tattoo of ink. It is he who, when the masturbator strikes – peeking naked from the dingy curtain of the hotel window opposite – stakes out our room to see what the fuss is about, gets us to avert our eyes, and within thirty minutes, like a ferret down a drainpipe, has got it sorted.

I have never lived life more in the now. Now, and now and now. Too much happening to think forward or back. Everything is part of a story that unwinds as fast as it is written. Even the redundancies and the man with undertaker hair who explains the pyramid system, the concept of natural wastage, this is a drama that plays out like a Catherine wheel upstairs and mostly doesn't touch us.

But someone has been sending authors' post to the wrong addresses; has been using the post-room for private purposes to send off pieces of underwear to other people's boyfriends. Neve is the only casualty from our office. The rest of us are relocated to a smaller but airier room overlooking the garden square, where, on the opposite side, once the trees have shed their leaves, we watch the strip-cartoon of hospital windows, reminding us, should we need it, that we are the lucky ones.

iii

Sometime in that first year I move in with Polly to the flat she shares off the Holloway Road. For a while she is between boyfriends and I tag along on her coat tails. It's painfully apparent that I have no life of my own, whereas she is Audrey Hepburn in *Breakfast at Tiffany's*. In the Old Red Lion, everyone is pleased to see her, to buy her a drink. We sit on scaffolding boards in a room upstairs to watch a friend of hers, a woman from Glasgow, doing stand-up, a brawny girl you wouldn't want to be on the wrong side of. Her act turns on the difference between 'a wee cough' and 'a week off'. 'Have you got a wee cough?' we regale each other all the way home, doubling up, and when we tell Mary the joke in the morning, it will seem, finally, as if I have arrived.

Polly and I have been invited together to the first of what proves to be a rash of weddings. Two of our former workmates, flung together by redundancy, are getting married. The venue's no more than a mile or so from the flat and we set out that morning with plenty of time to spare.

Polly's shoes are too tight, and she clutches my arm for support. It's a perfect spring day, a gentle breeze, the sunlight in our eyes. We're halfway along Upper Street when a voice calls out ahead of us: 'Crazy?'

Sometimes my brain plays tricks: I've seen Ardu, for instance, in the back of a man climbing the escalators. Two bodies saunter out of the sun towards us. 'Crazy!' The voice is nasal, northern. Blackpool Kevin! And next to him, more substantial and more exotic than I can ever depict, is Ardu.

'Where are you off to?' Kevin asks.

Polly looks to me to make the introductions, intrigued: she has never met anyone I know. 'This is Polly,' I say, as Ardu runs his eyes over her.

'Nice to meet you,' she says, a little curtsey.

'Crazy!' Ardu says. 'Time for a drink?' Polly looks at me with a grin on her face: always time for a drink.

We cross the road to the Hope and Anchor and sit in one of the big arched windows. Kevin goes off to the bar. My heart is running so fast I can barely hear what Ardu is saying: a job Kevin thinks he can get him. 'Anyway,' he says. 'Boring. What wedding?'

Polly explains about the redundancies, how we're going out of solidarity. Kevin sets down a tray of drinks. 'Doubles,' he says, winking. 'Isn't Clare in publishing?' he asks Ardu.

'Mon? Far as I know,' he says.

'Where?' I ask.

'Covent Garden somewhere?' His vagueness makes me wonder if he still sees her. 'What's it like, publishing?' he asks, pronouncing the word with his usual disdain. He stuffs a cigarette paper with a dab of tobacco, pulls it expertly into line.

Polly and I make faces. The schtick in the office is that everyone wants to be doing something else.

'Polly wants to go into theatre,' I say.

'Crazy did a spot of acting once,' he tells her, sending his tongue along the cigarette paper.

'Did you?' Polly asks.

'She was a natural, I heard,' he says, pressing the paper down. 'A natural Miss Prism.'

'Thanks,' I say.

'Another?' Kevin asks, collecting empty glasses in his fingers.

'Go on,' Polly says.

'Is there time?'

'Plenty of time,' Polly says.

'Where are you staying?' I ask Ardu.

He twitches, takes a drag. 'At Mon's,' he says, 'for the time being.'

It's a blow.

'She's my landlady,' he says, watching my face. 'It's convenient: close to the bookies, the station.'

This time the drinks have straws in them. Polly's eyes are bright.

'I'm going to give up booze when I'm thirty,' Ardu says, helping himself to his pint.

'When I'm forty,' Kevin says, 'I'm going to be a teacher: I'm going to give something *back*.'

'Give up fags someday,' Ardu says, raising his glass. 'Crazy! Cheer up!'

'Flower!' Kevin says, more kindly.

'Cheers,' Polly says. 'Well met.'

I can't help myself. 'I thought you hated London,' I say.

'See how it goes,' Ardu says.

'Shit,' Polly says. She's pulled the wristwatch out of her pocket. 'I should have checked.' She makes a clown's miserable face. 'Sorry,' she says.

I've been relying on her, which is a mistake.

'Take it easy, Crazy,' Ardu says.

Polly sucks on the straw until her cheeks cave in.

When we arrive, an hour late, there's a little boy sitting on the steps in a cream suit bawling his eyes out. The ceremony's over, the boy's mother tells us. I wonder if it would be better for us to disappear.

'No one'll notice,' Polly says, yanking my hand. There's a seating plan on a blackboard in the entranceway, and she uses her finger to find our names. The lights in the hall have been dimmed, the tables in their white cloths shine like lily pads and in the corner a three-piece band strikes up. A girl in a sequinned dress begins to sing too close to the mic, 'Nights in White Satin'. I follow where Polly leads to a table with two conspicuously empty chairs.

My head is filled with sand. I take hold of the tablecloth to lower myself. The man opposite is someone I recognize, Tony, the man from the Production department. There are tears running down his face, but he's pleased to see Polly. 'This song,' he says, explaining, 'it does my head in.' Polly slips from her chair to perch on his knee, smoothing the grizzled hair above his ears.

When we get home, Polly makes us whisky and hot water. 'It's good for you,' she says. 'Come on.' Her room is up in the attic.

'I still think they must have noticed,' I say.

'Drink up. Hair of the dog.'

'I feel terrible,' I say.

We sit on the floor in front of the gas fire, which she lights, the smell of sulphur.

'So,' she says. 'Ardu.'

I pull a weary face.

'Come on. It's obvious he likes you.'

'Is it?'

'Of course he does.'

I'm like a dog after a ball. But it's hard to come up with anything concrete. 'Nothing really happened,' I tell her.

'Really?'

'He said I was obsessed, that all I did was projection.'

'What does that mean?'

The blue flame is turning orange. 'I think it means that I was using him to displace something else.'

'He fancies you!'

I flare at the thought, but squash it. 'He doesn't. He told me that. And anyway, he's moved in with his girlfriend.'

'I thought he said she was his *landlady*?'

'He'll never admit to *girlfriend*.'

'Oh, fuck him,' she says, losing interest, digging about in her bag for fags.

'I can't believe we missed the wedding!' I say. 'I think it might be the worst thing I've ever done.'

'No one should get married,' she says, tartly. She lights a Marlboro and sticks it in my mouth to shut me up.

I reach for it and suck too hard, cough.

'They're all shitheads,' she says, cheerfully. 'You do know that?'

We draw on our fags together, blow the smoke out in a stream. She is watching me, smiles, draws herself up straight, cross-legged. *Look at me*, she seems to say, sets her hands on her knees, the fag drooping from her fingers, a thin trail of smoke. She shuts her eyes, as if to meditate. 'Fuck. Fuck. Fuck,' she begins, speeding up. 'Fuck, fuck, FuckFuckfuckfuckfuckfuck-fuckfuckfuck. Fuck. Fuck Fuckfuck,' slowing down. 'Shit. Shit. Fuck. Fuck,' like the blades of a helicopter coming to a stand, 'fuck.' Her eyes pop open, gleaming. 'Try it.'

9. Wreckless

The last time I'd seen Ardu was that night with the Iranians, when it had looked unlikely that I'd ever see him again. In the morning I didn't go home; I hadn't wanted to admit to the others where I'd been. Instead I'd headed straight into college, trying to reconcile the encounter in the pub with the disaster of what had followed.

The journey was mostly downhill, and I'd biked recklessly, with no heed as to how I'd stop if I needed to, content if it came to it to run under a bus. It was lucky, I suppose, that the route so early in the morning was relatively clear. I parked my bike outside the porter's lodge. As I passed the windows to the library, the usual suspects were already stationed at their posts, and I kept walking, heading instead for the Fellows' Garden.

We never knew whether the garden was out of bounds. It was generally empty, the rarefied atmosphere of precision-cut grass and colour-coded beds. In the far corner, by a bank of purple rhododendrons, there was a bench glistening with dew, and I took a seat, stretching out my legs, closing my eyes.

And then, a disturbance: from out of the rhododendrons two blackbirds came hurtling onto the lawn, two dark fists, launching themselves at one another, scattering dew as they fought, so intent they didn't notice me. I watched the furious contact and then the backing-off, and as I watched, some instinct told me that although it looked like a fight, it was in fact a stubborn kind of courtship, all bluster and fuss. I took it as a sign.

There was a pattern to how things went with Ardu. After the annihilation, which was wipe-out, there was numbness, despondency, and then, in a prickle of smarting, the tender, amoebic shoots of new life pushing through. It was possible from this vantage to see the process as a cleansing one, a burning off of old vegetation. And having survived it – knowing I was in some way better equipped, more resilient – it wouldn't take long before the story would kick in again.

Before our father left, Mum had started writing poems. She would bring them to him like a cat brings a mouse (her metaphor), to show how much she loved him, to get him, she imagined, to love her in return. Instead of doing any work that day, I wrote a poem about the blackbirds, labouring over it so long and hard – it was fourteen lines, it rhymed – I had it by heart. In the first flush of enthusiasm, I left it, handwritten, in Ardu's pigeonhole, innocent or arrogant enough to think that a poem might tip the balance.

Because I can still recite it, I see it for the *jejune* thing it is. But I can't dismiss it as a piece of evidence. *What I wanted you to be*, the poem ends,

> *Had taken refuge darkly in a tree*
> *And left me wreckless in the scattered sea.*

Ha! I wasn't stupid, I'd known it all along, the discrepancy between what I wanted Ardu to be and who he was, but such was my faith in story, my belief in my own powers to shape it, that the more hopeless the situation, the bigger and more enduring I imagined the pay-off would eventually be.

But *wreckless*, what did that mean?

The word had arrived as if from nowhere. Although the prevailing sense was the recklessness with which I'd ridden my bike, the spelling insisted on that 'w': *wreckless*, which, in the context of a scattered sea, meant, presumably, 'without a wreck', a shipwreck. At the time, I was happy enough with the pun, imagining, fondly, how Ardu might approve it. Only now do I see how intimately the two meanings are entwined: that feeling of recklessness the result of being without a wreck, as if my life depended on it.

But what, then, is the wreck?

I see in a flash that it is Ardu, or, more strictly, the peculiar conflation of Ardu and story: *what I wanted you to be*. The story was mine, but it depended entirely on his being there, and without it, without him, I was lost: no imperative or occasion for daring, for love, ambition or any number of those qualities by which we test ourselves as human.

ii

The subject this week is Life Writing, or, more precisely, 'writing from life'. There's a general nervousness among the other seminar tutors, who wonder if such a week is really necessary, or appropriate, even, in what purports to be a *fiction* module. They worry that it will merely give licence to students to reveal too much about themselves – anorexia, self-harm, sexual fantasy: who knows what they might come up with?

But I have so little faith in fiction at the moment, particularly in relation to my own capacity to produce it, that, quite the opposite, I look upon the week as a reprieve. And isn't all writing life writing? I argue.

Perhaps I am just covering my back. Perhaps my problem all along is that I've never understood or recognized the difference between story and life: my desire to write yoked inextricably to my desire to make things right – *to right it!* – a deeply inculcated belief in the restorative powers of story, which, in spite of any and all evidence to the contrary, will ensure that everything turns out happily in the end; it must. At the very least, I tell myself, writing is a chance to make something out of life so that it doesn't appear entirely to be the wreck it is, like a Piranesi print of the Roman ruins, a souvenir of the Grand Tour.

Meanwhile, something has been going on down there in the hold, some slow-working mutation, a sinister creaking of floorboards, the popping of metal rivets. I have been making a series of dives and raids, which at present seems to be the only way I have of keeping going, a way of writing, *faute de mieux*, because not only is writing a condition of my employment, it is, like a kind of graffiti, a condition of my very existence. What or who else is to say I was ever here?

Wreckless. I was reminded of a poem I once read, easy enough to dig out: I knew it was about diving and about a wreck. 'Diving into the Wreck', it's called, and now I read it again, I can only wonder whether, in reading it the first time, I was blind. Or has it lain in my subconscious all these years only waiting for the right moment to be realized? (*For now we see through a glass, darkly; but then face to face: now I know in part; but then shall I know even as also I am known.*)

This is how it begins:

> First having read the book of myths,
> and loaded the camera,
> and checked the edge of the knife-blade,
> I put on
> the body-armor of black rubber
> the absurd flippers
> the grave and awkward mask.
> I am having to do this
> not like Cousteau with his
> assiduous team
> aboard the sun-flooded schooner
> but here alone.

Here alone: a shock runs through my nervous system, because it is an aloneness I recognize, one that talks to itself aloud in the mirror. The difference is that, being addressed, I am the mirror image, quite ready, where I wasn't before, to slip into that 'I', to zip up the diving suit of black rubber.

On a whim, because I'm curious as to what they might make of it, I take copies along to this week's class, the Life Writing week, get them to read out a stanza in turn. The poem is a marvel, I think, hearing it again; it's about everything, truth and reality, story and history, about who gets to write it and how, and yet voiced – this, the most marvellous – by a woman who's able to describe herself as an insect crawling down a ladder.

'What do you think it's about?' I ask when they're finished reading.

'Is it about *Life*?' one suggests, drolly. There's a pair of boys who are friends and rivals and unusually eager to please. 'About *Writing*?' the other supplies.

'All right. How?' I ask. Apart from the two boys, getting questions answered can be like drawing blood from stone. I tell them who Cousteau was, that I used to watch his expeditions as a child on the TV, the beautiful gang of half-naked men who'd go diving for sharks or sunken cities. 'What do you think the significance is,' I ask, 'to the poet being "not like Cousteau", but being alone?'

Ellie is studious and thoughtful but doesn't contribute unless directly addressed. 'Ellie?' I ask.

She starts and takes a moment to collect herself. 'Because she's not used to doing it?' she says.

'Why might that be?' I ask.

She is nervous. 'Because she's a woman?'

'What do you think?' I try to involve the others.

'It seems real but not real,' another girl says.

'What makes it real?' I ask.

'The flippers, the mask?'

'What about those *absurd* flippers?'

'Is she slightly taking the piss?' the first boy says, and then reddens. Both, however bold, wear V-necked jumpers their mothers might have bought for them.

'There's a disarming self-awareness, isn't there,' I say. 'An ability to laugh at herself and how she looks in this get-up.'

'Isn't it a metaphor?' one of the boys asks, as if to get us back on track.

'What makes you think so?'

'Well. The diving, the going down, the wreck. Is *that* life?'

'Anyone else? What about that ladder?' I ask. I read the second stanza out for them again:

> There is a ladder.
> The ladder is always there
> hanging innocently
> close to the side of the schooner.
> We know what it is for,
> we who have used it.
> Otherwise
> it is a piece of maritime floss
> some sundry equipment.

I get up with my red marker and draw a ladder on the whiteboard, stand back. 'What might this ladder be if, as she suggests, it's more than some piece of *sundry equipment*?' There's a rush to avoid my eye. 'What about the shape of the poem?' I suggest.

'Is it a ladder?' one of the boys hazards.

'In what way?'

'The length of the lines? The length of the poem?'

I scan the room. 'Anything else about the ladder?' Silence. '*The ladder is always there*: doesn't that feel a bit odd – superlative?' I ask. 'What kind of ladder is *always* there? What kind of ladder hangs *innocently*? Are we included in the *we* who know what this ladder is for?'

I am losing them. I try another tack. 'Does anyone know that poem by Yeats where he talks about the "foul rag and bone shop of the heart"? The place, he says, "where all the ladders start"?' I draw an elongated red heart at the base of the ladder.

'Metaphor,' the boys say almost in unison because they've been trained to spot and label such things.

'I wonder what metaphor and ladders have in common? What do they allow us to *do*, for example?'

'To travel between things?'

'Like what?'

'Go down? Go up?'

'And if we were to think metaphorically, where might the ladder be taking her in the poem?' I count the seconds, my back turned from them because sometimes it's easier if I don't look.

'Into the past?' one says, and, happily, I write it down: 'the past'; 'Into herself?', another, which again I transcribe. Everything is put cautiously as if I am a very tricky customer to please.

'What does the diver tell us she has come for?' I ask.

They shuffle their pieces of paper.

'To explore the wreck,' the mousey girl says.

'Read us what the poem says,' I say.

The girl takes a moment to find her place, then reads: *'the thing I came for:/the wreck and not the story of the wreck.'*

'Go on,' I say.

'the thing itself and not the myth.'

I draw two circles on either side of the ladder. 'What do you think the difference is between the thing itself,' I point at one circle, 'and the myth of the thing?' The drawing, now I look at it, has turned into a lewd piece of graffiti. Hastily, with my sleeve, I rub it out. I've approached this all wrong. I should have split them into groups from the start.

There was a picture book we had when I was little, about

filling a bath for four children – it could have been us. The bath doesn't stop filling; it fills until it spills over the top, and then it floods the room, the house, and the children find themselves bobbing about in an emerald green ocean. At some point in the story, they sink to the ocean floor, and the sea rises up before them to form a vertical wall; the children have to push with all their might to hold it up.

'Is it, like, history?' This is the girl with orange lips, who speaks with the drawl of extreme boredom. 'The stuff, like, we're told about stuff?'

'Yes, good,' I find my balance, 'as opposed to?'

'Stuff that, like, maybe she can see for herself?'

'And why might that be important?'

'Because it isn't mediated,' one of the boys again. 'It's first-hand.'

'What does mediation do?' I ask.

'It dilutes it?'

'In what way?'

'Maybe it isn't as immediate?'

Ellie puts her hand up. 'It tells us how to read it?' she says.

'Good. Very good.' I find myself welling up when there is a spark, the least sign of something catching on, something I hadn't even thought of. I swallow. 'And what sorts of things have a bearing on how we read?'

'Power,' she says. She's on a roll. She has her finger on the page and she quotes, '*the sea is another story/the sea is not a question of power*: it's like the rules are different here.'

They are waiting for me. I come back to my seat. 'Good. Brilliant.' A scepticism has begun to settle in their faces; I don't have long to win them over, to arm myself from the crime of irrelevance. 'I think,' I say, deliberately, 'that this poem is a useful way of approaching what it means to write from life. It gives us a blueprint that shows us how valuable and possible it is, how necessary, even, that we take responsibility for and tell our own stories.' My chest is tight. 'It's about being brave, about being alone, about being prepared to go out of your comfort zone into an element you may not be used to. It's about confrontation, with yourself, maybe; with the stuff or the people around you; about telling the story in the most clear-eyed way you can. Which is why' – I can see my way out now – 'it's important to prepare. That is what the metaphor is doing: this is not you, it's a version of you, a more professional version, one who has equipped themselves for the job in hand, which is to explore the story as you find it, to report back, without worrying in that moment about anything else.'

The sheer volume and over-the-head weight of water has begun to bear down, I hear it buffeting my ears, a deafness to whatever is happening in the fake light of the room. 'So,' I say, grasping the edge of the table as I get up. 'Before we do any writing, five minutes. While I'm gone, I want you to turn yourself as the poet does into an investigator of some sort – a diver, astronaut, adventurer, you choose. Think specifically about how you'll dress and what key pieces of equipment you'll need; be prepared to talk about it. I'll be back.' The heat rises like an underwater volcano. It's hard to move in this constrictive suit, or to see where I'm going, the flip-flop of my feet.

I'm too far away from my office to return to it, but in the corridor find a kitchen to which they don't have access, shut the door behind me, run the tap in the sink and cup water in my hand to slurp up. A wash of sweat breaks along the hairline of my brow: *the wreck and not the story of the wreck*. Never mind the story, the thing itself, the carcass, the bones . . .

Do you know what they're talking about in there? It won't take them two seconds to work out:

THE THING THAT IS A WRECK IS YOU.

10. *I Know Where I'm Going*

'Crazy!' He has found me out at work. Mary and Polly are agog: they can tell by my tone of voice that this isn't an author, but a personal call.

'Who was it?' they ask, eagerly, when I put the phone down.

'Ardu,' I say, and my face cracks at their interest.

'Ardu?!' Polly says.

'Who's Ardu?' Mary asks.

'Told you,' Polly says.

Something must have happened with Clare; I don't know what and I don't dare ask. The last time I'd seen her was years ago, after their finals. She'd come to meet them with a bag of cherries, a white scarf in her hair, like a girl from an Impressionist picnic. They were sprawled on the grass, covered in foam, stinking of beer. Aidan was trying to find out how Ardu had done, and Ardu was being cryptic, winding him up. After a while, she'd given up offering the cherries round, had risen to her feet and taken off. Ardu hadn't batted an eye, and I remember in a rush of hopefulness realizing then that I had something Clare didn't: no squeamishness about drink or smoking or being ignored, I could put up with anything.

This time Ardu is staying with Blackpool Kevin, who has a flat in Gipsy Hill. Though it's a pain to get to, I can't resist the invitation to meet them after work, if only to prove to Polly and Mary that some part of my life is my own.

The word has got out. Another friend of Ardu's from Oxford, a tall, skinny Welshman, has brought a friend of his to meet him: a Welshman and a Yorkshireman. When I turn up and find them in the Colby Arms, they're in full flood, chain-smoking, the two men, sitting in their raincoats, telling Ardu earnestly about the comedy script they're working on, which they intend to submit to the BBC. *Maybe he could come in with them?*

'Jones the steam,' Ardu calls the Welshman behind his back. They spar in a competitive quick-fire and I'm not expected to contribute. I sit and listen like a moll; drink and smoke too much, staying long enough to make a night of it, but not too late to miss my train.

'It all kicked off when you left,' Kevin tells me later in the week to explain why the two men don't turn up again. At Last Orders, he says, because Ardu had been taking the piss out of them all night, the Welshman tipped beer over his head, and had to be dragged away by his friend. Ardu was asking for it, Kevin admitted, the only witness later to the shopping trolley incident, a trolley let loose at the top of Gipsy Hill to go crashing into cars either side of the road, setting off alarms, bringing people out into the street in their slippers and pyjamas.

The next time we meet, it's just the two of us, and Ardu appears chastened. He sniffs, has a cold, he says, buys me a drink, tells me the Welshman is a windbag and he's had enough of him. Which happily enough I take to mean he hasn't had enough of me.

'That script they've been writing,' Ardu says, 'they've been fiddling with it since we left college. *Years*. Two men in a bicycle shop. Can you imagine anything that pair has to say that you'd want to listen to?'

It's easy to agree. I have spent the day, I tell him, at the photocopier, copying thousands of Philip Larkin's letters. 'I think I must have ozone poisoning.'

'Did you get a chance to read them?'

'Only to see how different he is with different people. The ones to Kingsley Amis: he goes on about porn. But he's nice to the women.'

'Skunk was a sucker for Larkin.'

I don't admit that once I thought I'd marry him, the man who wrote 'An Arundel Tomb'. I say: 'I recognize that kind of' – trying to find the word – 'rebarbativeness?'

'Rebarbative?' he says, as if I've caught a fish in my mouth. 'What does it mean?' he says.

In order to fix it, I picture the word as a castle on a wave-swept island. 'It's peculiar to men,' I say. 'A sort of intellectual armoury that's used to dismiss everything and everyone?'

'Crazy!' he says. *Well done!*

The next round, I tell him about Mary, how she's planning her holidays. 'It's like a military operation,' I say. 'Twelve of them. She's on the phone all day.'

'Where?'

'Italy. They're renting a villa.'

'Why aren't you going?'

'I'm not a friend like that.'

'So where are you off to?'

This is the rub. 'I haven't thought,' I say.

'I'll be up at Sonnadh at the end of the month.' *Sonnadh*: it sounds like a bell, a call to prayer.

'Have you seen *I Know Where I'm Going*?' I ask.

'The English Bakie and the laird? Years ago. The Corryvreckan whirlpool,' he says, flashing his eyes.

'I love that film.'

'You don't say,' his ironic blink.

My heart is racing; we both know I'm on a mission. 'Will your mother be there?' I ask.

'There's no heating in the cottage yet.' His eyes are on me as he tips his glass back. 'I'll be on my own.' He sets the glass down on the table. Is this the moment to ask?

'Could I come?' I blurt as if it's a joke.

He pulls a face, a thinking face. And in I rush: we're friends, I say. If we went up together, you could do your thing, I could do mine. I wouldn't interfere.

He's thinking. 'Okay,' he says, taps his fag. He smiles because I am playing up to the surprise. 'One condition,' he says (and already I'm thinking, I'll do anything). 'You take the Shite-rider up.'

(*If he'd said jump off a cliff?* Yes, I would.)

I've borrowed my brother's Walkman, and it has got so hot with playing, the tape has begun to eat itself. My book is buried in the rucksack deep in the underside of the coach. Nine hours, and I'm too wired to sleep, the smell of piss and burning rubber. The boy next to me swigs vodka from a bottle in his pocket and passes out somewhere north of Birmingham, setting his head for the rest of the journey like a croquet ball against my shoulder.

Ardu will pick me up from the bus station in Glasgow, he says, and we'll spend the night en route at his parents' house.

I've imagined this house, like something out of E. M. Forster – mahogany bannisters, a grandfather clock. And though I cannot hold him to it, I've remembered what he said: *The girl I take home will be the girl I'll marry*. It has the ring of a riddle. Clare has never been taken home, this much I know, and, though the understanding is that I'm here strictly as a friend (that no one in any case would take me for anything else), I wonder whether, without his even realizing it, some tiny part of the spell might be undone.

Standing in the queue to disembark there's a pigeon in my chest. It takes a frantic moment to find him out, but it can only be him, leaning nonchalant against a pillar, puffing on a fag. My knees are jelly, because although he's not my boyfriend, it's me he's waiting for.

'Is that all you've got?' he says. I can't control my face, and a smile escapes him. He takes the weight of the rucksack and I jabber after him about the boy and the vodka. When we reach the car, he throws the rucksack onto the back seat. I let myself in at the front, plug in the seatbelt. Next to me, the bulk of him, rattling the gear stick, his chubby decisive hand.

It's warm in the car, and he winds his window down, rests his elbow in the frame. It takes no more than half an hour to get out of the city, and the air is green and blustery as if we're flying. He points out the nearest town, which appears on a road sign, Cumbernauld, a new town, the place where *Gregory's Girl* was filmed.

'Clare Grogan,' I say, remembering the name of the actress who plays the girl who wins the boy by not being the girl he thinks he wants.

He's concentrating on the road, humphs. 'Piece of work.'

'Did you know her?' I ask, amazed and forlorn too, because instantly I can imagine them together.

'Everyone knew her,' he says, dismissively, peering over his shoulder as he takes a right turn. We're in a cul-de-sac of detached, box-like houses, an estate much like Granny's was, a new house in the seventies. He pulls into a gravel driveway at the very end, a house flanked by tall trees, stops the car. From the side of a garage a dog has leapt to the extent of its chain, barking hoarsely.

'He has to be tied up,' Ardu says, 'otherwise he chases cars.'

The dog is missing a back leg. Ardu calls to him and the dog whimpers and scrapes as he passes. 'Dumb dog,' Ardu says. 'Got himself run over by the postie.'

The house has large, brown-framed windows and Ardu walks straight past the porch at the front, round the side of the house, where there's a sheltered terrace. 'Mother!' he says, full of bluff affection. She sits with her legs up on a sun-lounger, in a sweatshirt, oversized sunglasses, a glass of white wine to hand, which she raises.

'Ardu!' She has her own way of pronouncing his name.

He leans in and plants a kiss on her forehead. 'Mother,' he says, straightening up, 'Jane.'

'Hello, Jane. You're welcome. Pleased to meet you.'

Inside it smells of Granny's too, of furniture polish and ashtrays. In the hall there are A4-size photographs professionally taken of the three children, one in a bonnet, one on his elbows like a seal, and the last, who must be Ardu with big brown eyes, a toddler in a pale blue cardigan.

From behind the slats of the open-tread staircase a man appears. He is slighter than Ardu, a full head of cropped grey hair.

'Faether!'

'Lovely boy! When did you get here?' He holds out his arms as if the arrival has been kept from him. Ardu offers himself up.

'And who is this?' His smile is a grille of teeth.

'Faether, Jane.'

'Jane.' He says my name as if to weigh it, holds out his hand. 'How do you do, Jane?'

'Hello. Thank you.'

Ardu has wandered off through a door, and Faether lifts his arm gallantly to indicate that I should follow.

I recognize the Art Deco lamp from Oxford, the sculptural woman in her flowing robes, and it's the lamp, I realize, from which I'd projected my picture of a doctor's house.

But not this one. The room is rectangular and functional, two modern squashy sofas, a TV, a stone fireplace. But the walls are a saving grace, hung with half a dozen intricate Persian carpets. How beautiful they are, I enthuse. They are silk, his father tells me, and very old; in them are dark forests, deep jewel-like colours, alive with flowers and burrowing animals.

'Two of these, one day, will go to Ardu,' Faether says, and watches my reaction.

'They're beautiful,' I say again.

Ardu has left the room.

'Have you come far?' Faether asks.

'London,' I say.

'London? That's a long way. And you are a friend of Ardu's?'

'We were at college together.'

'You were at Oxford?'

'I was.'

'And what do you do, Jane?'

'I work for a publisher.'

'Publishing?'

From another room, we hear voices, and Faether suggests we go and join them.

'Mother!' he says, as he enters the kitchen. Ardu is nosing into the fitted cupboards; his mother is at the table, her ashtray and her glass of wine.

'Are we having tea, Mother?' Faether asks.

On her feet she moves in small jerky movements.

'Lovely boy,' Faether says, hovering. He can't keep his eyes off his son.

'What are these?' Ardu pulls out a bulk-wrapped pack of Benson & Hedges. 'Not your usual, Mother?'

'Jazmine brought them from the airport for me, Ardu.'

'Did she have a good time?'

'She's here for her tea. You ask her yourself.'

'Mind if I take one, Mother?'

'Help yourself, Ardu.'

He tucks into the cellophane, rips the edge with his teeth.

'Lovely boy,' Faether says.

Faether makes rice, beautiful Persian rice. No one can make it as well as he can. It involves soaking and cooking just so, the pan lid wrapped up in a tea-towel, twenty-five minutes precisely.

'The rice is delicious,' I say as we sit down to eat. I tell him I have never tasted rice as good as this. Koresh, a Persian recipe made with prunes.

Jazmine is more Scottish than Persian, her accent gentle, lilting, her cropped hair sensible. She likes The Jesus and Mary Chain and is going out with a fireman, a big man who will protect her.

'When did you come to this country?' I ask Faether.

He is happy to be the centre of attention and tells the story they've heard a hundred times. 'I came with gold coins in the heels of my shoes,' he says. 'I came to study. Ended up in Wales. Do you know a Lady Erskine? She took an interest in me. I was working on the buses. As a conductor.'

'He looked like Omar Sharif,' Ardu says, 'didn't you, Faether?'

Faether savours the comparison.

'Apu,' Jazmine calls her brother. 'Apu, can you pass the ketchup?' The name softens him.

There is wine at the table and there's beer. Ardu has switched to wine. He opens another bottle.

'What do you think Ardu should do?' Faether asks, suddenly.

I glance at Ardu, who half-closes his eyes.

'He could have been anything,' Faether says, 'a lawyer, a barrister. Think how good he'd be as a barrister!'

'All right, Faether,' Ardu says. He's filling his glass; he fills his mother's too.

'Did you know, Jane, Ardu got the top marks in the whole of the country? He was offered a place at Oxford when he was sixteen?'

'Mother!' Ardu says, raising his glass.

Faether bares his teeth in a smile. 'Do you know a *Skunk*?' There's a glint in his eye.

'Aidan Skelton? Yes, I did,' I say.

'Oh, you did?'

'He was at college with us.'

'Oh, he was?'

'Has everyone had enough to eat?' his mother asks. She is on her feet, and Jazmine rises simultaneously to clear away the plates. I make a move to help. 'Sit down, Jane. You're our guest.'

'What is *Skunk* doing now?' Faether asks.

'I've no idea,' I say.

'You've no idea?'

'I don't know him now.'

'You don't?' He has a congratulatory smile on his face.

'Did I tell you, Faether, Jane's family have a castle?' Ardu asks.

'A castle?' he says, eyes round.

'Tell him,' Ardu says.

I am hot with the attention. 'It belonged to a very distant relative,' I say. 'Cousin of a cousin of our father's. We used to go sometimes when I was little, when we lived in Newcastle.'

'Did you ever see a Lady Erskine?'

Ardu rolls his eyes.

His mother has lit a cigarette and offers one to Jazmine.

'Tell Jane how we found the cottage, Mother,' Ardu says. 'Tell her whose idea it was.'

'Yes, Ardu, it was yours.'

'I've been telling Mother for years: that timeshare of hers was a bloody waste of time.'

'It needed a lot of work, Jane,' his mother says. 'It was a mess. No bathroom, no toilet.'

'We had a cottage in Northumberland,' I say. 'It didn't have water. We used to go there every school holiday.'

'How did you wash?' Jazmine asks.

'The swimming pool in Hexham. Though once, Mum took us to the river to wash our hair. It felt like brain damage.'

'That explains a lot,' Ardu says.

'Ardu,' his mother says. They laugh, I laugh.

'What is your work?' Faether asks for the second time.

'She works for a publisher,' Ardu says.

'Books? You like books? Do you publish any Persian books?'

'Why would she publish Persian books?' Ardu says.

'I work on poetry,' I say.

'There are wonderful Persian poets,' Faether protests. 'And what does your father do?' he asks.

'He's a critic.'

'I see. And he's married again?'

Though it is sugar coated, I feel the barb; I wonder what Ardu has told him. 'He is,' I say.

'Is this the first time you've been to Scotland, Jane?' Jazmine asks.

'She's stayed in a castle,' Ardu says. 'Keep up.'

'I love Scotland,' I say. 'We used to come to Edinburgh, in the festival, for my father's work.'

'Oh, the festival: thoroughly enjoyable,' their mother says.

It's Bijan, Jazmine tells me, who's the good-looking brother, who gets mistaken for the boy who strips to his boxers in the

Levi's ad. Remember? Their parents have gone up to bed, and we're at opposite ends of the sofa, less formal, waiting with mugs of tea for Ardu to come through.

'Ardu says you work for a paper?' I say.

'Aye, I'm a sub.'

'Do you like it?'

'It's not bad. Crazy hours, though.'

Ardu saunters in with a tumbler of whisky. 'Oh,' he says, 'okay, so, little-Miss-sub-editor, answer me this—' He slumps in their father's armchair, hitches up a leg. 'What's the difference between imply and infer?'

Jazmine sips her tea.

'Imply—', rolling his hand to cue her in.

'Leave off,' she says.

'Ha!' he says.

'What?'

'Why don't you admit it?'

'Admit what?'

He snorts. 'That you don't know the difference.'

She is a statue of herself, eyes fixed. And then she says, quietly, 'If you want me to say I'm stupid, I'll say it, save you the bother.'

'Your call,' he says.

She's up on her feet, and before I know what's happened, she's walloped him in the head, and the mug is on the floor, a bolt of tea across the carpet. She storms out of the room. My heart is stopped. In the hall she grabs her coat, her keys. She shouts upstairs, her voice strained. 'Night, all.'

The room is a vacuum, a black reflection on the TV screen.

'She shouldn't be driving,' Ardu mutters. And then he, too, is up on his feet, raging. 'This would never have happened if you hadn't been here. Why the fuck did I listen to you? You're a fucking nightmare. I don't even like you! If it wasn't so late, I'd send you packing.'

Though he's gone from the room, his portrait is still here, an after-image of muscle and thunder. The *I-know-nothing* furniture, the fireplace with its scorched chimney breast, those fathomless carpets. The house is crouched above me, ear to the floor.

I retrieve the mug from the carpet, its raised white lettering that spells *Jazmine*; set it down with a clunk on the coffee table, a clunk that proves I'm still here. The alternative is the street outside, the dingy cul-de-sac that leads nowhere: at this time of night there's no reason for anyone but rapists and murderers to be about. And what would I say if I was picked up?

If only I can hold my nerve, take control of the winch and haul us back to normality: this is a house, after all, with all the trappings of respectability. The stairs creak just like Granny's. On the landing, I pass his parents' door – not a peep – and around the corner I head into the bedroom where my rucksack has been put for me, the guest. I return to the bathroom, past his parents' door again with my toothbrush. The light activates a fan. A minute for my teeth, rinse, spit. But my bladder is less easily fooled, still in shock, I have to coax, to whistle. It's okay, I say, this is a house with a mother and a father who is a doctor, three children. I feel my way back along the corridor and into the bedroom, push shut the door. The bedsheets when I get to them are pulled so tightly across, I have to prise my way in, lie flat. He must have been hurt by the mug, I tell myself. It would have been a shock. And embarrassed, too. I hear my sister, Rose: *Cool wet grass, cool wet grass*, the mantra of firewalkers as they skip across hot coals, which, because it makes us laugh, we recite for each other in times of crisis.

The last time Rose and I were at the cottage, all the bourgeois things that Mum had wanted – a bath, a loo, central heating, a cooker to replace the tiny Baby Belling – they had all come to pass: the woman our father had secretly married wasn't going to spend any time there otherwise.

The baby, too, had been a surprise: they hadn't told us until it became impossible to disguise, and then our father had been sheepish. 'A sister,' he said.

I was a student; I'd agreed to come up in the summer holidays to look after the baby because his wife had to be in London for work. She was our half-sister and she was a baby and I wanted everything to be all right. I'd always looked after the babies, priding myself on how good I was at it.

It was my fault that we were here: it was me who'd persuaded Rose. After only a few days she is disgruntled, blaming me because she knew it would be like this: the cottage she says has been taken over, and, whatever I say, we don't belong.

Our father is working as always in his room, tearing at his hair, jabbing the typewriter in flurries of attack. The baby is just over a year old and I've taken her out in the backpack for a walk, intending to show her the places down by the river, the troll's bridge, the mill. But halfway down the track she starts pulling my hair, snatching and tugging so that it hurts: she thinks it's a game, and only shrieks with laughter when I tell her to stop. This is not the bonding I'd envisaged, but a kind of demonic punishment. She won't go down in the cot when we get back, and I leave her to shout.

'I won't be doing that again,' I say, finding Rose still in bed, the shutters unopened. She's reading an old copy of *Just William* with a torch, her chin set. I turn on the light and she squints with irritation. 'I don't know why we're here.' She is fourteen and she's bored and wants to go home.

At the end of the week, his wife shows up and makes a big fuss of the baby. I offer to help make supper, standing by the stove as she stirs the soup, confiding, trying to describe what the trouble is with Rose. 'He isn't very demonstrative,' I say of our father.

She looks puzzled, then she beams: 'Oh, but he is! He's terribly affectionate to us.'

She stirs and she stirs, that smile on her face. I should have known that it was we who were the problem.

She is pregnant again, that much is obvious, and I wonder whether she will carry on having babies until she has four, and each of us in turn will be overwritten.

Rose is not speaking. We spend a day keeping out of the house, retreading our old haunts – the reservoir, the graveyard, the river – but there is no evidence to say we were ever here, or that the place gives a toss whether we were or not.

Shortly after we're back, Rose bursts into the bedroom. 'Did you see?' she says, accusingly. 'She's wearing my tights. She must have taken them off the clothes horse. They're Mum's tights. I brought them up with me.'

We sit together on the bed to work out what to do.

'You'll have to say something,' she says.

'They're your tights.'

'Mum's tights.' She stalks out, and not long after I hear expostulation from the living room, shrieking. Rose thunders back into our room. 'She's thrown them on the fucking fire,' she says, tears flying from her eyes. 'I only said, *they're Mum's.* They went up in flames; it stinks of burning in there. Didn't you hear her?'

'We want to go home,' we say; his wife has shut herself in their room. Although there's a week to go before our train is booked, our father makes no attempt to dissuade us. 'As you like,' he says. 'I'll drive you to the station.'

And, in half an hour, without another word, that is what he does.

Morning arrives with clicks and starts. The last thing I remember is shouting down the staircase of the cottage at Ardu, who lifts his face and becomes our father.

Stop!

The motor of the shower gurns. A door is shut and opened, shut. A cistern flushes. In a lull of activity, I creep to the bathroom, send home the catch. The shower cubicle smells of zinc.

Downstairs, his mother is at the table in the kitchen.

'Hello, Jane,' she says. 'Did you sleep well?'

I pull out the chair opposite. She draws on a cigarette, exhales with concentration, fixes a smile. 'Would you like breakfast?' she asks. 'I'll make porridge, soon as Ardu is up.'

'Thank you.' Under the table I'm pinching the crook of my thumb.

She taps the cigarette, glances at her wristwatch, then takes another drag, which fizzles up short against the filter. She squashes the butt into a saucer. 'I'll put it on,' she says, decisively, because something has to be done.

My back is to the door, my neck in a heightened state of alert, a tripwire on the stair.

The silence is punctuated by the clatter of porridge-making, the measured scrape of a wooden spoon on the floor of the pan.

When it comes, I know by the heavy rhythm of descent that it's him. The room swirls.

'Morning,' he grunts, the weight and mass of him behind me as he moves around the table to stand by his mother, watching her stir a neat figure of eight. 'Mother makes the best porridge,' he says, throwing a rope in my direction.

11. Sassenach

When first I began to write in sentences, I got it wrong, writing an 'a' for apple when I meant 'I'. This is partly because 'a' is what I heard: *As a came doon Sandgate,* we used to sing in Newcastle: *As a came doon Sandgate, a heard a lassie sing.*

Long before that, when I was six months old, I lived in Nottingham for a while with Granny Georgie. Mum was at university, preparing for her finals. It was bad enough that she'd got pregnant, but Granny didn't think she needed the added distraction of a baby. Plus, she wanted me for herself. 'God bless,' she said every time I was put down to sleep, 'sleep tight!' She fed me, bathed me, clothed me, blew raspberries into my toes. So determined was she to feed me up that when they came to collect me, they barely recognized me as theirs: I was round as an apple, the apple from the alphabet book which I pointed at and scribbled over with my blue crayon. Granny got Grandpa to come out into the garden with the cinecamera: there, in the dappled sunshine on a brown flecky rug, I've rolled over trying to capture the big green apple, which has been placed just beyond my reach. I lunge, straining with all my might, toppling onto my front. But however hard I reach for it, I only manage to push it infinitesimally away. I try again, this time furiously, as if otherwise – in a leap of understanding – what I reach for will

be lost, as if we are a mirror image, me and the apple. 'Apu,'
I say to a chorus of approval.

We are like Bonnie and Clyde, except that I am no Faye Dunaway,
the sort of woman I imagine he'd drop everything for. He drives
with one hand on the wheel and doesn't mention his sister or
last night, and I am sensible enough to let it go. We stop off at
Asda for provisions: Vimto, oats, haggis, neeps. I concede to
everything he wants, enjoy his housewifely delight in two-for-
one, spotting the yellow stickers of reduction. We're unlike the
regular shoppers, dour and pasty-faced. The trolley to us is a
joke with its dud wheel, and we steer cack-handedly towards the
booze, which has an aisle to itself, wide and glinting. Ardu tilts
his head: this particular malt, he decides, three bottles, four. At
the checkout, though no one bats an eye, it must look as if we're
having a party: a dozen bottles of wine; tinnies stacked in their
stiff plastic wrap, in tartan: this is Scotland!

We have one tape, Van Morrison, and I am up, cross-legged
in the passenger seat, singing along. The song Ardu likes is the
skippy, religious one about souls, so incongruous I tease him
about it, teasing he takes in his stride as if the requirement for
brooding and scepticism has gone.

At the last town before the Highlands we fill up the tank and
take the only road out towards Glencoe. Soon we hit a small
caravan of cars and trucks heading in the same direction, and
it isn't long before we're reduced to tiny cogs, the hillsides
either side of us rising sheer and monumental as iron hulks.

It's a heroic journey, and the final part, to save from going
the long way round, involves a crossing on the ferry from one

peninsula to the other. Though strictly we'll still be on the mainland, by crossing water it feels as if we're crossing to an island and all the magic that being on an island might entail.

When we're deposited on the other side, the road becomes narrow, narrower, single-track, skirting along the long edge of a mirror-surfaced loch, each turn in the road a viewpoint in blues and greens, vivid as a postcard. There seems to be no end to the driving, and if we drove for ever, I'd be happy. But he knows the way, is heading for a particular doorstep. He says, if we're lucky, we'll find what he's after in a bucket.

I've not heard of langoustines before. 'I don't even know what they look like,' I say.

We draw up on the road outside a house and Ardu gets out, disappears into the porch. When he comes back, he's carrying a bulging plastic bag, which he sets down in the footwell of my seat, pleased with himself. The briny smell of the sea rises off it. 'You're in for a treat,' he says.

We head inland, stop for a herd of lumbering rust-coloured cattle to pass us on the road; otherwise the landscape is bare, jagged along the horizon with rocky outcrops. The bungalow is up a pebbly track to the right, not far before the road gives out to sand. He reverses alongside the wire fence, pulls up the handbrake. We've arrived, unload the car, back and forth into a kitchen with its yellowing Rayburn, the smell of soot.

After we've unpacked, we sit out on the concrete apron at the front. There's a ruffle in the air, the sun low down, bowling straight at us from over the dunes, casting a burnished light over everything; sand that's worked its way up into the garden, a scrubland of grass and coils of old fencing. He has the plastic bag of shellfish at his feet, a child's seaside bucket for the shells;

shows me how to pull at the tailpiece, peel back the orange plating from chunky white flesh.

The tweed jacket he's wearing is the one his mother rescued from round the stovepipe when they bought the cottage. Whoever it was must have been a big man, Ardu says, stretching his arms to show how well it fits. She has patched the elbows for him and put a band of leather around the cuffs.

It doesn't take long to settle into a routine. Oats are soaked overnight on the Rayburn for porridge in the morning. Sometime after, we'll head out for a walk, setting off with a knapsack full of tinnies and cheese and onion crisps. In the evenings we'll sit in the front room with its brown-tiled fireplace and read our books. As a child I believed in Jesus, that he would come again. *Suffer the little children*, the caption read in the Bible Stories book, and there I'd be, first in line: he'd read to me, let me sit up on his knee. Ardu is a determined reader and I have to make an effort not to distract him. Attention-seeking, is what he calls it when I interrupt him.

The fourth day we climb to the top of the ridge of rock that skirts the coastline, follow it round, up and down, keeping parallel to the sea, stopping for a break when Ardu decrees. I'm useful as a windbreak as he rolls the fag that is passed between us, soggy from his lips to mine. How thrilling to hear the seabirds wheel and shriek as if we're one and the same – the sea with its razor blue that fuses us together.

Haggis and neaps are what he cooks, and I enthuse, content, I say, to eat haggis and nothing but. He's good at playing games, knows all the trick words: E.R.S.A.T.Z. he spells, arranging his tiles, and grins. The bedroom at the back belongs to his mother. We sleep in the room that's been made out of the roof space upstairs, where on two single beds tight into the eaves our sleeping bags are splayed. I keep my clothes on, breathing a fug of air down into the bag to get warm, waiting for him, the fine stripes of light between floorboards, where below he sits and drinks, conks out on the sofa, so that in the morning his bed is still empty and cold.

It's not until the fifth day that the weather turns, the sky leaden. Even so, it is as likely, he says, to turn again. We set off later than usual, heading inland this time on the plain between hills. It's boggy going. I get stuck, and where he might have stayed to yank me out, he has no patience, marches on.

The rain has set in and he's headed towards one of the old bothies, the rectangle of a doorway, an empty window frame. Rain spatters on a piece of corrugated metal. There's no roof, but a certain amount of shelter. Ardu crouches next to a rudimentary fireplace and I join him there. He pulls up the collar of the jacket.

'I could live here,' I say, cheerfully. 'You in your place, me in mine.'

The muscle in his cheek twitches. His eyes bore inwards. If we wait for the rain to stop, we could be here all night. The rain is my fault. Without a word he gets to his feet, kicks the metal, which buckles where it has rusted. I let him go, but follow at a distance, careful not to lose sight of him.

By the time I get back in, the onions are cooking. Cooking is what he does, and I hope it's a good sign. He doesn't want to talk, which is fine; he's drinking whisky; I help myself to a glass of wine. The pan is jostling with potatoes, the mince bubbling. I go through to the other room, and set about making a fire, twisting sheets of newspaper as he does into doughnuts, a tent of kindling, lumps of coal. I hold a full spread of newspaper over the chimney to help it draw, the fire licking and spitting until there are flags of orange; hold as long as I dare, the paper turning a parchment colour, smouldering, and then, as I've seen him do, snatch it away, sit back on my heels to admire the flames.

He doesn't comment on the fire when he comes through. He has a plate of mince in his hand and points it at me. Goes back for his own, which he eats in the other room.

Barometer is the word I'm looking for. Granny had one by the front door, with a clock face at the bottom with words instead of numbers: Change Rain Stormy.

The scrape of a kitchen chair. My smile is weak. He wraps his tongue around his teeth and takes up his usual spot in the corner of the sofa, glares into the tumbler which he swills on his lap. 'I knew it would turn out like this,' he says, talking as if he's talking to himself.

The walls are lined with planks of chestnut-coloured wood. It's like a barrel, the pressure in the room unbearable; the slightest wrong move and it will blow. I get to my feet, make a point of not looking at him. 'I'm going out,' I say, watching myself moving in the black reflection of the window.

ii

I pull the tweed jacket from its hook, put on his mother's gumboots, hoping that once I'm gone he'll feel compelled to follow. I can hear the churning of my heart, the night air curious, muscling round. I make for the empty car park, its board of instructions like a flag, and then head out. I'll show him the extent to which I've made the place my own, keep going till the tarmac fails, till I reach the dunes, beyond the dunes, the beach, the open sea.

A sea fret balloons towards me with the stench of old sponge; there are no stars. How easy it would be to lose a foot in a pothole, to twist an ankle. I shuffle in the sand like slippers. He'll bide his time, I think, long enough to give me a fright, and then, when I least expect him to, appear from the gloom like a piece of the landscape broken off.

We've been out here in daylight a dozen times: *machair* is the word for this no-man's stretch of sand and marram grass. It's a different word in the dark, *machair*, furry as a jumper I could climb into.

Keep left, further to the left: avoid at all costs the gully with the sheep we found, legs upturned, drowned in its own insulation. This is a test of my mettle. My chest bangs. I rake at sand that gives way, crumbling like damp sugar, scrabbling down a ridge, shin deep, the wind bowling straight in off the horizon. The bay is flat as an ice rink. Above the sea clouds momentarily part and a yellowish glimmer picks out the turn of a wave.

He'll find me, I say, believing it. And the night will disarm us both and knock our heads together.

But there's no sign, of him, of anyone.

Ardnamurchan Point to Cape Wrath. The jacket smells of peat, a kind of magic cloak, I tell myself, and the air blows through me as if I'm not here. What's to stop me walking till I'm up to my neck? *Plat, plat*: I steer a course between tarry patches of bladder-wrack, and, to the left, a bank of rocks asserts itself in the gloom. Something solid to get hold of, cold and grainy. I glance back towards the dunes: no blip, no footfall. Keep your wits about you: I'm on all fours, making for the high spot where I've sat in the day, clambering slantwise, the sea below me rattling its cans.

Here is the place, though, in the dark, more like a saddle than a seat. I take my wrist and hold it, hug my knees round the tops of the rubber boots. He's bound to come, it's human law: that saunter of his, no hurry, his eyes far sharper than mine that will detect me sitting proud on the rock like a thumb. I pray for it like Jonah in the Whale, the sea battering at the door.

In the arms of the jacket, still damp from rain, I smell the ruined cottage. Was that what started it? A switch in the air like a shoal of fish. Later, the panels of the room closing in, the cackle of the fire, its poker.

Let's be clear: you're not his girlfriend – not beautiful or mysterious enough: you're a limpet with your limpet stamina, as if that will ever be enough.

The sea slithers off and then returns, slithers off, then throws its scorn like gravel in my face. Water everywhere, bitter tasting, nothing to prevent me being carried off like a girl on a white bull. I edge backwards and down, barely breathing, drop my foot too soon, plunging into water that spills over the top of the boot. Hours from anywhere, from anyone, not welcome here, a splinter, an icy sock, *Sassenach*, *Little-fucking-Bo-Peep*.

I trip and stumble across ground that rolls like a bolt of flannel, a travelator that does strange things to distance: where there were dunes ahead, now there are mountains. My radar is defunct. There's a fence to negotiate where there was no fence, a ditch. I give up, fold into it, whimper out of wind-shot. If only I could be picked up and carried, the sea and sky a gyroscope of roaring: so this is where you choose to build your house, on sand, on air, on a vacant lot.

Here's the story: I brought it on myself, and no one will come to gather me up, to take me home, tell me everything's all right.

When animals first crawled out of the water, they moved like this: flippers turning to elbows, their tails dividing down the middle to form legs. The process of heaving inland is what changed them. Watch her on her elbows and knees move along the irregular line of the fence. Millions of years pass before she can work out how to be upright. Up she gets.

There's a smudge of light, though she can't be sure she hasn't conjured it. No matter. For want of anything else she follows. And just by walking on her own two legs, she comes to remember who she is.

Never mind the humiliation, I'll throw myself on the mercy of the first stranger. All this, whizzing through my head when I hit tarmac, recognize the sail of the notice board at the edge of the car park. I surge forwards and off to the right, up towards the halo of light that is the storm porch, tripping over my boots, the plastic door shuddering as I manhandle my way inside, stand in the doorway, *here I am.*

He hasn't shifted.

'I got lost,' careful to strip any accusation from my voice. 'It was like *Moby Dick* out there,' I say, trying to get him to laugh.

He raises the glass and tips it towards his lip, sups, lets it drop, swallows.

On my knees I stretch the clumps of my fingers to the fire.

His eyes are heavy. Something flits across his face. But it is not relief, and it is definitely not love. I edit it out.

Part Three

Mum and Dad

12. Mum and Dad

January, 1996

What's the point of a diary? It's a wretched, dismal thing. How many times over the last ten years have I written, *Never Again*?

Ardu is a figment of my imagination.

I am angry with myself for letting myself be prey to him. He is the stuff fantasies are built on. But he plays with me. I know that I do need someone to love me – and I know really that Ardu would be wrong from that point of view – arrogant and surly, too unpredictable and fickle. But at the same time, it is not enough to have someone love you. I need to love as well.

Ardu is a two-faced bastard. I am a silly cow.

Oh Jane, why can't you love someone who loves you?

Ardu is too much like Richard Burton in Look Back in Anger. *How could anyone like that still exist?*

I am supposed to be pleased that although he is charming to everyone else, he is sometimes horrid to me – it shows he respects me he says.

'Premier Sheds?' is how he answers the phone.

'Hello, premier shed,' I say, ringing him from work, normal service resumed.

'Sheddie' is what they've taken to calling him in the corridors, intrigued, because no one has yet met him, this man who sells sheds, who appears, in spite of everything I've said, to be living with me.

He's an expert on cockney rhyming slang, which he has from the old man who hangs around the yard and in the colder months sits on a stool in the shed that is the shed office complaining about his Hampton (*Hampton Wick!*). Hamptons happens also to be the name of an estate agents in South London, and, much to Ardu's delight, the place is populated with signs that proclaim, *Hamptons: For Sale*. The puerile stuff is a cover, I know it is, like a play by Pinter, and I'm good at the game. *Trouble and strife.*

'If I said you were *Mum and Dad*, what would I be saying?' he asks.

'Sad?'

'Nope.'

'Bad? Glad? Mad?'

'Bingo. So, if I say someone's *mum*, it means—?'

'They're mad.'

'Well done.'

His is the ultimate anti-bourgeois stand; he's the only one who has the guts to cock a snook at getting on, working-your-way-up: losers, arse-lickers, suckers, schmucks.

'When are you going to get married,' the Chairman asks, 'to your bit of rough?' There's no question but that marriage is the way to go. Last year Mary was married in splendour in the city to 'Zadok the Priest'; Julia, who is new, in Publicity, is about to get married in the Brompton Oratory. Young, ambitious men, who'd once have turned their noses up at our jobs – secretarial, admin – are lining up to replace us (they won't be secretaries for long): everyone knows, however much we protest, that unless we are unnaturally ambitious (which none of us appear to be) marriage and children will see us off.

I have moved into my own flat, not far from where we were brought up. It's the attic floor of a house in Tulse Hill. There's a kitchen with a sink and an old gas cooker, a bathroom with a huge dimpled glass window, where from the bath I can imagine I am out at sea, that same spangled light you get on water, *Dogger, Malin, Finisterre*.

The flat is not far from where Clare once lived. Convenient for the shed, for the bookies, as Ardu tells me – as once, presumably, he told her.

'I bet you tell them I'm your landlady,' I say.

'What do you think?'

I cannot count on his being there. Sometimes he will take umbrage at something I've said or done, or not said and not done, or the fact that I've been out too long, wasting my time and money getting a haircut that makes me look, as he says, like a Sloane. He will disappear for days on end.

I'm not blind; I know that the reason I've snagged him at all is that he's on the downward turn. By any bourgeois definition, he is a wreck, determined to make a wreck of himself, and only lucky, though he may not realize it yet, that he has met the one person who can sustain and tolerate the descent. This is how it has to be, because otherwise, if he'd fulfilled his early promise, he'd have taken off and left me far behind. And so we are in league. *Who's Afraid of Virginia Woolf?* I need this chance to prove my worth, my resilience, because although I'm not the one he thinks he wants, some resistant part of him will come to know I am the one he needs; determined that this is a love story, and that like the most rewarding love story, it will be the hardest won. I will break him; he will break me, and when we are broken, we will be even, and then we can be put back together again.

ii

His mother has asked me to call her Pauline, which marks some sign of progress. There is less ceremony now when we come to stay. She's in the kitchen, smoking, her ash-white hair scraped into a bun at the top of her head. 'Morning, Jane!' she says, staring into the vacancy above the table.

Though Ardu can afford to be a sloth, I cannot.

'Looks like a lovely day,' I say.

'Lovely,' Pauline says. It sounds like clucking when she says so: 'Lovely!' She taps her cigarette, takes another drag, exhales.

Faether is in his pyjamas and slippers. He shuffles into the kitchen, and then out again, like a man in a Swiss clock. If Ardu isn't in there, he's not interested. He has a leather reclining chair set up in the living room with a table at his elbow, and a coaster ready to take a drink, his medical journals tucked within easy reach. Down the corridor behind the stairs he has a small dark office, where he keeps his doctor's bag, enough diamorphine to kill an elephant.

The fact that he is in pyjamas I take to be a kind of acceptance. I plot my moves, not wanting to be left in a room with him alone.

Ardu has his own bedroom, the bedroom he's had since he was a boy. It's full of his things, his Russian Penguins, bookie slips on a spike, and a birthday card, two years old: a big bear holding a balloon with 30 on it, signed, *Jazmine*. I am put in the narrow room along the corridor, her old room with its posters and desk of troll dolls and necklaces.

I sink or swim. There is no special attention. Faether is less willing than Pauline to give up on the dream that something and someone better might come along. Those beautiful girls in the Persian embassy! He's baffled by the way Ardu avoids what has been so neatly plotted out for him, his handsome, clever son.

When they were small, Faether kept the two boys busy by giving them the task of moving a pile of bricks from one end of the garden to the other, then back again. It would keep them out of trouble. None of the stories are open to question, they are laid down, and re-laid like a ton of bricks: this is how it was. Ardu came up with the stair-jumping competition. He and his brother would take turns to jump from the stairs to the hall, each time progressing to a higher step. Ardu was always the winner, the stronger and more daring. He was the only one who could jump the whole flight and end up on his feet.

Jazmine and Duncan have come over for their dinner and we're gathered in the doorway with a pre-dinner drink to watch. Though there is no one to challenge him, Ardu is going to prove that he is still the king of stair-jumping. He stands on the landing, bends his knees, leaps and, with a thump that shakes us on our feet, lands on the hall rug, a zigzag of limbs.

'Ha!' Faether says, and claps his hands, looking around at us as if this proves beyond doubt how much his son is capable of.

Jazmine and Duncan applaud in turn, Jazmine rolling her eyes at me.

'Do you want to hear a joke?' Duncan asks when we sit down to eat.

Jazmine puts a hand on his arm.

'Go on, Duncan,' Faether says. 'Tell us your joke.'

'It's clean enough,' he says to Jazmine. 'I heard it at the station. It tickled me. Hang on.' He raises a finger to think. 'Okay. Here goes.' He takes a breath. 'A man is walking round Glasgow, comes across an old school friend, Jimmy McManus. *Hey, Jimmy, long time, no see. What are you up to now?*

'*I'm away studying,* Jimmy says.

'*What for?*

'*My PhD in logic,* he says.' Duncan moves his head from side to side to differentiate the two voices.

'*You've done well for yourself. What is logic, anyway?*

'Jimmy scratches his head. *I'll ha'e to explain by gi'ing you an example: have you got a fish tank?*

'*Aye.*

'*You must like fish?*

'*Aye.*

'*You must like water?*

'*Aye.*

'*You must like the sea?*

'*Aye.*

'*Then you must like shellfish?*

'*Aye.*'

'Are we allowed to eat?' Ardu asks, raising his fork.

'Go ahead, Ardu,' Pauline says.

Duncan takes another breath. '*You must like oysters?*

'*Aye.*

'*You must like pearls?*

198

'*Aye*.

'*You must like glamorous women?*'

'Finally,' Ardu mutters.

'*Aye*,' says Duncan. He stutters on a smile. '*You must like sex?*' – he flashes his eyes: a huff of acknowledgement from Faether and Ardu –

'*Ach, aye,*' he says.

'*Briwiant!* the man says, *So that's logic!*'

'Not bad,' Ardu says, deposits another spoonful of curry into his mouth.

'Hang on,' Duncan says, 'not finished yet. The man takes himself off to the pub along the road, and he says, *Guess who I bumped into?*

'*Who?*

'*Jimmy McManus—*'

Ardu is about to interrupt again and Duncan holds up his finger, says, '*He's got a PhD in logic!*

'*What's logic?*

'*I'll gi' y'an example. Have you got a fish tank?*'

'*Nae.*' Duncan sets his fists on the table, eyes wide. '*You poofter!* he says,' throws his hands up to show he's done.

There's a brief hiatus, and then Faether claps. 'You poofter!' he repeats. 'Oh, I like that. I like that joke. Poofter.'

'Steady on, Faether,' Ardu says.

'Well, it amused me, I must say, when I heard it.' Duncan picks up the kitchen towel in his lap and wipes his mouth, suddenly self-conscious. 'That's all folks.'

'That's a funny joke,' Pauline declares. 'Thank you, Duncan.'

'I'm surprised you can remember it all,' Ardu says.

'I surprise myself, sometimes,' Duncan says, good-naturedly.

'I can never remember jokes,' I say.

'How about this,' Ardu says. 'There was an Englishman, an Englishman and an Englishman—'

A glance threads the table. I'm under no illusion: the Scots hate the English like cats hate dogs.

'Honorary Scots,' Jazmine says, raising her glass in my direction.

Faether is running his tongue around his teeth. 'Both your parents are English, Jane?'

'Yes.'

'How old is your mother?' he asks.

'She's fifty.'

'Fifty? How young she is!'

'She was young when she had me.'

'Pauline was young, too.'

Pauline steers clear of the conversation, concentrating on her wine.

'I imagine your mother is good-looking?' he says. Pauline reaches for a cigarette.

'How is your mother's *boyfriend*?' he asks, savouring the ridiculousness of the word.

'They're getting married,' I say.

'Really? How long has it been?'

'They've been together a few years now.'

He tries another tack. 'Did you know a *Skunk*?' he asks.

Ardu will not help me out. *It's your own fault*, he'll say later, *you shouldn't indulge him.*

That night I go to bed before everyone else. I leave them playing cards, listening to the reel of their conversation. At some point, Pauline excuses herself, her smoker's cough, and then Jazmine and

Duncan, who bicker on the stairs. They're married now and have been given the twin room which is Bijan's. Ardu and his Faether are left alone, drinking; I listen to the rise and fall of their voices as I lie between Jazmine's sheets, wonder if Ardu, when he comes up, will dare slip into the room to say goodnight. But the voices show no sign of abating. I doze, though I can't drop off.

'Her mother is a HAW!' I hear it like a clay pigeon hurled into the house: a gunshot. It takes a moment to translate what I hear and spell as Haw to *Whore*. (*'Tis Pity She's a Whore.*) The echoes reverberate. *Her mother is a whore.* Her mother, my mother. What am I to do? The sheets are cold as plastic. There is stomping downstairs. I hear Ardu, his raised voice, but not what he says. I have crawled into the far corner of a shell, when I should be up, and on my feet, refusing to stay a minute longer.

But where would I go?

There must be a B&B?

But it's late, past midnight. How would I get there?

I swallow it down like poison, *whore*, as if swallowing is the only way to make it disappear.

In the morning, when I come down, I am surprised to find them all gathered in the kitchen waiting for me – Pauline, Faether, Jazmine, Ardu, Duncan – standing in a semi-circle. I'm invited to walk in. Faether says, querulously, 'I am being asked to apologize. And I will apologize for anything that I might have said that offended you.'

I am aghast. *But I swallowed the poison*, I want to say. There's no need for any of this. I can't look at him, this small man, handing out medicines to his depressed and constipated patients. 'It's fine,' I say. I can't bear to be seen to be the one who's been offended, whose job it is to accept an apology, who has no backbone, who should have left, who has betrayed her own mother. I don't want there to be anything to apologize for, I don't want to hear it or to know it.

All along I've been made to feel how inadequate and morally dubious my family is. By contrast Ardu's is what? Upright, whole?

But wholesome, it is not. Suffocating, repressed, fucking nightmare. I have been party to it, and in some ways it's a relief: I imagine that this can only bring us closer together. I can't wait for us to be on our own.

'He was pissed,' Ardu says lightly on the train home. 'He shouldn't drink. Persians are constitutionally unfit to take a drink.'

'But what he says about women?' I say.

'No one else takes any notice. I don't see why you should.'

iii

Julia from work has a face like a fourteenth-century Madonna, tenderized by a life spent ministering to the wounds of crusaders. In the great vaults of the Brompton Oratory she is a tiny figure, shafts of light bearing down on her as she is led to the altar by a father who couldn't be more proud, the red stripe of his military uniform flashing between pews.

This is the first time Ardu has appeared among my friends at work; the first time, given that we're been invited as a couple, that he's publicly acknowledged we bear any relation to one another. Afterwards at the Polish Club, he stands at the end of the long bar, a waitress supplying him with free shots of vodka. I keep an eye out but take care not to cramp him. When Julia comes over to insist that he dance, she is impossible to refuse, and amiably he follows her to the dance floor, ambles around to 'Gimme Shelter' like a Russian bear on a chain.

Not long after they're married, Julia and her husband buy a flat at the end of the road. It seems that we are bound to be friends. I've never known anyone within walking distance before, and sometimes she and I manage to get the bus into work together, finding a seat upstairs at the front, swaying high above the park, the lido, above the ticker-tape of shop fronts along Coldharbour Lane. We are born just a fortnight apart, we discover; she too is one of four, the eldest sister. We rail against the pettinesses of work, about how difficult men can be some-times. The journey is over in no time. She is full of grace and humour and understanding, and it feels as if we could go on talking for ever, that by talking to her, as long as I talk to her, I am known.

One morning I can see in her face she has something to tell. She's dying to tell me, she says, but waits until we're upstairs, looks round to check we're not overheard, and whispers, fixing me in her excitement, 'I'm pregnant.'

Even Ardu can't find fault with Julia. I tell him her news when I get home and I let it sit with him. I have to leave the room. When I come back in, I ask him how it would be if I stopped taking the pill. He knows this is what I want, the drip-drip of my enthusi-asm for children, how they give you the chance to start again, to see the world again from scratch. And all those books!

But now I can't wait, there's an urgency about it. Suddenly Julia is my twin and I panic she will leave me behind, it will be too late.

'It's your body,' he says. 'Do what you like.'

Which I take to be a yes. *Yes*. He's right, the one thing that isn't finally in his control, that is in mine, that makes me equal to bird fish dragonfly lion. *Yes*, by the light of a silvery moon, a phosphorescence, the gentle pitch and creak of a bed on water as he follows me in; *yes*, to being in the boat together, held, and being held, this long history of will-he-won't-he madness lain aside. Reptile marmoset phoenix bat. The pin hole of a universe through which the silken night is pushed and spread to cover everything, all creatures great and small, salted with stars, with planetary influence, the pollen shaken from flowers, dustings from wings of bees and other insects that sink straight into the pistil, the holy grail, well met, well met by moonlight, that silver kernel, that pip, which must have been there and you before I knew it. *Was it?* Whatever happened that night, something did, and for the first time in a long time I wasn't making it up.

13. *Formative Piece*

I call Julia from my desk upstairs at work and ask her to meet me in the basement loos. She knows it must be important. I can't contain myself, hopping for her and no one else to get down here. As soon as she does, I shut the door behind us, bring out the unopened box.

'You're not?' Her eyes are alight.

In the stall, because it's so deathly quiet, and because she's waiting for me outside, it's impossible to pee.

'How do you do this?' I say.

'Wait. I'll turn on the tap,' she says. Water splashes the sink. I let the sound enter the top of my head and trickle down. There's a dribble, a false start. I'm half-standing, the wand held approximately underneath, knickers snagged round my ankles. I try again, breathing out this time as I squat, and now, shyly, the warm snake of pee plays on my fingers; I can smell the pickled onion of hormone. When I finish and lift the plastic wand, there are beads of dark urine on its window, which I wipe with loo roll; pull up my knickers one-handed.

I am convinced already of what the stick will say. I draw back the bolt.

'Well?' Julia can hardly contain herself.

I turn it over, and she peers to see. There's no question, two distinct lines of pale blue.

She grabs my elbows and dances on the spot. 'We'll be pregnant together!'

In the yellow light of the mirror, we are anointed, as if the golden bough has touched us on the head. We are initiates, instant members of a secret cult, and truly yoked: our babies when we have them will be two weeks apart.

I can't risk ringing Ardu from the office, so I nip outside to the phone box on the corner of the square, the smell of warmed-up Bakelite, the hint of pee, which might be me.

I poke out the number.

'Premier Sheds?' he says.

'Premier shed.'

'Crazy!'

'I am,' I say. I can hardly contain myself.

'Crazy?'

'I've done the test. It's positive.' The railings of the garden melt beyond the glass.

'You sure?'

'Yes. I am. Are you pleased?'

He blows into the phone. 'That was quick. Yeah. Suppose so. Yeah.'

'Be pleased,' I say. 'I am.'

ii

If she turns up at all, Kathryn sits between the only two boys in the class, Tristan and Sam. She wears a pink hoodie from the English Society which reads, PROSE BEFORE HOES, slumps low on her chair, resisting eye contact, more often than not chewing gum. She can't remember the last time she read a book for pleasure she says. Does Harry Potter count? *The Great Gatsby*, which she did for GCSE, that was good. Two weeks late she has emailed me her 'formative' piece. It's about a boyfriend and girlfriend who live on opposite sides of a street. They meet up ('where?'), and after four hours ('of what?' I'm compelled to ask), there is, as far as the narrator remembers, only silence: 'a telepathic conversation of silence'.

I take my pen to it like a trowel. Some of this is automatic pilot saying, 'it's not interesting *not* to remember'; 'detail?'; 'how does feeling reveal itself?' My hand is bored and tired.

But that night the cadres break into my dreams. In their black body suits, they've come to hold me to account: 'Do you have any idea how sensitive this girl is? How on the edge?' I wake with a start. 'He told me I was a nightmare': was that from her story, or mine? My body is pounding. I resolve to give her work a second look.

As soon as I'm up, I turn my laptop on and fetch her story to the screen. The beginning of the story is perfunctory and distant as I remembered it, begging all the questions I felt obliged to ask. But then this next paragraph:

I was looking at him and he was looking at the ceiling. I willed him to look at me, I wanted to know what he was thinking. The silence between us was unfathomable and his not looking at me made me think he might never look or speak to me again. Maybe I've remembered this all wrong. Maybe he did say something and I've swapped what he said for silence. Maybe we did have a conversation. You're a nightmare is what he once said to me, and I didn't want to hear him say it again.

Perhaps I've been fooled by the use of the first person into believing this must be a true account, because suddenly I hear her voice. Here, in the middle of the story, I believe her – a voice that conveys the inarticulacy of not remembering exactly, of not wanting to know exactly, the clunkiness and repetitiveness of memory whose first thought is not for language and detail, but feeling, the awkwardness and inadequacy of words; not remembering, because it is too awful to remember. Fiction will tell us to do the opposite: stand back, make something of it, find the concrete image. But I've lost my nerve for it, and who am I to say how it works?

iii

Rose says I must have blanked it out; she remembers far more than I do. Carmen and Lola are the names of the old ladies who leased them the apartment in Santiago. They lived downstairs with a grown-up child who had Down's Syndrome, and the summer after we'd visited, the lavatories got blocked, the cockroaches arrived.

I'd booked the flights before I realized I was pregnant, and though I was feeling horribly sick, it seemed a pity to waste them. This was my grown-up younger sister with her own life, a boyfriend and a job in an orchestra in Spain. I wanted us to be grown-up together. And I wanted to go abroad with Ardu in the way that couples did, in the way he'd once done with Clare; I wanted to show that we were together, and by being so with Rose, to make it real.

Ardu is better at getting on with people he doesn't know, people in the street; he's uncomplicated, easy-going, makes an effort. The first two nights my sister and her boyfriend are at work, and he leads me in a trawl of the bars. This particular barman has taken a shine to him. They discover that they both speak Italian. He pours a glass of Aguardiente for Ardu to try. 'Ahh,' Ardu tosses it back, breathes an appreciative fire, shaking his fingers as if he's been stung. 'Bene. Bueno.' *Could he manage another?* The barman fills the small glass, tipping the liquid with care, wiping the neck with a cloth which hangs from his apron. I wait for him in the corner. The bar is streaked with ribbons of smoke: if I breathe through my nose, the air will be filtered for the baby, I think. I take tiny sips of water and let them sit on my tongue. This is Ardu's holiday as well as mine, I have to remind myself.

The next evening, I tell him I want an early night and let him go off on his own. I don't remember him coming in, except he is there in the morning, a stertorous heap. When I get up, Rose and her boyfriend are standing in the kitchen; they have arranged a set of empty bottles on the table.

'What?' I say.

'He's drunk all this,' Rose says. 'He must have drunk it when he came in last night.'

'Are you sure?'

She gives me a withering look.

'He'll pay you back,' I say. 'I know he will.'

'That's not the point,' she says.

I suggest we take them out to make amends. They are more or less fluent in Spanish and know where to go and what to order. Calamari, patatas bravas, gambas al ajillo. The earthenware dishes appear, and we help ourselves. The talk is of food, of where Ardu and I might go, if we take ourselves off for a few days along the coast, which seems in the circumstances to be a good idea.

It's my fault that Rose is wary of him: I've told her too much over the years. But at least tonight we can be convivial, the four of us. Things will be different. Perhaps the next time, we'll have the baby with us?

'Are you doing any writing?' Rose asks.

'Maybe I will when the baby's born. When I'm off work.'

'You shouldn't give up,' she says.

Ardu huffs, and says, as if to himself, 'What's the point? Why bother?'

I can see the fix of Rose's jaw, her chin working.

'If you can't be Beckett—' Ardu says.

'Why would anyone do anything then?' Rose says, and I hear the flint in her voice. 'If I'm not Jacqueline du Pré, are you saying I should give up?'

'That's different,' he says. My chest hurts. It's no use trying to catch her eye, he's off. He throws down his paper napkin, sits back. 'There's far too much mediocrity in the world. What's the point of adding to it?'

'Beckett is Beckett,' I say, half-heartedly, crushed because I know he's right.

There are flowers on the tablecloth and in a second Rose has risen from them to her feet. *Please sit down.* As if she were me and, by thinking it, I could call her back.

'I'm sick of this,' she says, and the acceleration is instant. 'We're going.' Her boyfriend sees that she is serious, and he, too, gets to his feet. Before she leaves, she turns on Ardu, her eyes spitting tears. 'You don't love my sister at all. Not one bit. I don't think you know what love is. I'm not going to stay and watch you treat her like this.'

Ardu fixes his eyes on the bread, blinks a laugh.

'You make me sick,' she says.

You can't speak to him like that, I'm thinking. You can't. He'll never come back. *Don't*, I'm thinking, *please don't*. I know how to deal with this. He's only joking, I try to tell her, he's only winding you up.

'He drank everything we had in the house,' Rose remembers. 'He told you you'd only ever be mediocre.'

'I do remember that,' I say.

'I screamed at him,' she says.

'And that.'

'You were obsessed,' Rose says.

And hard though it is to hear her say it and know she must be right, still I am convinced that there was more to it.

'I never saw the attraction,' she says.

'Other people did,' I say, defensively. 'It wasn't just me. Men and women.' I try harder. 'There was something about him. He made you feel that if you had his attention you could live, that if he stopped being interested you might as well not exist.'

'You just fancied him. You thought he was Heathcliff.'

To which there was no answer; it was exactly what I thought.

iv

'He wanted us to be together,' Kathryn writes. 'That's what I told myself, what I still tell myself.' I hand the story back and ask if she'd like to sign up to see me in my office hour so that we can go through it properly; it's promising, I say. But I'm saved the trouble: she has netball practice. The story is what it is, it's written, it's done. Nothing can change it now. She knows this better than anyone.

14. *Indelible Ink*

Ardu's up first, which isn't usual. The sheets are rucked and soft with warmth his side of the bed. Though the room is dark, there's a gold crack where the curtains join; outside the birds are peeping, and there's a steady grind of engines up and down Knight's Hill. I set a hand to the pumpkin of my stomach, drag like a metal detector until it registers the tick of a response. Although this is not the story I envisaged, it is something like. And I am here and in it.

I listen out. It's an effort to stay put – hot already – I throw off the bedclothes. There are coloured lights in the backs of my eyes – blue, gold, pink – all the colours of the Cinderella dresses we used to fight over, which one would be whose.

He's on the stairs, and in a moment through the door, sliding a tray onto the bed, in his vest, pyjama bottoms. 'There you go,' he says. I shunt to my elbows. 'Breakfast in bed!' I say, to register it. There's a mug of tea, a heap of pale scrambled eggs. Here he is in his pyjama bottoms, his vest: this is how it will be, I think, this comfortable *Steptoe and Son* domesticity. No need for the ridiculous theatre of separate establishments, of vicars and flowers and 'Zadok the Priest'. I've been quite happy to forgo the usual fuss.

'Thank you,' I say. I don't want to betray the full extent of my gratitude; I don't want to cry; I busy myself getting upright without upsetting the tray.

'Eat up,' he says. 'It'll get cold.'

Before I can keep him, he's gone, the hollow drum of his feet on the stairs. However casual he can be, he's done this to please me. This is the morning of the day we will be married, the beginning of days. Let it be enough.

We've agreed to have only one friend each; his parents are coming but not his brother or sister; mine are coming in their separate parties, one brother, one sister, but not Rose, who has made her excuses.

The eggs are silky soft, baby food, old lady food. The reassuring *plink* of the fork scraping round, tidying up.

'How did he propose?' someone will have asked.

Faether had been on to him over the phone. 'You'll have to marry her,' he'd said, demanding that the best be made of a bad job. 'A shot-gun wedding,' I hear myself joke. Ardu puts up no resistance, hands up, his whole being a shrug, which I take to be his uncompromised way of saying, *I will, I do*.

From the bathroom the taps shriek. The *cluck* of his razor in the sink, working upwards from beneath his chin, around the corners of his mouth, along the tops of his cheeks, his badger stripes.

I hoist my legs over the side of the bed, legs that have turned to girders shoring up the monument I've become. As soon as I'm upright, the weight of liquid presses in a bottleneck. I work my way around the bed frame, out into the corridor fit to burst. *The splendour falls on castle walls*, a glorious release of pressure amplified in the funnel of the tiny loo. I follow him into the bathroom, find him in the mirror, two press studs of blood on his chin. The pink bath steams. He pats his cheeks with a towel, and I pull my nightie up and over me like a trick.

For a second, he looks amazed. Someone has taken a pump to me and blown me up. He presses the towel into my hands. 'I need a shit,' he says.

The water gulps, an operation to lower myself, the skin over my belly taut. My belly button is turned out, the place where the glass once blown has been twisted off: I daren't touch the place I was cut from my mother, and she from hers, and so on, Great-Granny and her suitor Mr Poulson, reciting for her at Christmas, as Ardu once did for me, 'The Convergence of the Twain'. How do I know that?

There's an explosion from next door, slurry hits the sides of the bowl, his guts are shot. He coughs irritably. The intimacies of being together for good, I think, fondly enough. The smell of newsprint as he shakes out and turns the *Racing Post*, silence as he re-engages with it.

I paddle my hands and watch as the baby responds, tapping on the walls of her cell. She is a cloud of mistletoe, of luck. I take the soap and coddle it, watch my hands perform their ministrations, smoothing my arms, that dome of belly, the buried region between my legs. My skin's a tarpaulin, and as I splash to rinse it, more flutter from within, more friendly knocks on wood. And then I push forwards crooking my knees, lean back and under to wash my hair, listen to the glooping communication of tanks and pipes, remain just long enough to imagine him above me, bearing down, holding me under for a laugh, holding me and, by mistake, holding me a tad too long, longer than he might have intended—

I woosh up and water laps over the side, soap stings my eyes.

'Ardu?' I call to check where he is. No answer. A cascade of water falls from me as I rise. I swing like a crane over the side and pull the towel from the back of the door, tuck it round. My face is pink. A blushing bride.

Oh Rose thou art sick. Stop.

'Ardu?'

Flat-footed, belly-first, I wander back towards the bedroom, and find him pulling down the cuffs of his shirt. He's borrowed the suit from Will, Will whose favourite song was 'Reach Out I'll Be There'.

'It fits,' I say, as if this were an achievement, a sign of good fortune. There are buttons at the waist of the trousers for braces. The white of the shirt brings out the blacks of his eyes, the silk of his hair. He looks as exotic and beyond my ken as he did when I first clapped eyes on him: never in a million years could I have dreamed that all these years later his name would be more familiar than my own. Here I am with his baby packed inside me. We have a house together, a bed. He's made me scrambled eggs. Look at this! I want her to notice, see how tenacity, patience, endurance have paid off.

'Can you believe it?' I say out loud.

'Cab's booked for ten,' he says. 'Better get a move on.'

Sahara the label reads. The dress, pale blue, sleeveless, voluminous, is made from the pulp of trees. It's like a dress for Mary in the nativity play, has no fastening but slips over my head with a hole for neck and arms.

'Ready?' he calls up the stairs.

The dress swings as I move. And now I'm like the peasant doll who used to jiggle on her plastic stake on the window ledge at Granny's.

The minicab is waiting with the engine running, my heart turning over. Ardu gives instructions at the driver's open window. I let myself in at the back. The driver's hair is oiled, jet black. Although it's hot out, and hotter in the car, he's wearing a tight brown jumper. Ardu joins me in the back, the car sinking as he gets in. His hands are turned palm-up like boxing gloves.

The cab smells of pine air freshener, there's the cut-out of a Christmas tree and two miniature footballs dangling from the mirror. I wind down the window an inch, not enough to risk getting grit in my lenses. The street peels from either side, and the cab intercom crackles with the criss-cross of other days and other journeys.

We haven't got far before Ardu leans forwards. 'Here, mate, over there.' The driver pulls in at the kerb, a parade of shops. Ardu isn't going to explain. He gets out and saunters off in his suit, past the Co-op, the prissy clothes shop. Do I panic? He turns in, between tiers of greenery, buckets of flowers.

'Big day?' the cabbie asks, glancing up in his rear-view mirror.

When Ardu emerges he's dangling a bouquet; there's a white flower pinned to his lapel. He bundles back into the car and hands me the flowers. They're tied with raffia, their stems stiff – cornflowers, sea holly, delphinium, scabious, my favourite flowers. The lenses in my eyes float. Those feathery green stars around the heads of the scabious.

The car has taken off again, and I'm swamped by what rushes into my head. *He loves me, he loves me not, he loves me!* The traffic is slow-moving down the Croxted Road, a conveyor belt of stop and start. We nose under the railway bridge, past the lido at the corner of Brockwell Park. 'We used to swim there before school,' I tell him.

'You tell me every time,' he says. But I can't get over these curious repetitions, back in the vicinity of where I grew up as if there is a design to it all.

The cab pulls over in a sudden dart between bouts of oncoming traffic to the opposite side of Brixton Road. Ardu sends a note past the driver's ear, which he secretes in a zip-up purse before getting out, and, in deference to the occasion, opens the cab door for me, bowing his head.

'I'm shaking,' I say. I pull on Ardu's arm.

Behind the thick glass doors there are people I recognize in little bursts, and as the doors open it's impossible to know where to turn first. My brother steps forwards with a spray of garage flowers, makes a noise somewhere between laughter and greeting. He's on his own, gangly in an unaccustomed suit. Our father is with his wife. He smirks as he approaches, approving entirely of the ironies of this wedding, grasps Ardu by the hand. Pauline and Faether are trussed up in their wedding gear and hold back. Their other children have both been married recently, entirely different weddings, white dresses, a hundred relatives and friends: it's difficult for them to gauge what the form is here, and how and at what given moment to look pleased. Amelia, too, has recently been married. She runs about with her camera and the confidence of being loved. Mum is in a corner with her soon-to-be husband, intent on avoiding the twin panics of her life: our father, and her mother, Granny, who's in conference-blue, handbag clutched underarm, and the video camera, which will be evidence, which will be proof.

The foyer is a-murmur with reasons certain people couldn't make it: Bijan, in Australia, Jazmine can't get the time off work, neither can Rose, who will tell me later how she sobbed down the phone to Mum, the terrible mistake she knew I was making.

We're waiting for the party ahead. When they emerge, they're like an aviary let loose, flutters of red and gold and green, laughter, a sheen of joyous sweat on foreheads, the bride beaming under her floppy hat. In contrast we are painfully subdued, moving inside, not sure where to sit. The chairs are clipped together at the sides, too close. 'Don't all sit at the back, now!' The officiator appears, big window specs, a sandy moustache.

He makes an effort to instil a degree of humour, a beam to show that he's aware, no doubt, that this is a happy occasion, but a reminder that he's also here in an official capacity and is obliged to point out certain things, 'the solemn and binding nature of marriage', for instance.

'Indelible ink?' Ardu jokes as he takes the pen and makes an illegible scrawl. There's an embarrassing hiatus. Is that it? The registrar raises his hands. 'All done.'

Out into the dusty garden, Granny's fine white hair lifts in the thermals. She scowls: none of us like having our photograph taken.

I have Ardu's hand, and lean into it, my dress ballooning like a pantomime. Our father takes charge, corrals. Faether is brought over, Pauline, Will. Mum, who has been moving around the perimeter as if she's being hunted.

It's like an injection: look away, and it's done. I rub my arm, continue to rub my arm as another photograph is taken, me in every one, a different configuration. My smile has begun to hurt, fixed as wood and plaster.

Our father's contribution is lunch in a restaurant in the square behind Morleys. It's a five-minute walk, and we set off in straggles, past the man declaiming the devil from a loud hailer, Faether with his tie flipped over one shoulder, deep in conversation with Granny, who's telling him earnestly about the journeys she's made to Asia; how one of her best friends is from Pakistan.

The square behind Morleys is unexpectedly gracious with white stucco buildings. We head for the green awning tucked in one corner. In the entranceway, tied to the leg of a chair, there's a fistful of heart-shaped balloons, silver and pink. *Congratulations, Wedding Day*. A small envelope attached, which I open. 'Hope you're having a wonderful day!'

'It's from work,' I say, and I can barely speak: all those years, all the talk of weddings, and I'm stung to tears by what they might be imagining they're missing.

A waiter in a green waistcoat appears with a tray of fluted glasses.

'The only thing I don't like,' Amelia is saying in her adamant way, 'is chlorine.'

'Cheers!'

Ardu is sotto voce, talking to his mother, slippery as a fish. They smoke a last fag together before the food comes out.

As the camera pans around the table and lands, it's as if they've each been tapped on the forehead, looking up, in surprise, dismay. Granny and Faether are still deep in conversation, picking their words carefully. Granny is explaining that she taught immigrants in a college of further education; Faether, deferential, his teeth charming, as if he recognizes in Granny a respectable woman, someone who keeps a clean house.

The arched windows are stuffed with plants – rubber plants and miniature palms, which slice the light in pineapple chunks. My lenses are dry and weigh on my eyes. I can't afford to be seen to be at a loss, to be anything less than happy, and I blink, punch-drunk on the requirement. Mum has given up trying, staring askance because our father, who, as far as she's concerned, has ruined all our lives, has no right to be on his feet and making speeches.

'Every August, it seems,' he says, 'I'm called upon to make a speech. This one – ahem – is, a little premature.'

Laughter.

'But it's traditional, I gather, to say a few words about your daughter. So, I wondered whether I should talk about Jane and her striking sense of décor . . . About the day in 1971 in her bedroom in Newcastle—'

'No!' I say. (*Fox, stag, moose.*)

'If you want to ask her afterwards how the Artex effect was created – a very cheap way of redecorating a room – I'm sure she'll oblige.'

There's a form to a father-of-the-bride's speech, I know it. *Joking aside*, he's bound to say, and this is the part that will be the hardest, that will bring tears to everyone's eyes: how to express the love, the pride—

'She ruled her siblings viciously and aggressively,' he says, drolly. 'Her younger sister moved to Spain to avoid this wedding. Ardu, who has known Jane for some time, must know what he is taking on. And so, let's raise a toast: to the happy threesome.'

Chorus: 'The happy threesome.'

Ardu gets to his feet. He hasn't mentioned a speech, and now I'm thinking, perhaps he'll surprise me as he did with the flowers.

He raises his glass to our father. 'Thank you for the nosh-up,' he says. 'And Will,' he nods in Will's direction, 'for my whistle. And, while we're on the subject of couture and threesomes: I'd like to thank whoever designed Jane's dress – on the Tardis principle – a toast: *multum in parvo*. That's it,' he says.

Our father interjects, 'That's French!' Laughter. And then he says, 'Perhaps Jane should defend herself? Why don't you put the record straight about the Artex?'

'Speech!' someone cries.

Granny can restrain herself no longer. I was the baby she fed and loved and who she cannot bear to see throwing herself away on a man who, as far as she can see, is doing nothing about getting himself a proper job. 'Come on, Jane. You're more than capable. Come on, Jane.' Her voice is Wigan, she beats the table.

I move in slow motion as if remotely controlled. This is not going to happen. I am not going to make a fuss or show that in any way I cannot take it. This is who I am: I can take anything.

Mum is stung into action: why, in any case, should *he* have been the one to make a speech? 'I was going to take a feminist stand!' she declares. 'But I was going to talk about the Little Mother, too.' Her eyes are firing. 'Why don't we swap stories about Jane? *Nice* stories.'

'Let's not,' I say, looking to Ardu. *I do, I does, I did, I done.*

'There were nice memories,' Mum insists, 'good memories.'

'Jane made my life an absolute hell,' Amelia says from her corner.

Our brother pipes up. 'She did try and leave once before—'

'Oh, yes!' Mum claps her hands. 'She took a stick and a red and white handkerchief, a bottle of whisky.'

Laughter.

'When no one went to fetch her, she stayed at the top of the road – took a swig – then she came back.'

Laughter.

'Faether?' Ardu is quiet but pointed.

Faether gets to his feet as if reluctantly, clears his throat. 'My son is forcing me,' he says, casting around. 'Do you know Avesta? It is a sort of blessing.' He is floundering. This is the speech he has given at the proper weddings of each of his offspring; it has been important to him, to remind everyone of the links they have to their ancestors, to his mother, who is a hundred and three, and still living in the house outside Tehran in which he and his brothers were raised. He is a little tight in the collar. Whatever he has been expecting to contribute now feels inappropriate, the tone of proceedings all wrong. But he ploughs on because this is what he has prepared and rehearsed, and Ardu expects it. He speaks haltingly, translating as he goes.

'Let there be good health,' he reads. He is a nervous interpreter, as if, unwittingly, he might get something wrong. His speech goes on and on, and where only a year ago, the idea of him saying anything in his native tongue at my wedding would have brought me to my knees, now I know him well enough to know his heart isn't in it, that inside he is weeping: a girl from a broken family where even her own father doesn't have a good word to say of her. He reads his notes aware of the camera trained on him, as if he's reading from a hostage's script. 'Let there be good luck . . . Let there be goodness . . . let it continue . . . to the agreement of God.' He reaches for his seat. 'I hope Ardu is satisfied,' he says at last.

Later when everyone disbands, we set off with Ardu's parents for the pub. My dress clings to my sides and my feet are swollen in the blue fabric shoes. Ardu walks ahead with Pauline, and

Faether trails, locked into the disappointment of a son who should have done great things, a son who was supposed to make his sacrifice, all these years in a godforsaken land, make sense.

At the back of my heel a spot of damson blood begins to seep. It's like a fairy tale, though I try not to think it, the ugly sister, who's prised her feet into a slipper too small. Ardu is on a mission and walks faster than usual. He needs a drink. Pauline keeps pace by walking twice as fast in her narrow dress: she needs a drink too.

Afterwards, though they are staying elsewhere, Pauline and Faether agree to return with us to the house, where they can watch the Olympic Games.

I am exhausted, I admit to Ardu. If I go to bed, perhaps they will leave? This is no different from any other night, except that we are married. It *is* no different, what did I expect? The words slide off. Husband. Wife. I know it isn't real. The rosy band on my finger which I've coveted is like dressing-up.

From the other room the TV cheers, the hyperactive patter of a commentary. Ardu will not stir; he'll never be the one to say the day is over, done: I should take it as a compliment, he'll say, that they're content to sit it out.

But in the austerity bed I am beyond sleep, having imagined us, sleeplessly together, picking over the detail, the speeches, the embarrassments. It is my wedding night, I goad myself, the night of nights, trying to squash the disappointment that turns their presence to a curse.

15. Little Monkey

One of the many literary nuggets Ardu passed on to me is the story Thomas Hogg tells of his friend Shelley. How Shelley once so full of Plato was skipping with excitement at the idea of pre-existence, and accosted a mother strolling across Magdalen Bridge.

'Talk to me,' he says, gleefully, craning his neck to address the child. 'Tell me something about the world before.'

The woman raises a protective arm.

'Speak,' Shelley insists, peering at the infant.

'Let us be, Sir. Leave off,' the woman says. He has her trapped up against the parapet of the bridge, and she's envisioning a push or a leap, or that he might snatch the child from her grip.

'Has he forgotten how to speak?' Shelley exclaims. 'Forgotten already?'

He has a theory about the tongue – that worm, that snake – itching from the moment it exits the womb to seek out the engorged nipple, addled by this ecstasy of sucking, which continues all its life, content for sucking to put that miraculous brain in hock.

The woman, seeing her pathway blocked, lifts her elbow around the baby's head, and like a caber to a door, barges her way past, off into St Clement's, determined not to cease until she's run out of breath.

Shelley removes his hat, rakes his hands through his hair, staring after her. His elbows bear down onto the stone parapet. Look! he counsels his febrile brain, lifting his eyes from the shapely balusters to view the cool slop of the river – ribbons, counter-ribbons – allowing it summarily to wash through him as if he's down there, fanned and soothed under the nonchalant surface of the water.

The pale grey walls of a tanker somewhere thousands of miles out at sea: I sense it as a dull ache, a tugging sickness in the base of my spine that won't let me be. There's a heavy fog, the mournful pulse of a horn. I sit with my back to the wall, wanting to get down as low to the ground as possible, onto it, into it, through it, the pull into the earth like an umbrella turned inside out.

When are you due? Words have started to slip from their moorings: 'due'? Something owed? an obligation? something deserved? Or is it 'dew', as in early morning? In any case, the 'due date' has come and gone, and now it feels as if we might have missed the boat.

I've stopped work and lie in the long dead hours of the day, grown used to the idea that what is supposed to happen never will. We've struck up a way of being that suits us, communicating in a Morse of punches and kicks. For the first time I have breasts that I can weigh in my hands, fruits of solid marble. Soon I will be quite immobile, as if someone has put his mouth to me and blown me up, my thighs like the pillars of a bouncy castle. I am not frightened: this is the strangest thing of all. As if fear like a dangerous toy has been gently taken out of my hands and packed back into its box.

Next door Ardu is sleeping so soundly I know it will be an operation to wake him. The room is pearly grey from the streetlamp outside. Beyond it the terraces are under wraps, the sounds stratified: a lorry pulls away, a night bus, and in desultory front gardens rats drag their tails from where litter collects, a fox's eyes flash infra-red.

I crawl along the corridor, following the wall, an old carthorse, a sea-slug. These are my stations. In the loo, I haul myself up by the walls and sit in the halter of the seat. It is the worst sort of period pain.

Before: here is a word. Examine it. This is the only version of *before* that will ever matter. I sit on the moment, watch it from a vantage of zero-gravity, turn it into a pole on which the whole earth appears to turn.

When I get to my feet again, a pitcher in the cupboard of my insides topples with no warning, streaming down my thigh, splashing the floor. It isn't pee, it's like the watery milk from a coconut. This is it. By the rivers of Babylon. The waters are broken. It is 4 a.m. I will clean myself up, put on clothes. There is no panic, though the tanker is here again, the sheet-wall of its approach. I must begin to count this, to measure it. I instruct my dim assistant: find a pen, write it down.

She is cow-like and I have to be firm. Send her along the corridor with the back of an envelope and a biro. Seven minutes, she writes down. There's a paroxysm of machinery, of pulley and wire. Another five minutes, and dutifully she notes it down.

'Time to wake him,' I tell her. She makes her way round to his side of the bed, takes his shoulder. 'Ardu?' whispering. 'Ardu?' louder. 'It's started. You need to get up.'

He is groggy. He moves from sleep as if the sky is on top of him, as if he's coming out of hibernation, clumsy, stunned. His mouth is gummy. He can listen but he can barely speak. He manages to pull on his jeans, get his arms into a shirt. She has a bag ready, a nightie, a towel, a sponge bag.

The car doors, opening and slamming so early in the street, are an affront; the grind of the engine magnified. As we drive, a dim light begins to break over the serrated edges of the city. There are so few cars it doesn't take more than twenty minutes to reach the river. Ardu drops me off where the ambulances arrive so that he can park. They bring a chair, and wheel me off along electric corridors into the grey box of a lift. Upstairs, more corridors, and at the end, a bare rectangular room with a bed in the middle of it. I'm handed a gown to get into with slits for arms, exactly the same pattern as our old school blouses, those little blue diamond shapes. I clamber onto the bed. On the trolley next to me, there's a grey cardboard tray, just in case, the nurse says, her busty uniform, her stopwatch.

By the time he finds me, they've taken blood pressure, poked about under the gown as if down a hatch. Ardu's sleeves hang loose. It's so hot in the room he sets to rolling them up. His chest is a bruised purple. I am propped up on pillows. I've brought no book to read, we have no music. Ardu had been to one of the NCT meetings and refused to go back. The other men, he says, were just too fucking earnest.

The midwife has disappeared. *Remember not to push*, she's said. *Just breathe.* Ardu decides to go in search of tea. The force arrives again but this time like a water cannon, enough to

227

knock me from my feet if I were on them. 'Don't go again,' I say when he comes back. He sits down but is at a loss.

I've forgone the epidural, imagining the spike thick as a knitting needle. It's too late now. When the machinery cranks up again, I grab his arm, dig into his flesh, groan like a creature from hell. He holds steady though he looks aghast, his cynicism burning off.

A different midwife enters. She has a freckly face and stolid limbs; wheels over the canister of gas and air as if now we're preparing to dive. 'How are we doing?' she says. 'Take a big breath on here,' she says, 'when you feel the contractions coming.'

I bite so hard on the mouthpiece I think it will split. I make my knees into a bridge, arch my back.

'You could try standing up? Or sitting, squatting, whatever you like. Sometimes it helps?'

I can't move from the table, cling to it like a life-raft. If I move, I'll be washed away. I haul at Ardu's arm, a branch from the flood. The midwife has taken over on the other side, strokes back my hair. 'Nice, deep breaths for me, now,' she says. The tanker is screeching in its approach, high as a tower block. The noises that come out of me are from the swamp; I'm on the rack, guttural, possessed, and he is ashen, his eyes full of the terror of being forced to witness and do nothing.

If it doesn't end soon it will kill her. A camel and a needle's eye. The sea wall is mounting, terrifying because there's nowhere for the mounting to go and she's exhausted with swimming, not strong enough to keep her head above water.

A doctor is called. He ducks his head, prods with his fingers. The monitor is bleeping. 'Foetal distress,' someone says. 'You need to push.' As if I've not been pushing hard enough, as if I've not been trying. 'We're going to need you to push as hard as you can this time,' a blunt edge to the voice. But my limbs, they will pop out of their skins. I heave on the gas. The water in my ears bubbles and distorts, down here in the flood I can hear the scrapings of the ark. 'Save your energy for pushing,' the midwife instructs. She's at the bottom of the bed, peering. 'Good girl. One more time. Push. I can see baby's head!' She lifts her bright burning face. 'One more go!' The machine is out of control, destroying itself, shaking free of its mooring. There is blood. *Push.* There is shit. *Push.* I'm a drone, a bagpipe with all the air pushed out. *I can't*, I drone. *I can't.*

Picture the head as an eyeball in a socket, the cervix and its clamps, this precious matter of a brain. So much pressure, an engine from a tunnel shrieking, a black flower breaking to the leopard-spots of its interior.

'Here it comes! We've got her. Here she is. It's a girl. A little girl.'

Ardu is standing, he has been handed the shears; he will cut the cord that joins us together before the midwife hurries her off into a corner, smoothing away the worst of the gunk. There's a tiny cry, a seagull mewl from a voice-box small as a pea, an inrush of air that whizzes to the ends of arms, and legs, and toes.

The midwife gazes at the baby as she hands her over. 'Take her, Mum. Hold her.'

She places the curled-up creature on my belly: *There you are!* Little monkey, so hairy, eyes tight for it to be over, crusty fingers that aren't yet used to the air's rough exposure. What possible blueprint is there for this?

I bring my hand to the baby's fairy buttocks. She has eyelashes, the darkest hair slick with vernix; a feathery down on her back. Already the little purse of a mouth is pulling open, working. She elbows, soft-pedalling, worrying her head from side to side. 'Look at her go,' the midwife says.

Shell shock. All that is left of me takes refuge in my head, watching from this ledge as the baby crawls, muddied, blind, following her mouth.

'Clever girl,' the midwife says.

The breast, which does not seem to be mine, is swollen and numb. The baby has found the nipple, hangs on.

'She's doing great,' the midwife says. 'Isn't she, Mum?'

A pulsing jaw, a mashing. And when she lets go, the midwife turns to Ardu. 'Do you want to hold your daughter?'

He doesn't know what to do with his arms, arranges them approximately, and the midwife tucks the baby in. I've never seen such a look on his face. My body leaks and deflates. He glances across at me, eyes unshielded. 'I don't know how you did it,' he says. Everything Will Be All Right (this is what I thought). The three of us. Nothing will ever not be this.

The midwife returns with a metal dish. She takes my arm, 'Up you get, that's it,' and I stand, legs trembling, picturing the purple-black of a trampled flower. She pulls, and something gives. Into the dish in a greyish caul, the clot of the placenta.

As soon as I'm on my back again she takes a look. 'There's a sort of triangular flap, here,' she says cheerfully, poking. 'We'll push it back and hope for the best, shall we?'

Ardu leaves at four for me to get some rest, he says, off he goes to wet the baby's head. The baby sleeps. The lights are dimmed.

We have a view of the Thames, dark and oily, and every now and then the sky bursts with pops of light, because there are still fireworks left over from Bonfire Night.

I wander the ward in my thin white nightie and bare feet. There's a bloodied sanitary pad in the corner of the shower. I wipe the loo seat with a wad of loo roll. When I return to my bed, I think I must be mistaken, on the wrong ward. The baby is gone. Where is the baby? I set off again to the nursing station. 'Where's my baby?'

The nurse tells me not to worry. The baby hasn't been feeding too well, she says. She needs a tube down her throat to clean her out. She's swallowed meconium, they think. I hear the bleating of babies and try to differentiate my own, following the thread to a room with transparent cots. I'm ushered away: 'We'll have her back to you as soon as we're done,' they say.

Across the way green curtains have been drawn around a bed, and someone is sobbing. A nurse click-clacking purposefully. There's no one to listen, though I don't know what I'd say except to bleat, *Where is my baby? Where is my baby?*

The nurse arrives pushing a cot, and I daren't think what I'll do if the cot isn't mine. She parks it by my bed. 'She should do better now,' she says, briskly.

As soon as she's gone, I take you up and lie you next to me so that no one can come and take you again. There's a feather on your breath. How will I ever sleep for watching? I push the tip of my finger into your fist, and your fingers take hold, tight as a fern. Though it seems beyond imagining, I make the leap: one day, you'll be eighteen, and I'll tell you about this first conversation: how you listened to everything I said with a concentrated expression that told me you knew exactly what I was saying.

16. Don't Say a Word

My crumpled belly pines for what it has lost, for what all these months it has fed and watered. Flesh of my flesh, we had no secrets, and with your Prior Knowledge – a little anchorite in your cell, a little cricket – there was nothing you didn't know. It had only been us, me, privileged above all others to be entrusted with the job of conveying you round, and in deference to which Ardu had cooked when I came home from work, had got me to put my feet up, sat and watched with me episodes of *Inspector Morse*. There had been no rancour all this time, no wrong foot.

You were the hardest thing I ever let go of, and now I cannot bear the thought of losing you further, or the thought of losing the thought of you. These arms, the crook of my neck, hands, eyes, ears, it seemed they had no use till now, the moving parts of a cradle designed exclusively to keep you close.

I am nine and I have given birth; I am Mary, stunned by what I have produced, the shepherds, the kings, rejoicing. By Jove, this is what love is, a whole religion turning on it, love incarnate, something a woman did that was good.

He couldn't have done it, Ardu admits.

In this relation he and I are newborn, too. I am mother and

he is father, and being so, together, we override whoever went by those names before.

I have her slung across my ribs, the shark-frenzy of her feeding. I don't appear to have a knack for it, trying and trying again to match my unfamiliar swollen breast to her irritable plughole of a mouth. I'm intent on proving to him what a natural I am, singing with half an ear for him: *Hush little baby—*

Breastfeeding is what a mother does, it is the first thing she does, the first test of how natural or not she is.

If that mockingbird don't sing—

The nipple is angry and raw, weeping.

Daddy's going to buy you a diamond ring.

They call it latching on, as if nothing could be simpler or more inevitable, and yet the pain – *Ring!* – shoots through me like a bolt to the head – a bolt to the head! – until, eventually—

Hush little baby, don't say a word—

The suck-suck is some form of anaesthetic.

When she turns from my nipple to sleep, it is the sleep of angels. I watch the easy rise and fall of her breathing and it is as momentous and soothing as a sea of barley.

But it can't be healthy to begin to long for her to remain asleep like this, to eke out the times between one feed and the next, which, as the day drags on, draw only closer together. I have pads to stem the leakages; like a religious painting far too profligate with my tears of milk. She chews her lips, fists her mouth, presages of a full-on wail. She has discovered her voice, writhes in my arms. And not being sufficient to her, not being able to contain her hunger, this is my greatest fear.

After a few days I've begun to stink. I don't dare inspect myself or wash, because I worry that those bits of me that were stuffed back in must have come to grief. Every evening I break out in yellowish weals that radiate across my chest and up my neck. The midwife recommends a deep hot bath of salt. My body, she says, is still in shock.

At the end of a week, the health visitor pops round, a plump man with hairless skin. 'How's baby? How's Mum?' He doesn't meet my eye. *Breast is best*, he repeats, when I tell him it's getting worse. Someone has suggested cabbage leaves, which lie about the room soft and wilting; I have been down on all fours, I tell him, like a wolf.

Julia is two weeks ahead of me. It hasn't been easy for her, either. She's developed mastitis and is on antibiotics, one breast swollen and throbbing. 'It's hell,' we can agree, a conspiracy of silence: no one ever warned us about this. And agreeing is such instant relief, we are shocked by it into laughter. Thank God there are two of us. I don't want to let go of the phone, we are like Pyramus and Thisbe whispering through the crack in a wall. But when the phone goes back to its cradle, as it must, the silence is unbearable, the room, as it was before, working away at the evidence that will impeach me for impersonation and failure.

Colic kicks in routinely at the end of the afternoon and the baby is inconsolable. Ardu can't bear the noise and disappears downstairs to the kitchen to smoke. His admiration is wearing thin. I trundle about the room, the island of the sofa to the window, joggling, patting. 'Look at the tree!' I say. 'Look at the pussy-cat!' And eventually, hot and fractious, she will judder into sleep.

On Friday, when she's a week old, Mum and the man who is to be her husband come to visit. We sit next to each other on the sofa, and soon I recognize the prickly bubbling of my skin, the plague-like blisters.

'All babies look the same,' her about-to-be husband says, standing aloof and uninterested.

Mum is absorbed in whatever is going on between them. She isn't entirely happy about being a grandmother, she says. The baby is on her lap, but she's not looking at the baby, she's looking at him. 'We could have a baby?' she says, half-jokingly.

The story isn't mine, it is hers. I sit at the end of the sofa, a tear like an ant prospecting down my cheek.

At night in bed I plead with Ardu not to go into the shed the next day because he is my family as my mother has hers. But he'll have no truck with this kind of talk. 'You're mad,' he says.

I've run out of credit. In the morning he's off, and, later, because it can't be as bad as I think, Mum and I set out with the baby for a walk. It's the first time I've been outside, and though I'm bundled up like an old woman in shawls, I feel naked and exposed as if I've forgotten how to conduct myself in the outside world. The machinery grinds on, the whizz of a bike, the low roar of traffic. I use the pram as a prop. We make the circuit of the block around the patch of wasteland at the back of the terrace, dog shit squeezed like oil paint in variations of the same shitty colour, past the swings where at some future time beyond my ken, surely this is what I will be doing, pushing you, and pushing you higher.

In the second week, Faether comes down. He has heard about the breastfeeding problem and is sure he can solve it. He tips out a bag of ointments. Carefully I read the contents on the box he hands me. *Codeine.* No. No. No. I will not have it. She will be a drug addict! My left nipple is raw and weeping, an open scar the glassiness of fluorspar.

'Undo your shirt!' he says, a more radical approach. 'I'll show you how I used to treat the girls in the Gorbals.' He's rolling up his sleeves. I do as he says, because he's a doctor, though it feels wrong, my rack of breasts, their butchered animal teats. Ardu has backed off to the doorway, where he watches half-in, half-out. Faether's hands come twirling towards me like propellers. His fingers on my skin, welded. He twists. 'You have to toughen them up!' he says. He twists one way and then the other, firmly. 'They used to have a go at them with a wire brush,' he says, as if I should count myself lucky. My voice is in the rafters of my head and won't come down, wants no part in this. Faether is concentrating, casting a professional eye.

We've seen the cinefilm of his honeymoon: the dream-technicolour of Super 8, a long close-up, not of Pauline, but her breasts which are held voluptuously in the stretched harness of a ski-jumper.

'You're engorged,' he says as if I've done this to myself. He keeps up the twizzling and the breasts begin to leak. Ardu makes no move to intervene, and though I try to fetch him with my eyes, he will not read me. It is too shocking this proximity and I vanish, down into the well that opens where I sit.

I won't, I can't come out.

It's only when Faether has gone, a day later, that I find my voice. 'Why didn't you stop him?' I ask.

'He was trying to help,' Ardu says. 'It's pretty obvious you don't want to feed her. Textbook psychology. Clear to anyone, you've got a problem.'

Ardu's most faithful drinking companion is Bo'heid, Ardu's name for him. He teaches chemistry at a minor public school, and though he was brought up in Essex, speaks with the Glaswegian accent he had as a young boy. He rarely addresses me at all, except to nod, *All right?* He comes to the house to pay his dues to the baby, nods, retreats downstairs again. What do they talk about? Football, horses. *Minging. Midden. Carnage.* Claps of laughter up the stairs, where I keep out of the way, feed the baby, who wants feeding every twenty minutes, through *Coronation Street*, *EastEnders*.

There's a code among men: however much Ardu takes the piss out of Bo'heid, he is one of the brotherhood. Though Ardu brings me up my supper, he leaves it for me, returns to eat with Bo'heid downstairs.

One breast dries up, the nipple has never healed. Now I am ridiculously lop-sided, the other breast hot and hard as a bomb. I keep going, and when it works, take pleasure in the fist raised like a fencer's above her head, the intricate vaulting of the inside of her mouth.

'Once you start the bottle, it's a slippery slope,' the health visitor says. And it is. We buy bottles and a plastic container to sterilize them in the microwave.

I'm ashamed to appear in public with a bottle. The powdered stuff is like plaster of Paris. I read the information on the carton again and again to convince myself that there is no harm but worry that if I don't breastfeed, I'll lose all prior claim. How can I call myself a mother?

In the night, when I go to fetch a bottle, I have to be careful where I tread. The slugs are out in force. Under the dazzle of the fluorescent light they're colourless and easy to miss; they freeze. It takes a while to tune in, but when I do, I find there are at least a dozen, on the lino, the skirting, there's three on the draining board by the sink. As the microwave gurns, I can hardly bear to make contact with the floor, as if too long a connection will allow me to be taken over, slugs plugged to my legs, emerging from behind my ears. The machine pings. I test the milk on the inside of my wrist: this much mothering I can do. It is the middle of the night. On his side of the bed the breathing is heavy as dockyards. I hug the baby to me like a float. The radio is on low, 'Sailing By', a slow, anachronistic waltz that taunts me with a future I was fool enough to have dreamt: two lovers dancing by moonlight out on deck.

17. *The Fury of Men's Gullets*

No matter how slow and lumpen I am, having a child is some sort of surety, a circuit of familiarity that binds us together. She is his child and she is mine and she is ours. This is my belief, but I begin to understand that it is not his. He can see that if I were made to choose, I'd have to plant my flag here, nothing more precious or vulnerable than this miraculous eruption of my flesh, whose larval heat has cooled on me to form an igneous layer, an exoskeleton. And nothing before has come between him and me that could not be put aside. Where once it was his, she has all my obeisance; a love that has no need for tricks or secrets, ancient as a white globe warmed to attract a swarm of bees and swung from a chain in a cathedral. And being indivisible, isn't subject to the ebb and flow of his humours.

At eight months she's begun to sit up by herself, is sitting on the sofa, and we witness her delight in discovering the kinetic power of wobbling, watching together until in a moment of abandon she lurches forwards and there's nothing to stop her from tipping over the edge.

I am furthest away, but rush, when he doesn't, to catch her. 'What are you doing?' I ask, my voice in a panic.

'She has to learn sometime,' he says.

He does it to wind me up, I know he does, to break my idea of a magical ring. It wouldn't be the same if I wasn't there

– he'd be the first to rush in. Now she's crying at the shock of being snatched up, the experiment ended. 'Look what you've done,' he says.

When the time comes, we have always agreed that since I have the full-time job, it will be me to go back to work. It makes the transition easy for me, knowing she will be with him, because whatever he is like about anything else, she is a part of him and in that part, beyond compare, and something to pull himself together for.

He has got me to take a photograph of them to show just how alike they are, the two of them in the armchair. He apes the exact angle of her head as she lies in his lap, thrown back in a state of sated abandon, of which he has become the giant version. He calls her 'pup'. While I'm gone, he trains her to recognize the creatures in her pen: ladybird, teddy, and a little painted Indian god he calls the flying gimp.

She is a genius, I agree, when I come home, and he gets her to perform, pointing out each one.

I work in the week, he at weekends so that we barely overlap; the arrangement appears to suit him. We have joked that he is the househusband, a joke that neither of his parents takes seriously, because they cannot bring themselves to think it, too demeaning and domestic for a boy who could be king.

On Saturday morning when he's gone, I sit and stare. The house is chaos. I drive us to the park in Dulwich in order to get out; trundle the pushchair purposefully along gritted paths, talking as we go to make the best of it. I'm the only mother on her own, or so it seems, because this is prime time for cosy outings, nappy bags, dads with babies strung to their chests. We go through the motions, the two of us. *Look at the ducks!*

Quack, quack! Distribute crusts from the bottom of the bag. She hurls, and then is terrified, beaks honking and crowding at her feet. I cajole her, unbuckle her from the pushchair and scoop her up. It is touch and go, because I am only an extension of her: there's no one else to confirm that there's nothing to be frightened of.

At the swings, I'm with the dads, who do all the chasing round, the pushing and the encouraging. At a certain point one of them will draw breath and shade his eyes, wave: *Look at my wonderful wife!* There she sits in her fancy dark glasses, safe in the knowledge that, having given him something of himself so thoroughly to love, he will always be in her debt.

But before Shirin is a year old, we too go on holiday. A friend at work has put us in touch with someone who'll rent us a cottage cheaply. It is out-of-season, early October, and the sea on the east coast, on the other side of the wall, is rough and unwelcoming. Briefly we meet on the promenade to be handed keys, and I see the look of doubt in the woman's eyes.

The cottage is dark and sparsely furnished. There is no fire. The night storage heaters are tepid. We bring the things in from the car. I sit in my coat and Shirin in her padded bodysuit. Ardu goes to the pub, because otherwise he will go mad, he says, cooped up in this depressing hole.

Shirin is out of sorts and refuses to sleep in the travel cot; comes into our bed, where she wriggles and bats for attention the rest of the night. In the day we go to the beach and stumble over the pebbles, we eat in a café, though she is tired out now and will not be still or quiet. We pass her from one to the other so that we can bolt our food, try to shush her, though she will not be shushed. We are a menace: we are putting off customers. I think, we will never be able to have a holiday again.

But in the afternoon when she is carried on his back, a little Chinese emperor, she is swept into a sudden fit of laughter that erupts from nowhere, so happy she can't stop, and because I am her mirror, I am laughing too, ashamed at how unhappy we have been, how ridiculous. And even he is infected, and now we are laughing together, all of us, and we look for that moment as if we belong together, like other families, as if everything and everyone else can go to the end of the pier and hang.

Nonetheless, it's a relief to get back, we admit.

A mistake to go on holidays, he says for future reference.

On my birthday, he cooks. I have come in from work and the food is all done, lamb chops and red cabbage. We sit in the room downstairs to eat with plates on our knees. There's a candle on the windowsill. I choose my moment to tell him what I've found out today, and say it, coyly: Julia is pregnant again.

He chews, has found a rhythm, and before the next mouthful, he says, 'No way.'

'No way what?' I think he is joking, that this will only be the prelude to a conversation that will end in bed.

'You were a fucking nightmare.' He slides his tongue around his mouth. 'I'm not going through that again.'

'Everyone finds it difficult,' I say, my throat so tight I can't swallow.

'You said it yourself,' he says, ' "never again".'

'Everyone says that.'

The dull feeling in the pit of my stomach, at the back of my head, knowing the wave is coming and I will have to ride it.

'You're a joke,' he says. 'Your ambition. It's completely pathetic.'

'I want us to be happy.'

'You'll never be happy.'

He clatters into the kitchen and I follow. 'I'll wash up,' I say.

Outside, on the window ledge, two eerie stumps of geranium appear in negative in the glass; behind me the click and fizz of a lighter. What saves me in these moments is the thought of putting a lid on it, and, tomorrow, racing into work, where I'll repeat the conversation word for word, kneeling at Julia's desk, her absolvent Madonna face, knowing that a sympathetic hearing is all it will take to restore me.

'I don't know what makes you think you'd be any different?' He's standing in the corner, narrowing his eyes as he drags on the fag.

'She'll be an only child,' I say.

'So what?'

'It's mean.'

'Bollocks.'

'Why are you being like this?' I say.

'This is nothing to do with me,' he says. 'You brought it up.'

'It's my birthday.'

'You can't help yourself.'

'What did I say?'

'Oh, absolutely nothing.' He heaves on the fag. 'It's never you.'

'Stop. Stop. I don't know why this is happening.'

'Because you just can't help yourself. You're a fucking nightmare.' He squashes out the fag in a dish.

'And you're not?!'

There's a dullness in his eyes, which look straight through me. He moves from his elbow, and the way he's moving, it doesn't appear that he has a place in mind to stop. I imagine a fist like a bird loose in the room. My eyes are in his chest before he stops, a bitter laugh: 'The only woman I'd hit would be the woman I loved.'

The only woman I'd hit would be the woman I loved – It's a record that jumps, as if there's no other way to stop it and to prove that he loves me but, please, please to hit me. *Hit me!* the voice in my head, hopping, *Hit me!* Rumpelstiltskin in a rage.

'Did you hit *her*?' I ask, grimly.

He registers a kind of disgust, turns away. 'If you really want to know, Mon only ever saw you as an incompetent ingénue with a crush.'

ii

Answer the bloody phone!

'Did you look it up? The fury of men's gullets?' Ardu asks.

'I didn't,' I say.

'The fury of men's gullets and their groins: take a guess, go on.'

'MasterChef?'

He snorts. 'Your friend would know.'

'Which friend?'

'The friend that knows.'

'I've told you a hundred times, he's not my friend.'

'Did something happen?'

'He doesn't work here any more.'

'So you've said, but I thought he came to stay. Have you fallen out?' (No one can live with your mother, he tells Shirin, when she and I argue.)

The Professor story is old news and so far I've managed to hold off telling him. But something catches me off guard. Perhaps it is the sense of déjà vu. This is how it always was: though he was the source of all hurt, he was also the only one who could make it better.

'I responded to a tweet,' I tell him.

'Serves you right.' And then his curiosity kicks in. 'What did you *tweet*?'

'It doesn't matter.'

'An apposite little aperçu?' I know the way his lips dance.

'It was about politics. I shouldn't have got involved. He went mad.'

'Classic,' he says.

'I've come off Twitter,' I say. 'It's the work of the devil.' And now I'm cycling in thin air. 'He wrote an email the next day,' I say, perversely, because I can hear the danger in my ears.

'Saying what?'

(The line between abjection and alleviation is so thin.) 'The worst things he could think of to say.'

'Like what?'

I have the line by heart: '*The way that all this habitual behaviour is affecting your life and prospects is its own punishment.*'

There's a moment's delay as he takes the weapon in his hands.

Instantly I see my mistake. 'It's a gift, isn't it?' I say.

'Knowing how to choose your enemies?'

(*I am the enemy you killed . . .*) 'Did you ring for a reason?' I ask.

'Knock, knock.'

(Can he hear me breathing?)

'Ben Jonson,' he says, 'for your information.'

iii

On finding no proper object, grief rebounds, folds over, subsumes you, until all you can be is the sum of your failure to have been what you ever imagined yourself to be.

When our father left, Mum said that it would have been easier if he'd died. Her grief then wouldn't have had the air of failure about it, or of disproportion. Had he died, it would have been respectable to have gone on and on as she did for years, head in hands over the pull-down kitchen table, her face wrung out with crying, eyes permanently swollen, and to have expected an ever-ready supply of succour and kind words.

Would it have been easier for us, too?

He was still our father. She was the only one who'd lost anything, everything. What had we lost?

We stood to one side, ashamed of ourselves.

I am the worst, the biggest thorn in her side, because, according to her, I am just like him. And I was the one who tried to get the others to behave, sitting, at those once-weekly visits, at the heavy mahogany table. There was no reward for this. I was the eldest, eighteen, recruited to be a grown-up, to understand, and needed only to prove how understanding I could be.

Our father didn't cook so we could assume the stew was hers, Rose and Jack turning their mouths down at it, spooning it under the table to the Persian rug on the floor. I didn't have the luxury of being childish. 'Don't,' I hissed.

'Go and live with him!' Mum yelled because she heard how bossy I'd been. 'Go and live with them, if you're such a fan.' The split ran down my middle like a zip.

18. *The Swimmer*

Mum's husband is big in AA. There's a serenity prayer, which she's taken to heart, and recites to me down the phone as if it will help: *God grant me the Serenity to accept the things I cannot change; Courage to change the things I can; and Wisdom to know the difference.*

Accept the things I cannot change.

'Do you think he's an alcoholic?' I ask.

She will not be drawn. But whether he is, or he isn't, she suggests I ring Al-Anon, which has been set up, she says, for the friends and relatives of alcoholics.

'Then you do think he's an alcoholic?'

'It's not for me to say.'

I wait until Shirin is asleep, until there is no danger of being disturbed. I dial the number and a woman answers almost straight away, comfortable and kind. 'Good morning,' she says. 'Al-Anon. My name is Sally. Can I help?'

'I don't know why I'm ringing,' I say.

'That's fine. Take your time.'

'Someone suggested it. I don't know if my husband is an alcoholic,' I blurt.

'Well, thank you for ringing. Maybe I can ask you a few questions?'

He doesn't drink all the time, I tell her. He doesn't get up in the morning and drink. She tells me it's not necessarily a question of when or how much the person is drinking. It's more a question of what the drinking does to them, if it changes them in any way.

'Does your husband's behaviour change when he drinks?'

Her question is like a closing and opening of blinds. I know that when I say 'yes', there is my answer. I hear myself say it, 'Yes,' and my voice fails.

She explains to me that if the drinking is having an adverse effect, then there is very likely a problem with alcohol.

'Thank you,' I say. 'Thank you for your help,' and I hang up. Thank you. I am so well behaved. So civilized.

I had convinced myself; he has convinced me. He says he can give up if he wants, has given up for a week or so in the past. He isn't drinking meths; he isn't curled up on a park bench.

But all those times when I've had no idea why, out of nowhere, the air will switch. Something I've said, something I've done or not done, not anticipated something he's thought, been thinking, not sensitive enough, not agile, not clever enough.

How stupid, how blind.

Shirin has learned to stand in her cot, she will not sleep, cries out, recognizing my step. It's as if a whole new planetary system has invaded us, its own bleeping pulse, disrupting, in a way that nothing else could, the ley lines of the house.

He will not have it. This is all to do with my ambition, which he is as sensitive to as to daylight.

'You used me,' he snarls. 'All you wanted was a baby.'

'Why did I marry you, then? Why did I do that?'

He's dragged down the armchair from upstairs, its horizontal wooden arms convenient for an ashtray and a tumbler, and has taken up permanent residence in the kitchen. When I walk in, his heavy head tips forwards; he barely moves, if only to prove he's not a corpse, tapping the ash, lifting a tumbler to his lips.

I write a letter to his parents. I tell them that I think he needs help, that I think, apart from anything else, he is an alcoholic.

In ten days, when there has been no answer, I ring them from work. Faether answers. 'Four-Five-Two,' he says.

'It's Jane,' I say.

'Yes?' He is short.

'Did you get my letter?'

'We had a letter from you, yes.'

'I can't deal with him myself.'

He won't hear of it. 'All this nonsense. It takes two,' he says.

They are closing ranks. Expelled. You were no good. Never good enough. No surprise. Broken family: no moral compass. I could have told you that. Trapped. She wanted his child.

Although I don't know her very well, but because we've always seemed to get on, I ring Jazmine.

'Hello,' she says, surprised. 'Good to hear from you.'

I ask her how everything is going, though I know she knows I must be ringing for a reason. 'I wrote to your parents,' I say. 'I don't know who else I can talk to.'

Her voice stiffens. 'You knew what he was like.'

'I thought he'd change,' I say.

'You knew what he was like when you took him on,' she says.

'I thought when we had a child—' And then I give up.

Where once I used to love the beery, honeyed smell, I begin to dread it. The sheer liquid volume, the way a wave can turn as big as a house. He comes in from the park one Sunday with his back roasted to crackling; his skin is preternaturally sensitive, and he'd fallen asleep under a tree with his shirt off. He lets me smear cold cream over the burns, wincing under the touch of my fingertips.

Though we've been sleeping in the same bed, we've kept to our own sides, and usually he comes up long after I'm asleep. But this night he follows me. He climbs up from the bottom of the bed. He says, 'We could give it another go, if you like.' And then, like a man over the top, waving a hankie, he says, 'I love you,' and it's a shock to hear, because I've lain in wait so long to hear it, I don't recognize the words. I am a door, and he is upon me. I can't push him away because I can't reject this straw of his relenting, which for him is more than mountains. I am wooden but I let him in, no sense of anything, but that this, I tell myself, will be the last time. Crank, crank. I watch over his shoulder in the dark. This is how it feels, a marriage, conjugal rights, no connection, no love, ridden, unresponsive. The thread breaks. He falls away like a baby on his back and breathes blackness, ending, rope.

ii

'How're you?' Ardu asks.

'Fine.'

'What are you up to?'

'I'm at work.'

'What are you teaching them today?'

'We're looking at Cheever. Did you want something?'

'John Cheever? I like Cheever,' he says.

I don't remind him that it was he who put me onto Cheever in the first place. 'Have you read "The Swimmer"?' he'd asked, when I was nineteen or twenty, knowing more than likely that

I hadn't. He explained that it was about a man who set out to swim home from a party by using only his neighbours' swimming pools. It sounded to be a tale of machismo like one in the long line of books by American men he berated me for not having read, and I wasn't going to make an exception.

It was years later when finally I got round to reading it, and I must have read the story a hundred times. When I give it to students, it takes some unpacking: more often than not, they can't identify with this middle-aged, apparently full-of-himself man: why should they?

But it isn't them I'm thinking of.

If the audio-machine is working, I'll play a recording of Cheever reading the story himself, his voice so ravaged by fags and booze he can't reach the end of a sentence without coughing, clearing his throat: it doesn't endear him to them.

Isn't this a great pattern for a story, I might say, this diving into different pools? He dove, he dove, the story goes, down into the dive.

They aren't particularly impressed. One of them points out that Cheever appears to have got his timescale and his seasons all wrong. I say, 'Well spotted.' And I'll ask, 'Do you think it might be a deliberate effect?' It takes a concerted effort to get them not to read things literally, and, if not literally, not to want to ascribe an $a = b$, as if they can't help but be repelled by ambiguity. Perhaps, their age, I was the same, a resistance to anything that smacked of decrepitude. Don't we all start out as heroes of our own lives?

I can't help wondering what Ardu made of the story, whether it carried for him the slightest hint of a warning, or whether, more likely, it was just an example of a perfectly executed conceit.

Perhaps it only means so much to me because I read it in hindsight, knowing what I know, recognizing the tell-tale signs of an alcoholic. And perhaps I read too much into it, that heart-breaking shift when Cheever deserts his swimmer's point of view to extend an invitation to the reader to take a look:

Had you gone for a Sunday afternoon ride that day you might have seen him, close to naked, standing on the shoulders of Route 424, waiting for a chance to cross. You might have wondered if he was the victim of foul play, had his car broken down, or was he merely a fool.

It is a shock, any illusion that the man is in control of his destiny, abruptly shattered, a narrative sleight of hand all the more compelling given that Cheever was an alcoholic, too.

Students generally refuse to see the pathos. Alcoholism probably means as little to them now as it did to me then. Neither does the terrifying concatenation of years the story pulls off. They've barely lived: how can they yet know that time is not progression, but that it baffles, undoes as fast as it makes – those four children, that wife, the house all gone, it seems, in the dizzying space of an afternoon?

'Have you seen the film?' Ardu asks. 'Burt Lancaster is underrated as an actor, I think.'

'I haven't,' I say.

'Cheever gets a walk-on part. He was a terrible fuck-up, but he was a good writer.'

I zip up the rucksack on my knee. 'You mean he was an alcoholic?'

'Married, but preferred men.'

'How's *your* drinking?' I ask.

'I've stopped.'

'What, completely?' I'm searching the drawer for a biro.

'Yup.'

'How's that going?'

'We'll have to see.'

'Because you're an alcoholic,' I say, predictably.

'If you say so.'

'It's up to you to say it.'

'Okay,' he says, lightly. 'I'm an alcoholic.'

I'm stopped in my tracks. He's never said so before. All those years like cards laid out upon a table are thrown up into the air. *I am an alcoholic.* It's like a code: I know how significant the words are, the only way to begin to get beyond the assertion that it's everyone else who's at fault – *stupid cook, stupid maid.* The detonation is deep underwater, a wave of molten heat pulsing through me, a nuclear core sufficient, I imagine, to power the whole station.

iii

I wake, soaked through, and thankful for the small mercy that there's no one here to witness it. All night, jostling for position, the helter-skelter of visits to dark cities, the climbing of a crumbling rock face against mounting seas. Somewhere a stone has been rolled from the entrance to a cave, and I'm standing with a sponge of vinegar in my hand, having waited so long I don't know what to do with it.

Strictly I don't have to be at work until mid-morning. In the car, I put the radio on, *Woman's Hour*: they're talking about a production of *Jane Eyre*. *It's not a love story*, the director declares, *it's a life story*.

I perk up. Another woman, an academic, chips in: *It's a fearful odyssey ... Through the experience of a girl we have intimations of titanic structures: colonialism, patriarchy, the terrifying manners of the sequestered life ...*

Yes, yes! How many of us, listening, will cry, you are talking about me, you are talking about my life (*though, in the twenty-first century, how can that be true?*)!

But how many of those listeners are also called Jane, a proprietary advantage? I've had cause to give it thought: too easy to claim I was groomed by the book, groomed to persevere and suffer until the man I'd dared to love was brought so low I was allowed to think him the man I deserved. But this is a book that is subject to those same structures it suggests – romantic, patriarchal, domestic, whatever else – and manages to rise above them: that unprecedented example of a female voice – real, heartfelt, fallible, partial – that is the one thing that can light a way out of such prisons, inflicted or self-imposed.

Sometimes I wish I could write down what I think when I'm driving. Without even realizing it, I've come off the A30, driving along the back road on autopilot. Jenni Murray is winding things up, and in doing so turns her listeners' attention to a 'true story', she says, one with a touch of the Jane Eyres about it. Here is a woman (although her name is not Jane), who, after years of separation, has returned to her ex-husband to nurse him through his cancer. There is no one else to do it.

And do you love your husband – (Jenni corrects herself) – *your ex-husband?* There's a brief radio silence, and then the woman replies: *It's a different kind of love.* She won't elaborate.

I turn off the radio, *too late*.

What if he came to live with me?

What?

If, I said.

What are you doing?! Don't even think it!

What am I thinking?

You're thinking, Rochester. You're thinking, how would it be, after all these years, if the story were to come right, if it weren't such a wreck after all?

The background beeping of a horn makes itself heard, coming straight at me. We are crawling down the hill into town. I dart up to the rear-view mirror. A man behind lifts his hands from the steering wheel, *What's the hold-up?* I jump to it. *Sorry.* Wrong gear. The car stalls. *Sorry.* His shoulders are set in fury. *Bugger off,* I mutter, and lurch forwards to the lights, which, before I reach them, turn red.

As if all this time my head has been in a bucket, a home-made visor, and I've been stumbling around in the story impossible to write because impossible to *right* it.

When I was fifteen I worried I had Quadrophenia: *Dear Diary, I think I am quadrophenic. I want to make myself into a person who will be accepted and liked, and NOT one of those revolting neurotic paranoid feminist egocentric women, thank you.*

Too late!

1. *Have you forgotten everything?* I shriek. *Something is wrong with you, something is very badly wrong!*

2. I have gagged her and bound her hands and feet and locked her up in the wardrobe.

3. Here is the story of the man I met when I was the age my students are, the age my daughter (his daughter) is now, a man

who's separated from me, from everyone, by decades of drinking. He'll arrive with his army bag stuffed with the few things he'll need, take up residence in the spare room, where I'll cart up trays of food and water for him. Occasionally I'll catch an unguarded look on his face, the cynicism and the irony burnt off. Here in its fragile chick-like state will be the creature I banked upon, who under my care will revert to the marvellous boy he was.

4. I compose a letter on the subject of giving up drink: *For what it's worth*, I say, *I think it is a great and brave thing to do what you are doing. If it is of any use to you then I hope that you are able to feel that you can call upon me if you ever want or need to as your friend.*

He is staying with his mother at Sonnadh, I discover. I've made a package of the letter, including with it an old lead carthorse I've found on eBay, whose sturdy fetlocks and shapely neck I imagine will provide a talisman of fortitude and strength. How can this fail? I send the parcel recorded delivery to be sure it gets there and check hourly on the Royal Mail website to see if it's arrived. At 3.15, the computer reproduces the wild loops of his mother's signature.

I imagine her bringing the package through to where he sits, in the small front room, the room that is panelled in wood like a family-sized coffin. He might recognize the handwriting and will wait until he's on his own to open it. It'll take a few goes to get through the Sellotape; he'll use his teeth. First out will be the horse in its blanket of bubble-wrap. He'll curl his hand quite naturally around its body, whose metal will soon warm up, and with the other hand, he'll pull out the letter, lay it along his thigh to read. It's the last thing he'll expect from me. *Great and brave*: he'll be disarmed, and – though I've never seen him do so before – finally, I imagine, he might weep.

19. Fanlight Fanny

I take the bus to the hospital, H for hospital bus. The building is grey and labyrinthine; there are coloured lines on the floor to guide you into the right place, long wide corridors, trolleys, photographs on the walls of giant technicolour sea anemones, industrial laundry baskets, a half-hearted attempt at a garden, glassed off, no obvious entrance, the plants grubbily evergreen. It is the first time I've been in a hospital since Shirin was born. Radiography. I have the letter of appointment and pass it over to the receptionist. She signs me in, date of birth, address; tells me to follow the green line to the waiting area.

Blue-backed metal chairs are arranged in a square to one side of the thoroughfare. I take a seat opposite a young couple holding hands and at a remove from three others each of whom make sure not to sit directly next to anyone else. The only talking occurs between this couple who speak a language made in the back of the nose. In the corridor, there's a water dispenser with pointy cups. When I press the button, water gushes and won't stop. A cleaner appears with a mop as if she lies in wait for just such an eventuality.

I apologize. How stupid I am, I say.

'Jane Feaver?' The voice that calls the name doesn't sound convinced. Could there be any one of that name here? Even in my head it takes a moment for the name to attach itself to me. I stand quickly in case someone contests it.

'Hello, Jane, I'm Julie, your nurse today. If you'd like to follow me.'

I follow gratefully into a room with a bed and a screen. 'Hello, Jane, I'm the radiographer. I'll be performing the ultrasound today. Okay? If you'd like to step up onto the couch?' She is wearing a white housecoat, sits swivel to a screen. The nurse is in attendance, coal black hair.

'Do I need to take anything off?'

She casts her eye. 'Just your shoes. I think we'll be fine,' she says.

I lie back stiffly.

'Comfortable?' she says.

'The last time I was here I was pregnant,' I say. 'A long time ago,' I laugh.

The twelve-week scan, and Ardu has come with me, a sign – what joy! – that he takes his responsibility as father seriously. Waiting for the infra-red to kick in, focus the binoculars for a measurement of the nuchal fold, the heart-stopping moment before the heartbeat – there! – a submarine radar, the fan-shape that is my womb being swept, this creature, no bigger than a peanut, with pods for arms and legs. A photograph to prove it. I am the goose with the golden egg, so emboldened to be so I take his hand: this bit of us that is in both our interests to keep intact and safe.

The radiographer loads the sensor with clear gel, warns me, setting it down, it may be cold. On my belly it's a dog's paw. I look up at the ceiling, big square pitted tiles. The contact is silver. She begins to stir back and forth across my belly, her eyes on the monitor which is turned so that I can't see. She takes it up and sets it down again, into the dips either side, then climbs further up, pushes the edge of my T-shirt. Pauses. Presses. Revisits. Asks me to turn on my side. Presses. Asks me to turn back. Her face flickers with concentration.

'Did you know you had some scarring of your kidney?' she asks, incidentally. 'Ever had kidney stones?'

Scarring? 'No, I don't think so.'

She runs the sensor around and back up, over to the other side, back down again. I feel that she is looking too hard, that she is intent on finding something wrong.

'Well, there's definitely a cyst here,' she says. She beckons with her head for the nurse to have a look. 'About as big as a tennis ball, would you say?'

'A tennis ball?' I ask.

'Oh, believe me,' she says, 'I've seen cysts as big as melons.' She presses, she hasn't stopped moving the sensor. 'I'll just need to take some measurements,' she says, 'for the consultant.'

In part I'm relieved that there's something concrete, a legitimate pathology, but perhaps I should be more careful what I wish for. I swing my legs from the couch and tip to the floor, put my shoes on. Gravida: though I'm not pregnant, I feel that I'm carrying more than I did when I arrived. The two women raise their hands like ministrating nuns. Politely we say our goodbyes, and I retrace my steps along the lines to exit.

'Don't tell Shirin,' Ardu says.

'What happened?'

'The neighbour found me outside. I must have blacked out.'

'Where are you?'

'Hospital.'

'I thought you'd stopped drinking?' No response. 'How long are you in there?'

'They're doing tests.'

'For what?'

'Who knows.'

'They're drying you out?'

'Everyone's drying out in this place. That's standard. Do you know, there's an old bloke across the way, lost both his legs? You might laugh, but I'm one of the normal ones. The nurses can't get enough of me.'

On car journeys to the cottage, on the old tape recorder, our father would play George Formby. We all had our favourites and tried to learn the words off by heart so we could sing along or sing when the batteries gave out. The one I liked best was a jolly song about a jazz club singer, Fanlight Fanny. It seemed to me then to be about a woman defying her age, at home in the limelight of the stage, all the energy and glamour of the West End. I've since looked up the song and found I hadn't listened or understood it properly. She's not the '*Saturday* night club queen', as I'd learned to sing it, she's the '*frowzy* night club queen', fusty, unwashed, past her sell-by date. Every achievement of hers – I understand it now – is in one way or other undermined: 'She's a peach but understand, she's called a peach because she's always canned.'

In many ways she's no different from the swimmer, a raging alcoholic, embracing her dives with as much bravado as he does. Except one is a middle-aged man and the other a middle-aged woman, and this, of course, makes all the difference. Fanny is ridiculous, blotto, waltzing around with saucepan lids on her breasts, whereas the swimmer has, would always have, far more to lose: a family, wife, four children, a job, a house, a cook, a maid. His fall is epic because his author has the wherewithal to imagine it so, a man who can pat the bottom of a Greek god, allude to Shakespeare; he's a cartographer, an explorer. The swimmer's story bears repetition, and each re-reading the wash of dramatic irony works deeper. And I love the story for it, I have told you so, though I realize I can only love it as Jane Eyre might do, full of compassion for this man and his fate (even though he's a terrible snob and an adulterer, to boot). And the truth is, alcoholic or not, I can never be him, or be like him, not in the way, conceivably, I can be Fanny or Miss Prism, or any number of laughable middle-aged spinsters whose clothes would fit if I tried them on.

Lecturing is a kind of stand-up. Those fifty minutes in the spotlight of the overhead projector, which leave my body rattling in its cage, in need of a darkened room. And the indignity doesn't end. The lectures are recorded, and it's my responsibility to check – which I do, abjectly (Ardu's word) – to see that the recording is up and running. *Play*. Here I am credit-card-sized – *this is what fiction means!* – waving my arms like a farce from silent cinema.

One of those ninety faces – it only takes one – will report to MACE that the lectures were 'useless', 'they didn't teach me anything', the lecturer kept 'going off at tangents'. To which my head and its orchestra of castigating voices will explode.

'I don't know why you let it bother you,' Anthony says

when, having printed it out, I take the offending email to his room.

Because I can't see why we are subjected to it. What is the use? Not only do I not believe in treating students as consumers with customer-satisfaction questionnaires, but I'm convinced that their responses will be slanted. They've done research on it, I tell him. Evaluation is categorically gender biased. And it's racist, and I bet it's ageist too. It's abuse, I say. Why do we have to put up with it?

'What about the ones that were nice?' he asks, tactfully. 'Why don't you listen to them?'

'Because that's not the point,' I say. 'Either I'm good enough, or I'm not. I don't want to be subject to these anonymous poison darts.'

Half-past four on a Friday is a terrible time for a seminar. We arrange ourselves with the torpor of moving underwater. Since giving my lecture, the pain has wound tighter. I sit on a chair, but I'd rather be on the floor, under the table. I've asked them to bring in objects, but the request has slipped their minds. I produce a stand-by from my office: a toggle, pebble-sized with a hole drilled through the narrower part and on its flat base a winged creature roughly carved. 'Pass it round,' I say, air bubbles crashing from my mouth. 'When you have it in your hand, tell us something about it. Describe it in physical detail. Anything you like.'

The idea, as we go around the class, and as they run out of description, is for the thread of a story to begin to emerge.

Chance would be a fine thing. What seems to come from their mouths, every one of them, is 'pebble': 'pebble', 'pebble', 'pebble', 'pebble'.

Halfway into the second round, I ask: 'Is there a significance to the carving on the base?' my voice so distorted now, I might as well be drunk.

This boy seems far too big for his age, his T-shirt stretched to capacity over the tops of his arms. He's sunk like a statue of Hercules, the stone corkscrews of his hair. 'Pebble,' he says, moving the toggle from one hand to the other. Time moves slow as honey down here, and as I watch him, I enter his fist, back and forth, those pulverized limbs, that hole, straight through my side. Tick. Tock.

20. *Strike!*

'You won't believe the email I've had,' I say. And then, 'Did I wake you up?'

'No,' Ardu yawns again. 'What is it?'

'Guess who it's from.'

'Skunk?' he says, stealing my thunder.

'How did you know?'

'How many people do we have in common?'

'I'll read it. Hang on.' I have my machine in front of me and scroll down:

How are you? Not been in touch for years, and no idea if you still use this address.

Divorced here, but I guess that is true for most of us these days. I imagine your daughter (sorry, awful, but name escapes me) must be entirely grown-up?

I was wondering if you know what has happened to Ardu – as if anyone does you both presumably do? Number I had, not working. Is he still in the land of the living?

'Huh!' Ardu says.

'Are you?' I ask. 'How much is it worth?'

'You can tell him what you like. Why aren't you at work?'

'How do you know I'm not?'

'You don't ring from work.'

'I'm on strike.'

'Strike? How long's that been going on?'

'Two weeks, on and off.'

'I bet they're quaking in their boots.' The pop of the vape at his lips. He huffs. 'Do *you* remember writing a letter?' he asks. 'I didn't read it at the time, but I found it the other day; I've read it now. And I think you sent a lead horse, which, I must admit, I'd assumed was from Shirin.'

'I don't,' I say, although, of course, I do, and it chills me to remember how recently and utterly susceptible I was.

'I'll send it back to you, if you like?' He draws on the vape. 'Did you know,' he asks, 'she has a fantasy that her parents will get back together?'

'Don't all children?'

'I don't think you realize how clever she is.'

'I do realize,' I say, and add, defensively, 'She's other things too.'

'Things, I suppose, she gets from you?' He snorts. 'You know you can get the complete Balzac for 99p on Kindle?' He can't stop. 'What's the weather doing down there? There's thick snow here.' I feel the tug as he peers out of the window. 'You wouldn't believe it. In the old days I'd have gone into a cold sweat. I'd be thinking, how was I going to get out of the house to get hold of some booze?'

ii

When we were children in Northumberland it snowed every year. A couple of times the snow was so deep the snow plough couldn't get through, snow piled high as the hedgerow, a thick crust on the coping stones of walls and along the arms of trees. Our father dug a passage out of the front door which turned the cottage into an igloo. We couldn't wait to be first in, the first to lay our footsteps in that crunch of being new, the first into the Arctic, on the moon.

The best place to sledge was on the lane below the cottage, a clear and steady run straight down to the farm so that if you fell, it was unlikely to hurt. A plastic bag or a tray was more efficient than the old sledge from the barn, whose runners were so rusty it stuck like a donkey in its tracks. Amelia and I knew how to steer with our heels, and, depending on the depth and crispness of the snow, we'd take one of the babies behind us, pushing off with the deafening shrieks of two dissonant kettles. The light was far more dazzling than it ever was in summer. How could something so bright be so cold? The babies would be first to crack, hot tears of defeat as the chill set in, fingers and toes which at the tap of a hammer would drop off – a mitten iced and grubby where one of them had sprawled in the ditch.

It doesn't snow as often now so that when it does, it comes tumbling straight out of childhood, as if snow is what the past is made of, white and feathery.

This year, extraordinarily, it has snowed twice in a row. My car is encased thick as polystyrene. The primary school is shut, and already there are cries from kids on the hill, tiny and colourful as little plastic footballers. People emerge squinting from their doorways, disarmed because they are children again, too.

It seems more than coincidence that both times – *twice!* – it snows on those days when after striking we're due to go back into work. Not a paltry scattering, but the kind of snowfall, blizzardy and continuous, designed to shut down a campus: the snow is on our side!

There have been strikes before, a huddle of placards on the perimeter road that go to show how few of us there are. And I've only been there among the die-hards because I'm an anachronism, from a time when to strike was the only honourable thing to do. Whole generations since then, it seems, have been deactivated, neutered, caught up in a kind of Stockholm syndrome, too conditioned by the system not to achieve satisfaction.

But there's a rustle in the corridors. In what has been a long process of attrition, compliance has been overestimated. This latest insult is the last straw. This time everyone is joining in so that, far from being ignominious, it would be positively embarrassing *not* to appear on the picket line.

Against such momentum, it's hard for the cadres not to come unstuck. Emails are sent with blustering instructions not to disadvantage student learning, to make sure work and assessment-planning are on track, etc. An official loses his cool and is filmed on a smartphone shouting like Basil Fawlty: his Security Men, he bawls, are being intimidated by a handful of students who've locked themselves into the admin offices with guitars and packs of cards, who've hung a sheet from the window that urges in fluffy spray-paint letters, SUPPORT OUR STRIKE. As pizzas and cake and toothpaste are smuggled in, I swell with pride to pick out the blue hair of the kingfisher boy. Isn't this what any self-respecting student should be doing, protesting, marching, waving a flag?

There is something old-fashioned, a hint of wildness to what has been set loose. In the booming body of a church in town, the temperature is stone. The sign proclaims, 'Alternative University', which for the afternoon is what it has become. People are beginning to file in, staff, some students. There is a nervousness. How many will turn up? Sandwiches have been made. Someone from the church, a woman with a cardigan and scratchy hair, is demonstrating how the tea urn works. The pews begin to fill, the acoustics encouraging. It's a while, in fact, since the church has been as full. There is a microphone at the front, tested nervously. Mike is an earnest young man, all elbows and wrists, diffident, concentrated, wearing his Hi Vis waistcoat with aplomb. He blinks. He has a wife and a young child in a woollen strawberry hat who yelps at the back to the sound of his voice. There is daring and there is fighting talk. *Education has been taken by stealth, turned from pursuit into transaction: target, output, learning outcome. What is a university? What is it supposed to do? Who are they, and who are we?* It's as if, finally, we've woken from the spell, a decade of living each in our own narrow cell.

I thought it was just me, I thought it was because I was so hopeless.

If you felt like an imposter, so did I! In a reverse of fortune, it's a badge of honour to be so. The perimeter road is a fairground. A patchwork blanket is knitted to hang with its sickle and pink fist over the ziggurat of the university crest. I have never seen such animation in the faces around me. We have jumped the fence and it is exhilarating, the hubbub of warm flanks, the relief of moving through a landscape together.

Can you hear it in my voice? I worry that I'll give myself away, trembling with excitement, the hairs on my neck on end, because this strike has unlocked for me the deeper fault: where I've had no difficulty railing against the injustices of an institution, I have been blind – I know you have seen it! – to the Trojan horse that is in my head, loaded with those men whose interest I was bred to believe, it being so scant, was the only interest worth having.

And worse than that, I've been complicit: I've invited them in, have made them so much at home they sit and declaim and piss wherever they like.

('I had to laugh,' was something Granny used to say about our father when what she really wanted was to point out some offence.)

How could I have let it pass? One poor woman who crossed the Professor stank, he declared, of fish. *Ha-ha.*

Bakies are all the same is what Ardu used to say.

It's a tried and tested technique to keep us on the bite of not-being-good-enough, the threat of being ghosted, sunk – for what? A crumb of attention, a pat on the head.

Well, cynics, mordant wits, *pisseurs*, I've had enough! Go fuck yourselves.

I wake up drenched in sweat, disoriented, scrabbling to pull myself together. What day is it? How old am I? You have a child. Panic. Where is she? Next door? No, she is away. She is away at university, living on her own trajectory, and sometimes it's as if I've released her like a balloon, and at others it feels like a piece of the iceberg broken off.

Enough of that! heaving my limbs from high over the side of the bed, slipping unsteadily to my feet like a princess who's grown into a very old lady, making for the door.

By the time I get into the bath, I'm merely middle-aged, a woman on my own who has no idea what is wrong except that things are coming to a head, unattended things, habitual things, which have the additional weight of time attached, half a century's worth, tick-tock, tick-tock, the clapper jerking its head in readiness to strike: those footmen who'll be turned to mice, the carriage to a pumpkin.

21. Fish Tank

Our father's mother was far stricter than Granny Georgie. She didn't give us ice cream or ginger beer; we were expected to be quiet and well behaved, to have clean fingernails, to amuse ourselves until it was time to eat, to say our prayers. We were children from a book by E. Nesbit, *The Wouldbegoods*, *Five Children and It*, and perfectly good at disappearing when we should. On rainy days there was a drawer in the chest at the bottom of the staircase stuffed with the dressing-up clothes our father and his sisters had had as children, a suit of armour knitted from string, a milkmaid's skirt with a black velvet bodice. For lunch a gong rang, which we ate at the long dining table, Grandpa at one end, and portraits of older bishops all around to remind us how important he was, and why it was he said grace and had the skin off the custard.

For a treat, Granny took us to rub brasses in the cathedral; she did embroidery and French knitting with us, showed us plaits of real human hair that she kept in her sewing box for making the clever double dolls she was famous for: if you lifted Red Riding Hood's skirts and pulled them up over her head, you'd find a wolf, disguised in a pair of fuse-wire spectacles and dressed in Grandmother's clothes.

When our father left, the visits appeared to stop. Rather than impute blame to our father, it must have been easier to imagine that somehow we didn't exist. It wasn't until Granny became ill that we really understood what had happened. *Only close relatives*, we were told, when we asked to see her. And then she died, and it had been so long, it was hard to work out what dying meant in relation to her already being gone.

Granny wanted the cousins to look pretty for her funeral: she left money to buy dresses for them from Laura Ashley. But no one supervised what we would wear, Amelia in her home-made paisley trousers, me in a polka-dot skirt and DMs, the most sombre clothes we could lay our hands on. It had been four years since we'd seen anyone on that side of the family. We might have been living in Argentina, so incongruous was our return. We stuck together, four of us in a row, bowing our heads to whisper in the pew, *forgive us our trespasses*, listening as we had done through the years to our grandfather in the pulpit, intoning as he always did at breakneck speed.

But we were not who we were before, and unprepared for the peculiar familiarity of hymn books, the kneelers with their cross-stitch rabbits and bowls of fruit, exactly as they'd always been, too sharp a reminder of a history that was no longer ours. One by one our voices cracked, and we stopped trying to sing, succumbed along the line to quaking shoulders and snot that came in terrible quantities, no hankies. We were a weir of grief, embarrassing, disproportionate, hysterical, as if a lid had been lifted on a sewer in flood, unspeakable things in it, a grief that had been stockpiled, dammed, for not being able to say goodbye, for not being included in the flowery dresses, for not belonging, for not being loved, full stop.

There were waitresses in white pinnies handing round canapes and sherry in the drawing room of the rectory to which assembled mourners had been invited, a little man circulating in plus fours with a photocopied family tree to press on anyone whose eye he caught. We were taken to greet our grandfather who sat in his purple dress receiving condolences. The fusty smell of church and doormat. One by one he gripped us by the arm. We had grown, he said, holding on to Rose the longest: 'Weren't you supposed to be the pretty one?'

And then we were shown into the kitchen, away from the rest of them, a plate of sandwiches, a bowl of crisps, and the two pugs who'd been shut in, their wrinkled, congested faces snuffling at our feet for anything we might drop.

Not long after the funeral we heard that Grandpa was getting remarried, was marrying the woman who'd been Granny's best friend, with whom it turned out Granny had been worried he'd been having an affair. An affair! What a ridiculous word to bandy about!

But suppose that it were true, as his children clearly suspected: that our grandfather, whatever he protested, had been having an affair? That at the least he'd shown an undue haste in getting remarried? How outraged they were at being asked to accept it. And how outraged we were to be asked to be outraged on our father's behalf. Couldn't he see the correspondence?

The rules, apparently, were different for us, who were outside, beyond, too old to be children, to make a fuss, to be upset. We were like skeletons in the cupboard, I wrote, the one time I made a stand, though the letter, it seemed, got lost in the post.

I've been back and forth to the hospital enough now to know my way around. It's like the insides of an enormous space-ship, and not the sort of place to which you'd want to become accustomed: a spaceship with the threat of alien life on board, which might strike from a cupboard or a laundry basket at any moment. Deep in the bowels of the place, I'm in a waiting room that has no windows, immune to the weather that dissolves on our coats and shoes. There is a huge fish tank opposite the seating area, the seats, which are arranged in rows rather than in the round I've been used to. Everyone waits here: even a nurse in her blue trouser-uniform and plastic shoes is waiting. An old couple to the side of me sit melting, holding hands. There is the soft buzz like the engine of a fridge. We stare at the fish who come to the glass and gape, though it seems by their unselfconsciousness that they cannot see us. We wait and the waiting sucks us into the fish tank, where the world is bathed in a greenish light, more appealing than ours, which pulses from metallic squares in the ceiling.

Dim moon-eyed fishes: there are one, two, three flesh-coloured fish. They have transparent fluttery fins, fanning the water, swivel-eyed, in and out of greenery, above a bed of gravel, the plastic semblance of a rock, and a backdrop that, if you look closely enough, is a photograph of an ocean wall, a reef and, in one corner, the rigging of a wreck.

For whose benefit? The fish are oblivious: it is no more than a dappling of colour that might offer camouflage at most, though here, in this holding station, there is no threat, nothing to require camouflage from. And if they were at sea, how would they read a shipwreck except as a variety of holes and tunnels to swim through? There would be no sentiment, no story. Imagine it, a suspension that's the opposite of suspense, a world that is endlessly available, contained, perfectly balanced to a sweet spot of momentum that is swimming, flying, the glory days of wheeling back and forth through a puddle on a bicycle.

And then a leopard fish appears as if from nowhere out of the gravel, somersaults in a corner, eyes on either side of its thin protruding face. O, O, O. It is like a piece of leopard thrown into the tank, a limb that has developed fins, tiny fins to direct that hunk of a body, its proud crest. *Tyger Tyger*. This is hell, its mouth signs. If only you could have imagined it better. If only you weren't so dim.

'Jane Feaver?'

The nephrologist has some news. He shows me the screen with the X-ray and points with his pen to a tree with a bean-shaped cloud in its branches. 'On this side,' he says, 'as you can see, you have a nice, healthy kidney, if anything, bigger than we might expect. And then—' He points to the other side, which is cowed and shrunk. 'We can tell from the CT scan and from the yellow dye that this second kidney has practically no function at all.'

I can't help feeling responsible, and sorry, as if this kidney has been quietly taking all the blows.

'What's happened to it?' I ask.

'It's probably been like that since you were born,' he says. 'It's the sort of thing we'd catch in babies these days.'

'Is that what's causing the pain?' I ask.

'It's hard to know,' he says. 'It could be that, it could be the ovary. We could remove it—?'

'I'm having my ovaries removed,' I say, tensely.

'It's possible they could take the kidney at the same time—'

It feels, suddenly, as if I am under siege and that there will be nothing left in the bag to remove. 'Does it need to come out?' I ask.

'The problem with an operation is that you need to want it, to believe that it will do you good. It's perfectly possible that after an operation, you may find that the pain is still there. I must tell you, if we looked into anyone's body, we'd be surprised at what we'd find. No one is particularly "normal".'

My knowledge of kidney treatment is mostly gleaned from what I've picked up from *Coronation Street*, where, over the years, there's been a deal of kidney trouble. 'You can live on one kidney, can't you?'

'Of course. Absolutely.'

Far worse things happen, so much worse. But this kidney thing will not keep to facts. It's like finding out some fundamental secret – like finding out your father is not your father – a secret that suddenly makes sense of how unaligned to everything you've been.

But your father clearly *is* your father, there is no escaping that.

Like finding out, then, that the father you thought you had, you didn't. And although you've known it all along, you've refused to believe it.

22. Black Hole

Though we can't agree on anything it seems that he's accepted for whatever reason that it will be better if he moves out. There's someone at the shed who knows a woman who runs a couple of bedsits in Streatham, one of which may be available in a few weeks. For those weeks he will sleep in the spare room at the back of the house, the room above the kitchen, an extension that was attached at some point after the original house was built. There's a crack where the room joins the main building and it has expanded enough to allow rainwater to seep in, a brownish-yellow stain that spreads across the ceiling and into the corner, where it has acquired a dense silver fur.

It's a Sunday again. He hasn't moved from his bedroom except to visit the loo next door. He has a *Racing Post*, an ashtray and, on the floor, my old copy of *Where the Wild Things Are*. It's humid inside, but too rainy to go out, and Shirin is fractious. We've exhausted her three favourite books, got halfway through the video of *Snow White*, and she's tired but won't go to sleep. It is his turn.

I gather her up and we trot along the landing, jiggedy-jig. 'Let's go and see Daddy,' I say. 'Let's see what Daddy is up to.' Fat blobs of rain gather and fall from the sill where it is open to the side of the bed to draw out the smoke.

He is lying with his head propped up, irritated to be disturbed.

'You can have her for a bit,' I say.

Shirin is distracted to be up off the floor, to be in this room, and she is sick of me; she reaches out.

He makes no move to take her. I waltz over and dump her on his stomach, turn, and as I do he yells, 'You bitch!' I'm so incensed to be called a bitch in front of her I'm ready at once to take her back and have no more of it ever. He holds her up and away from his body, rigid. I gather her from him, her face, up in the air, and he is puce and thunderous and stinks of doused bonfire.

As soon as she's in my arms she begins to cry, full-blown, an air-raid warning, and I bind her to me, try to soothe her.

'You bitch,' he says again, trawling the floor of his voice as I make for the door. He is bent over himself.

'What's wrong?'

'Ring an ambulance,' he says through gritted teeth. And he mutters, 'Fucking bitch.'

'What have you done?'

'You threw her at me.'

'I didn't *throw* her. I wouldn't throw her. I put her down on you.' And I am scrutinizing my story: I wouldn't, I couldn't, of course I didn't throw her.

'Do it. Ring an ambulance. Now. Do it!'

'What's happened?'

'Just do it!'

I am shaky as I carry her down the stairs. I have to believe he knows what he's doing. The movement takes the wind from

Shirin's sails, but it doesn't quieten her completely. I have never called 999 before. 'Shh, shh,' I say, lifting the phone from its place on the wall, poking at the keypad. 'Ambulance,' I say, Shirin, a weight, arching away from me. They put me through. 'He seems to be in terrible pain,' I say. 'No. My husband. His stomach. I don't know.'

I give them the address and stay downstairs with Shirin, our two hearts beating like rattles one against the other. I think, by the time the ambulance arrives, he may have calmed down, that he was overreacting and the pain, whatever it was, is bound to have worn off. Already I'm rehearsing what to say when it becomes my job to explain, to turn them away.

They are burly in their fluorescent lime jackets. I lead them upstairs and wait outside. I hear him answer their questions in a quiet rumble.

'Can you walk?' they ask.

One of them comes to the door. 'It looks like a torsion,' they say to me. 'A twisted testicle. We'll need to take him in. Can you put together an overnight bag?'

I have done this to him. He will tell them what I did, and I will say, *I set her down. I set her down.* With Shirin, who is beady at this new development, I find pyjamas and take his dressing gown from where it still hangs on the hook on our bedroom door, the tartan slippers I bought him for Christmas. I stuff them into a carrier bag. Either side of him, with his arms around their necks, they support him sideways down the stairs. At the bottom we catch them up. Shirin is curious, she sucks her fist. I will stay with her, I tell them. 'Ring me when you know what's happening,' I say to him, and the tone of my voice is suspect; the ambulance men will think I'm unnatural: he doesn't answer, and there is no kiss.

'Thank you,' I say, handing over the bag as I shut the door on them. 'Thank you.'

Two days a week for the past few months, because it has been too much for Ardu, Shirin has been going to a childminder, the same minder Julia has found for her daughter. The few days that Ardu is in hospital the childminder agrees to take her so that I can go into work. The hospital is on my way home and I visit him with a plastic carton of grapes because I am supposed to be his wife and that is what visitors do. His bed on the ward is empty, and on the near side, a rheumy old man with no teeth shakes his head. The nurse suggests I try the smokers' room at the far end of the corridor.

There are three of them in there, on three sides, one in a wheelchair, making a serious business of filling the room with smoke. The ceiling, the walls are streaked with nicotine, the furniture, plastic-covered, scrawled upon. I am an imposter with my grapes. I set down the plastic carton in the chair beside him and he barely looks up.

'How are you?' I ask, aware that this is a performance for the benefit of the others.

He stares ahead, not interested.

'Have they operated?'

He grunts, pokes the carton. 'Are they seedless?' he asks. 'You can take them away if they're not.'

'I need to pick up Shirin,' I say. 'I can't be long.'

'You'd better get going then.'

*　　*　　*

After a few days, when he's ready to leave the hospital, there's no option but for him to come home. Someone needs to keep an eye on him. Because I'm at work, Rose and her boyfriend offer to collect him. They've come back from Spain, looking for jobs, and I tell them that if they can wait, Ardu will be moving out and then there'll be plenty of room for them. I want them to stay, I tell them; I don't want to be alone in that house.

When I get back, Rose tells me that they've put him upstairs; he'd got them to stop off at the newsagents so that he could buy fags. 'He went in in his dressing gown and slippers,' she says. 'Has he told you, they had to remove one of his balls?'

'Fucking bitches,' Ardu says when I go up with a tray of bread and cheese, a glass of water. His eyes are sheet metal, hair shaggy, face unshaven. 'You and your fucking sisters, you're all the same.' He's as strange and unpredictable as a beast, captive incongruously in our bed. I don't ask about the operation: I don't want to know or begin to imagine it. I deposit the tray on the wooden chair next to him.

'He says we're all bitches,' I say when I come downstairs. Rose is feeding Shirin apple puree from a jar, scooping the pudding from round her mouth. 'Did he tell you what I said?' she asks. 'Oh God, he was saying how, when they castrate dogs, they give them a plastic ball instead. *Good girl*,' she says to Shirin, loading the spoon again. 'And I said, because he seemed to be joking about it: *Hitler only had one ball*. I know, it sounds terrible, but I didn't know what to say!'

ii

All I've had to go on for years is his voice, which is more or less the same as it ever was, persuasive, plausible, sure of itself. When I picture him on the end of the line, it's in a room with a chair, a standard lamp. Everything else is dark; the point of focus is his face, which is unchanged, and the casual way he hugs the receiver one shoulder raised to an ear so that his hands can be free for fetching drink, for cigarettes; the way his eyes and mouth work together, his mouth as mobile as a frog's.

But this evening he sounds pissed, though he says he hasn't been drinking, says he's slurry precisely because he hasn't had a drink. It's true, even when he's been drinking, he rarely slurs his words. He mentioned diabetes among his complaints the last time I spoke to him and I'm so used to googling medical ailments, I look it up. I say authoritatively, 'You're either drunk or you're hypoglycaemic.'

'I'm not drunk. So, what do I do?' he asks.

'Drink orange juice,' I say. 'Have you got any juice?'

'Nothing in the fridge.'

'Well, if you feel really bad, you'll have to call an ambulance,' I say.

He seems to be laughing. Then he says, 'Those books of St Aubyn's, you've read them?'

'Yes.'

'He's a good writer.'

'I told you that.'

'He *is* a good writer. That scene where his father rapes him—' He breaks off, and for a moment I think that he's laughing, making chimp-like noises. But then I realize he's crying. I haven't ever seen him cry, but the tears sound so copious I see them washing in a veil over his face. 'I'm not the sort of guy who cries,' he protests. 'But it's written so well. It's just brilliant writing.' He carries on crying, breathing, but not, it seems, being able to speak.

All I can do is hold the line. If it were a film, I think, this would be the crux of it, something that might explain everything. I wonder if he is about to make a confession. I'm peering down at him and he is in a deep hole, his face blackened, the whites of his eyes blinking up at me.

'He was at Keble, you know that?' Ardu says. 'He was off his head on smack most of the time, and no wonder . . .' More crying, inconsolable. I don't dare interrupt.

'I can't sleep. They won't give me pills.'

'Why?'

'They won't give me pills.'

'Who's looking after you?'

'The doctors are shite.'

'You've got a counsellor?'

'She's ill. She's off sick. She's bloody useless.'

'Who's keeping an eye on you, then? Someone must be?'

'I've got a terrible cold,' he says, snorting. 'I can't actually breathe.'

'Ardu?'

The line cuts out.

I leave it five minutes and then I dial him back. I'm at the sink, filling the kettle, the phone jammed between my shoulder and my ear. The phone doesn't even ring, before he's got it. He cackles, 'I can see your bits.'

'What?'

'Sluicing out your fanny?'

'What?'

'I can hear you.'

'I'm filling a hot-water bottle.'

'The doctors are waiting for me to die,' he says.

'Can you talk to someone?'

'I don't want to talk.'

'I mean, ring someone?'

'Who?'

'I don't know. Your brother? Your mother? You could ring

Clare?' I say, because, according to him, Clare has never gone away.

'She's crazy about me,' he says, viciously.

iii

I come across the obituary of a Scottish writer in the *Glasgow Herald*. I tear it from the paper because the likeness is uncanny. The obituary quotes the writer talking about himself:

> *Scots are luckier than, say, Estonians: we have our own little quirks of character, namely obsessiveness, megalomania, suicidal guilt, paranoia, cowardice when sober, and loudmouth hostility in drink, a fetish for minutiae and unquestioning drudgery as a defence against headaches from using our brains.*

It is the fetish for minutiae that clinches it, Ardu's indefatigable interest, for instance, in varieties of toothpaste. The only distinction I can find is that Ardu never wrote a novel (as if writing a novel is a way to explain or excuse anything else). But I wasn't the only one who thought he would. Clare bought him a typewriter years ago, which sat in a corner of her flat gathering dust; an editor I knew, without having seen a word he'd written, offered to give him a contract for a book because he believed, having once clapped eyes on him, that he was the kind of man who could. (And, of course, I would have typed it up, as Mum did for our father, in a flash.)

'Why did you marry me?' I ask in one of our late-night conversations. I don't know why it should still matter, but it does. He treats the question as rhetorical and I am forced to ask the question that lies at the bottom of it: 'Did you ever love me?' It's hard to use the word, but I spit it out.

He has to think. 'In my own way, perhaps I did,' he says. 'But I'd have had affairs, maybe you'd have had affairs, too?'

I don't say that I wouldn't, because it sounds ridiculous, climb-every-mountain, and like a weakness.

'Why did you marry me?' he asks again, rhetorically, as if we are the same. And then he says, 'In a funny way, I think we *are* alike. You should write about it,' he says.

Are we alike? Is that what it has been all along? That he is one of the few to know – my father knows it; the Professor thinks he knows – how rotten and despicable I am? Or is it that I'm too good a chameleon, and will adapt myself out of existence?

'Mon never wanted marriage. She was sensible,' he says. 'She understood. Other people have asked me why I married you. And I've told them: I was passive; you seemed to want it.'

'What if you'd stopped drinking?'

'Then why did you marry me?'

We are going round in circles. 'I didn't marry you in order to split up.'

'Much as it's nice to talk to you, I'm going to have to go,' he says. 'Desperate for a fag.'

iv

Herschel identified something similar in the night sky off the Cape of Good Hope: 'a coal-sack', he called it, a 'singular vacuity'. The image I am shown is a black circle, the truest, deepest black, which has no notion of its own depth. The radiographer plots its size with two intersecting dotted lines. This black hole is inside me, I am its universe, and the best option, they've said, to be on the safe side, is to remove it, this cyst and the ovary to which it's attached, and the Fallopian tubes, which can be of no use to me now.

Mum has kindly come down from Scotland to be around. The taxi driver arrives for us in the morning from Okehampton with her over-dyed hair, a rackety smoker's laugh. In the forty-minute drive to the hospital she delivers the story of her husband's demise. This is how it happened, she says:

'He'd been out beating and had tripped on a hidden piece of barbed wire. He told me, *I fell a beauty*. He said there was a sort of liquid he could feel under his ribs, and then he said he'd peed out blood. I said, *get on straight to that doctor. Tell them: "You see me now!"* He said there were no appointments that day, and I said, *that's not good enough*. And I went round to the surgery with him, and I was stood there, saying, *I'm not moving 'til someone gives me an answer*. And my doctor came out, and he knows what I'm like, and he says, *better send him in*. Well, they took one look at him and he was off to the hospital.' She cackles. 'A week later, we had the nurse upstairs and she said, *I don't think he's got long*. And by some kind of luck, we was all there, his mum, his son. Up we went. He took a deep breath, he held onto it. Then he was gone. I never thought it could be so quick.'

'That was cheerful,' I say to Mum, on our way inside. I change into the gown they leave, weaving myself into its three armholes, and ease on the compression stockings. I lie back on a couch upholstered in sturdy black plastic, a curtain that pulls round like a child's bedroom curtain with faded cartoons of the city's buildings – the cathedral, the Guildhall. Mum is looking anxious, and I'm practised at refusing to be infected. It is keyhole surgery, there is nothing to it, in and out, the consultant has said. I'm borne off into a lift to see the anaesthetist. I've never had a general anaesthetic, I tell her. 'Nothing to worry about.' She has dark eyes, a chatty face. I lie on the couch, and her assistant, Clive, an older, unshaven man, beams at me. She taps the back of my hand; he says, 'You'll feel a scratch.'

'So, you're a writer?' she says. 'What do you write?'

'Fiction,' I say.

'What sort of fiction?'

I can only think, ruefully, of what it is not, not the sort of fiction people generally read. 'You may feel something cold,' she says. 'It's anti-sickness.' And my vein tingles as she says so. She's above me, her broad face bearing down. 'You may feel a little woozy. That glass of wine—'

I'm having a dream when I come round, though to call it a dream is to do it an injustice: *catachresis*, one of Ardu's words, floats into my head, and now I can tell you what it means: the wrong word for the wrong thing, because everything in this so-called dream was more fitting, more real and vivid than the whole of my life put together. If there's the tiniest window of opportunity, might I fold myself back in?

'Hello,' the nurse says. 'Coming round?'

'How long have I been gone?'

'An hour and ten minutes,' she says.

An hour and ten minutes for which I'd have swapped my life.

'You're in the recovery ward,' she says.

'It isn't done, is it?' I ask.

'Done and dusted,' she says.

I'm alive and it's over. She brings a jug of water. 'You'll need to drink this,' she says. 'Drink as much as you can.'

I'm wheeled back down to the day ward. 'Drink more water,' Mum says, anxiously. I'm a grotesque middle-aged baby, my mouth sandpaper dry, my lips stuck to my teeth. I drink, run the cool water over my gums.

The woman opposite is pretty and pale with golden hair; a man sits next to her holding her hand, soothing. Eventually our eyes meet. We smile. It's a chasm to reach across the ward to talk, but we begin to attempt it. She tells me she's a flautist. Her partner is a trumpeter. Her voice is a whisper. She's had an operation on her throat. Mum intervenes, she stands between the two of us. 'My other daughter,' she says proudly, 'she's a musician. She plays for the BBC.'

The girl is wan but a pleaser, too, with a face she is able to switch on in a smile. How I love strangers, I think, that connection based on nothing but the living moment of paths crossing, a flare of what it feels to be human without the burden of a past or the pressure of a future to look out for.

We are all waiting to be released; they just need us to pee, to prove that we can. I drink more: the more I drink, I think, the quicker I'll be gone. I feel nothing between my heart and the tops of my legs, but I get up and make my way to the patient toilet hoping for the best. Don't lock the door! I sit but nothing happens, the connection between my brain and the workings of my insides is lost. I sit for a while; I turn on the tap. I whistle through my teeth. Nothing. I come out, shaking my head.

'Don't worry,' Mum says.

In an hour, I try again. This time, taking my time, someone barges in. 'Hello?' quickly shuts the door, 'Sorry.' I'm beyond embarrassment. It's like being in some strange lunar colony.

'No luck?'

At five to six I produce two tiny drops, one with a pipette of blood in it. The nurse shakes her head. The ward is draining. The blond, fragile girl has gone. Mum looks worn out. This is a day ward, and now we've entered a new time zone, where nothing goes forwards, the minutes approximate as syrup.

Out in the corridor in my white stockings I walk, hoping that walking might set me off. A man in pale blue is there at the desk. Beyond him there must be another ward, and another. The toilet is mine, no need to stand guard, there is no one else here to use it. This time I manage a little more than a trickle. I take the trough to show him, carrying it like a crown on a cushion as if I've produced an elixir. 'I'm only the ward clerk,' he says. After a while the nurse appears with a scanner on wheels. She puts clear gel on the domed stick, and she moves it around just above the dressing, moves it back and forth and looks at the monitor. She goes away. When she comes back, she says they aren't happy. 'We may have to put in a catheter.' Surely the machine has got it wrong? I mistrust her; I think she must be getting the numbers back to front.

Mum rings my brother. 'A catheter for a week, they're saying.' She reports back to me, and to the nurse. 'That's ridiculous. My son's an anaesthetist. He says it's ridiculous.'

The nurse is boot-faced. I don't want Mum to tell them that they don't know what they're doing; I feel they will punish me for it. I'll try again. I'm desperate. The tray has the consistency of an egg box. I slot it into the toilet seat and reach for the tap, which I turn to keep it on the bite, on the point of release, trickle, whistle. *Shhhhhh*. Something happens, so delicate there's barely a sound on the drum of the pan. A little more. I stand to inspect. 'Well done!' I tell myself in the mirror. I lift my arms, tell myself that what's required is a rain dance. Gingerly – not Ginger Rogers – I move about, lift a knee, the other knee, return to the pan. A tiny trickle more. This is success, surely, a reservoir. The nurse returns with the machine: 600 millilitres. Not enough.

It's after midnight. The nurse is on all night, and this is not her favourite job. She strips open a pack, rubber gloves. 'You're not allergic to latex?' She brings out the blood-orange coloured tube. 'Open your legs, relax,' she says, a script. My legs are shaking. She bends with a look on her face that tells me already, this isn't going to work. I feel her stab with the end of the contraption. 'Relax,' Mum says, 'take a big breath.' She tries again, then lifts her head, exasperated. 'Sorry. I can't get it in,' she says. 'We'll have to wait for the doctor.'

In another twenty minutes or so, there is a doctor. 'We're going to take you somewhere with more light,' she says, as if light must be the problem. They lead me off to a room with a bed with raised stirrups. 'Pop yourself on the end, there,' the doctor says. I raise my legs and hook them into place. 'Now then,' she says. And in she goes. My legs shake. 'Bear down,' she says. 'As if you're doing a poo,' Mum says, and I am three years old. It is done. The nurse is busy securing the Velcro straps around my thigh. The bag is huge. I am dumb. The doctor explains too fast, handing over a blue catheter pack as if it is a party bag of goodies: there are seven in there, she says, bigger ones for the night-time. She shows me the lever. They stand me now over a cardboard collector and turn the tap; pale liquid gushes out. A whole cardboard container, and now another. 'It was the right thing to do,' she says. 'There's a lot of liquid in there. We need to give your bladder a rest.'

She is fresh-faced. No nonsense. 'How will you get home?' she asks. 'Can someone come and collect you?' It's 2.30 a.m., the house is twenty miles away. 'Have you got the number for a taxi?'

We go to stand by the sliding automatic doors in the entranceway. We are black and white as ghosts in the reflection. 'Once you're out,' they warn, 'you won't be able to come back in.' It's dark, cars at rest in the car park, a light just bright enough to see the shapes. I don't believe the taxi will ever come, or, if I blink, it will cruise around and out again. But here is a car. We exit the doors, which slide shut behind us. Apple Cars. He's a nice young man, he gets out to help us in. He is cheerful and he drives fast, nineteen years old, he says, from Cairo. He's going to university to read PPE. He has sisters, one a doctor, the other a lawyer. His father worked so hard. 'Your father must be proud of you,' Mum says. 'And we are proud of my father,' he says.

I use my phone as a torch to light the way in up the steps. It is far too late to be awake or to talk. We run into each other trying to go to bed. I have to attach the night-time bag. I work it out, hang the bag over the side of the bed in a basket that's full of old diaries. What will happen if it leaks? Good riddance, I think. I lie rigid on my side, imagine my wounds, three of them, and that I will never sleep.

In the morning, the assault comes bowling at me. There's a sack of pee heavy on my leg, which I detach from its strips, and carry on its lead to the toilet bowl. Golden piss, nearly two litres of it. I cut off the corner of the bag with nail scissors and aim it into the bowl, a tumble of liquid that rattles through the house.

I am a horrible invalid, querulous, tetchy, unloving and unloved. It is like being pregnant all over again, but there is no baby, just this sack of piss to look after. How will I ever walk further than the lamppost?

Mum tries her best. She will stay for as long as it takes, she says, this purdah for us both. She has been devouring books downstairs. She says, 'I gobble them up. Can you recommend another?'

'There are books all over the place!' I say.

'But something you've read?'

I can't read.

'Have you seen my phone?' she asks. 'My diary? My pills?'

A neighbour comes round. 'Is she a difficult patient?' she asks, teasing.

'Terrible!' Mum says. 'The scornful look she gave me this afternoon: it was just like her father.'

'I was joking,' she says afterwards. 'It just popped out. Two glasses of wine— I know you're worried.'

'I'm not worried, it's just a nightmare. It's boring, and it's waiting, and I'm not a saint.'

'I had a dream about your father and his wife last night,' she says. 'I don't like thinking about them.' And hearing her outside on the phone: 'I should just keep my mouth shut. I shouldn't say *anything*.'

Three days later, though I could never have imagined it, I've grown used to the plastic bag, which lays its warm cheek to my thigh. I walk around peg-legged. The bag is connected via a plastic tube that's threaded up through my urethra to the neck of my bladder where it's held in place by a little inflated balloon. 'Resist the urge to pee,' the doctor has said. When the bag fills with liquid there's a tap at the knee end like a keg of beer. I guide the end of the plastic tube into the bowl and twist, a gush of clear, pale liquid, and a thought enters my head: *this is what it feels like to have a penis.* How well-aimed and tidily achieved this peeing is, tapping the last drops from the end of the plastic valve. And on its heels, a sharper thought: *how much better at this I am than he is:*

The night, when we were still on speaking terms, the Professor elected to stay in my house, and managed – perhaps he'd drunk too much? – to piss around the seat, and on the wooden floor around the bowl. I had to get out rubber gloves to deal with it when he'd gone, down on my hands and knees.

23. Protracted Regret

I took it as a good sign, the curiosity I had about the man in the bookshop, a sign that, finally, I was moving on. He's overweight, but, because he's tall, he carries the excess reasonably well. He's good at recommending books. On his recommendation I've read the whole of James Salter. And now he's come up with a Norwegian who writes with such candour and shamelessness about his own life and relationships that most of his relatives will no longer speak to him. What's the point in making things up? the Norwegian asks, and at once I want to believe him.

There are days when the bookshop man is not at work and my journey – say it! – my journey is wasted. What has happened to me? When he is there – and his shape is utterly distinctive – I find my heart skips. 'I've finished the first one,' I tell him next time, 'the Knausgård?'

He's sorting out the 'recommends' table. He looks up from what he's doing, his hands setting straight a small pile of duplicate books. 'What did you think?'

'I loved it, the stuff about his father—'

'The house at the end—' he says, and between us we conjure the squalour of the alcoholic father's house.

'But I'm not sure he's right,' I hazard. 'I don't see that it's any different from fiction, really, in that it's something he's made from something else.'

'But it's his life,' the man says.

'I don't think the life bit is as important as what he makes of it. And being made, even if it isn't "made up", I'd call it fiction. Isn't that more honest?'

The man pulls a thinking face. 'If you say so,' he says, and he glances towards the till. *If you say so*, a shot across my bows. I hear Ardu, his voice, his huff. No matter how much I think I've weeded it out, those little thread-like roots are everywhere. I am red in the face and hot. *I do say so*, I say to myself. *I do*.

At the till I hand over the second volume. 'Glad you liked it.' He takes it from me and rings it up, pauses as he hands it back. 'My partner read it in one,' he says. 'She's onto the next already. Can't get enough of him.' I smart at his need to tell me this.

The man in the bookshop, what was I thinking? As long as he knows, and I know (I know it now) that I was thinking nothing of the sort.

ii

I made a note of this: In 1810, a boy called Charles Farrington practises his handwriting. He writes the same sentence in a large, loopy italic to the bottom of the page. The exercise is designed to help him master the mechanics of capitalization, of punctuation and spelling, as well as to direct and improve his character. His script is so beautifully even, it is like wallpaper, like the wallpaper you might hang in a room in your head:

Protracted regret weakens the mind and impairs the health.
Protracted regret weakens the mind and impairs the health.
Protracted regret weakens the mind and impairs the health.

Protracted regret weakens the mind and impairs the health.
Protracted regret weakens the mind and impairs the health.
Protracted regret weakens the mind and impairs the health.
Protracted regret weakens the mind and impairs the health.
Protracted regret weakens the mind and impairs the health.
Protracted regret weakens the mind and impairs the health.
Protracted regret weakens the mind and impairs the health.
Protracted regret weakens the mind and impairs the health.
Protracted regret weakens the mind and impairs the health.

iii

T. S. Eliot's summer house lies not far from the museum in a quiet suburb north of Boston. It's a fine old gabled house with a veranda, the same veranda on which Eliot as a little boy in a sailor suit sat and read with his pensive, fine-featured face. It is no longer the only house on the promontory, but has been built around, suburbanized. There are tidy raked drives, big enough for several station wagons, lawns clicking with watering devices, dense screen doors. I recognize it as the world John Cheever writes about, Sunday afternoon parties and quiet, tense rows, and I think of him, writing in a basement in his underpants about all those frustrated husbands and wives.

The house is surrounded by granite, whale-like forms of rock that remind me of Sonnadh, the same volcanic stock. It strikes me that we're on a similar latitude; that the waves that touch this shore may well have travelled all the way from Scotland.

I am out here on a rock, eating my lunch, watching a tiny piece of sponge-like substance navigate the blisters of pale lichen. Is it an ant, I wonder, carting off some trophy larger than its own body? Tentatively I give the creature a prod, I lift it on the end of a dried stalk. Barely detectable from the spongy mass, are tiny pale legs waving, not ant legs. And not a creature I have ever come across. I set it down. It freezes, stock still. It has a brain that tells it to behave like a worthless crumb. Behave like a crumb and no one will notice you, no one will do you any harm. The breeze stirs, and the creature anchors itself, sways gently on the spot. After an interval, which, as far as I know, has been calculated to the nth degree to represent the waning of my interest, the creature sets off again, marvellously heroic, like something torn from the corner of the packaging in which the world comes wrapped.

iv

It is the last time we'll take the path over the hill down to Sonnadh, setting out to see Jazmine, which we've agreed after all this time will be weird. We don't talk about it. Instead I'm telling her how there was no option when I was young but to find a man, get married. 'It was all we knew,' I say. She finds it hard to believe. '*Lezzer* was the worst kind of insult,' I say. 'I don't think most of us believed that lesbians existed. Apart from our teachers at school. But they were teachers, and none of us would have dreamed of being a teacher.'

'But what about feminism?' she asks. We're on the steep downward track towards the beach.

'Maybe it was because people were so terrified that feminism might actually take hold. Where would it end? And if you were a feminist of the hairy lesbian kind (which was the only kind they allowed us), you'd never get a man, that was the understanding. And getting a man was more important than anything else to us because we were girls, and all we knew was that boys were different from us, and might rescue us, if anyone could.'

'Was it really that bad?' She's stopped where we climb the fence. 'Everyone's bisexual: you know that, don't you?' she says, climbing over. 'At the least. You should get out more,' she says, holding the wire down for me. 'It's not too late.'

We clamber down to the beach, which is deserted, the horizon a vanishing point of palest blue, difficult to find a distinction between sea and sky. I tell her that when she was visiting her dad last summer, I was talking to an insect that looked like a crumb somewhere out there. 'I thought I might have discovered a new species.'

'And?'

'I googled *insect that looks like a crumb*. It's got a name it turns out: Breadcrumb bug.'

'Were you upset?'

'Devastated.'

I can picture the creature still, jiggling over the tiny blips in the rock with its pale lacy crumb. 'I loved that insect,' I say. 'Meeting that insect was the most meaningful interaction I've had in years.'

Her eyes roll.

'We were equals,' I say. 'I loved how tiny, but how thoughtful and valiant it was.'

'Like a pilgrim?' she says: how predictable I am.

'*Who so beset him round,*' I hum in her wake, '*With dismal stories, Do but themselves confound—*'

'Stop!'

We're near enough to see the bungalow from the machair, and outside, a little group on white plastic garden seats. They must know that it is us, though they can't yet make out our faces.

We reach the double gate. 'Hello!'

The afternoon sun is bronze against the wall. Jazmine is on her feet in a furry zip-up top and leggings, that soft putty-like voice, almost exactly as I remember her. Duncan, too, a little blown and ruddy. 'You haven't changed,' he says, 'not in your face.' I indicate my hair. 'We've all gone grey,' he concedes, those pale twinkly eyes.

'We're old!' I say.

'Ach, less of that,' Jazmine says. 'Sit down. Duncan'll get you a drink. What're you having?'

It's as if none of the Ardu stuff ever happened; after all these years, the stickiness of familiarity between us.

'We brought a bag of leftovers,' I say, and hand over a carrier bag to Pauline. 'No point taking it back with us.' Pauline puts her nose into the bag. 'Perhaps Ardu can make use of it when he's up here?' I suggest.

'Thank you, Jane. I'll take it inside.'

Jazmine doesn't respond to his name. 'You've grown,' she says to Shirin, who is the embodiment of the years gone by.

'Pauline says you're teaching now?' Duncan says.

'I am,' and I can't help pulling a face.

'Don't you enjoy it?'

'I've never been heard to say so.'

'That's a shame.' Jazmine takes a slug from her glass. 'I'm retraining. You'll never guess—'

'Teaching, no!?'

She laughs. 'They're a good bunch.'

'I bet you're a great teacher.'

'Ach, I don't know. I feel like an imposter.'

We all feel that, I say. The sun grows thinner, the air chilly, and we agree to move inside, gathering up glasses as we go.

'Sorry,' Pauline says. She's peeling off strips of plastic. 'It's only stuff from the shop.' There's pitta bread, salami and ham, multicoloured dips.

'Tuck in,' Jazmine says, and we do, passing things round politely. We talk about what Shirin might do next, and what her cousin Angus is up to now he's left home.

When the time comes to clear up, I follow Jazmine into the kitchen, just the two of us. The sink is in the far corner and we stand together as she runs the tap. I can't risk saying anything unless she does. She lowers her voice. 'You know I fell out with my brother?' She glances at me. 'I don't speak to him any more,' she says. 'He's a bully. I wouldn't mind for me, but he started on Angus. I wasn't going to put up with that.' Her eyes are full and sincere. 'I didn't realize when I was a child how manipulative he was. You don't, do you?'

'I'm sorry,' I say.

'You think it's normal.'

There's a charge in the air between us. Now we've broached the subject there's no end to what we could pour out.

I tell her Shirin went to see him in their old house, and she is aghast. 'She shouldn't have gone,' she says. 'Do you know how bad it is? It's derelict, it's in a terrible state.'

She moves towards me and lifts an arm which she lays around my shoulders. 'I'm sorry,' she says. She is shaky.

'Mother won't talk about it. He had such a brain; he just didn't know what to do with it.'

'Hello in there!' Duncan calls.

'We're coming.'

'Thought we'd lost you,' he says.

Pauline is in her corner, sucking on a cigarette. The sun has gone from the room. 'We'd better be getting back,' I say, 'before the light goes.'

They all get to their feet.

'Lovely to see you.'

'You'll stay in touch?'

'We will. Of course.'

With a flip of her hands Jazmine signals for her mother and Duncan, and by drawing them in, she brings us into the circle, too. 'Group hug,' she says, and it reminds me of the strike, the joy I shouldn't be feeling because such a warm, kind-hearted gesture is anathema to the cynics in my head. She folds us in. We stand for a moment with our heads bowed, bound by some unsayable acknowledgement of what in our various ways we have all undergone.

It isn't as dark as you think when your eyes adjust. When we reach the beach, we stop to watch the sea, made up of thousands of paper slits, cut and pushed upwards to form curves, whose angles catch the last scatterings of the sun. *Mull of Kintyre to Ardnamurchan Point.* It was a fairy tale, a prayer, a spell, which I'm reminded of most nights, the radio turned low, *falling, falling more slowly.* I'd always resisted the idea of coming back: too much to return to the reality of what I'd so keenly imagined and then lost. But long ago I'd pictured this, the two of us on one of these white deserted beaches, pictured how you would grow up.

'Little Mum,' Shirin says, suddenly indulgent, taking my arm. 'I'm glad we came.'

The light drains into the sea, the faint thumbprint of the moon, and then the stars, thickening like aquatint. I've never tried to understand or question them, but now – and maybe only as long as now pertains – they fall into place as if I've known all along what they are and what they're for, those tiny spots of solder: an instant when the original hurt is joined by its returning moment, a soldering in time, a cauterizing of old wounds.

24. Packing Up (epilogue)

Shirin tells me how her dad has told her that Bijan and Jazmine made a raid on the old house and took everything worth taking, the silver, the rugs.

'I don't know why they don't burn it down,' I say.

'Get the insurance,' she agrees.

We're driving back from Portbeag to meet Ardu in Edinburgh. I've turned on the satnav. 'We're at Loch Lomond,' Shirin tells him.

I can hear his voice. '*—wrong road.*'

'He says we're on the wrong road,' she says.

'Never mind,' I say.

'*She's mad,*' I hear him say. '*Tell her she's mad.*'

'He says it'll take far longer,' she says. Then she's saying to him, 'I don't think there's going to be time. Why can't we meet in Edinburgh?'

There is a lengthy explanation, which I don't catch.

'What's wrong?' I ask.

'He wants me to see his flat, and he wants to watch the Grand National.'

I fume. And some of it is selfish, because I've braced myself for this meeting. If I see him, I think, it will be a way of casting off. It's not seeing him that does the damage, that lets him into my head.

'Do you want to come to my graduation?' I hear her ask. 'End of June,' she says. 'Normal clothes,' she says. 'Okay, Dad, speak to you soon.' She hangs up.

'You asked him to your graduation?'

'He says he can stay with Bijan.'

'Is Bijan speaking to him?' I ask.

'Can I open a window?'

I fumble with the window controls, and when it's done, I say, 'So, he can get himself to your graduation, but not to Edinburgh?'

'He doesn't like Edinburgh.'

'And it's the Grand National.'

'Yup.'

ii

We've arranged to meet for breakfast in Caffè Nero, Shirin and her friend, Adrika. They have hired hoods and are trying to work out how they fasten on. Shirin is waiting for a phone call from her dad, but neither of us is holding our breath. Adrika's mother is anxious, too, that her three sisters, Adrika's aunts, have lost their way and will be late. 'They were only two minutes away,' she says. 'That was twenty minutes ago.' She covers her wristwatch with her hand. 'It was a good dinner last night, wasn't it?' We'd been given a formal meal in the dining hall, part of the passing-out cere-mony, and because I was nervous and on my own I'd drunk too much.

'I woke up with a bit of a headache,' I confess.

Her sympathy turns into a beam of relief. 'Here they are!'

The aunts arrive in a flurry of energy and warmth: Arya, Saira and Nur. Two in long scarves and the youngest, Nur, in a red top that reveals the pear drops of her shoulders. 'We got completely lost!' They are full of laughter. Immediately they take photos of Adrika and Shirin, who are off to assemble with the others outside the college chapel. Shirin says, looking at her phone, 'He's texted to say he's late. Sorry, Mum.' She looks up. 'You're going to have to meet him.' When the two of them are gone, I explain to the aunties, 'I haven't seen her father for fifteen years.'

Their eyes are round. 'Goodness,' they say. 'Good luck.'

I make my way over to the porter's lodge. Though it's midsummer, it's much colder than forecast, a stiff breeze passing along the queue waiting to go in for the ceremony. There are goosebumps on my arms and legs. People have put on their best clothes, silk dresses, suits, linen jackets, and stand affably in pairs and in groups. Maybe I won't even recognize him? He's joked that he might turn up in a dress or a burqa, and I am prepared for anything, but there is no sign. I ring his number. After a while he answers. 'Yes? I'm here.' That voice. He hangs up. *What's he doing?* I give it a few minutes, ring again.

'I'm outside the gates,' I say, scanning the queue for him.

A lone figure appears in the gateway of the college. His walking is slow and uncertain, he has to concentrate. Though he's nothing like the image I've preserved, there's no mistaking him for anyone else, shuffling like an old dictator, dressed in ill-fitting civilian clothes. He lifts his heavy head and spots me, sets a course. When we meet, he's radiating rage, speaks without looking at me in a volley of tics and starts: he'd stayed the night with his brother, he says, who insisted on dropping him off at a different station than agreed; the traffic was bad, and it's made him late. I let him rattle on; it gives me a chance to adjust – a huge adjustment – moving towards the end of the queue, where he follows. However I might baulk at it, he's less of a stranger than the people about us, whom I've never met, and who will no doubt identify us as being together. I am aware of holding very still, letting his rage expend itself. From the corner of my eye I register his thick grey hair, his beard, his glooming presence.

The Senate House building has been filled with chairs. He elects not to sit in the single seat at the end of a row but to follow me into the middle of the next. He talks into my ear loudly and I want to say, *please, don't*, fixing on the ceiling with its squares of ornately decorated plaster.

The Vice Chancellor enters dressed in scarlet, round as Father Christmas. He will speak in Latin, the officiator announces.

'Cod Latin,' Ardu scoffs, loudly. He turns. 'Did you ever pick up your degree?'

I shake my head.

'*Placet*,' a man calls earnestly.

The students in their black gowns are lined behind us in ranks and motioned forward by a small female official full of smiles. In groups of five, they take a finger each of a crow-like officiator, who draws them on to kneel in turn and receive their benediction. Shirin is at the end of the alphabet, and one of the last to go up. It is a strange ritual that only underlines where she is: the whole of her life ahead of her as he once had his, as I, mine. *In nomine Patris et Filii et Spiritus Sancti.*

'Short and sweet,' Ardu says, calmer now as the officiators are led out with their golden maces.

Having accepted my role as his minder, I make an effort to adjust my pace. We are shepherded out to the green in front of the building. He warns me that he can't feel his feet; that they may pack up at any time. I don't offer my arm, though am primed for the possibility of doing so.

Shirin is a butterfly and it's impossible to pick her from the crowd that gathers and dilates, moving in the general direction of the college in order that the next body of supplicants and their attendants can be ushered in.

In the court, people are taking photos against the backdrop of the chapel. A boy holds up his certificate, a fixed smile on his face.

'Did you cry?' Shirin appears, and I hug her.

'She did,' Ardu says.

'I had a lump in my throat,' I say. 'Let me take a photo.' Ardu and she move together and stand to face me. In the shoes I've lent her, she's nearly as tall as he is. He squeezes her shoulder with his puffy hand, pulls a smile. The ire has lifted. His trousers are turned up at the ankles to reveal a tartan lining like Rupert Bear's.

'Show me how to work it,' he says, reaching for the phone. I move off with Shirin so that he can take us together, stand with my arm hooked about her, but find it hard to face the eye of the camera.

'Do you want one together?' Shirin asks.

'No,' we agree, instantly.

When we reach the Fellows' Garden, the aunties are in a huddle. They whisper, 'How is it?' peering across to him, where he's sat down on a bench. 'I'm sure I recognize him,' Saira says. 'Is he an actor?'

It reminds me that when she was little, Shirin used to watch *Oliver!* 'When Bill Sykes appeared,' I tell them, 'she'd point at the screen saying, "Daddy! Daddy!"' I wonder if they've seen the film? 'Do you remember what Oliver Reed looked like when he was young?' I ask.

'Oh yes,' Arya says, checking for the resemblance. 'He was very handsome.'

Ardu comes bearing a glass of white wine. Is he drinking again? Has he been driven to drink by this? He holds it out: 'For you.' My head still hurts, and, though I've vowed not to, I accept the glass from him, thinking, otherwise, he might drink it himself.

'She's standing like a tragedian,' I hear him tell Shirin, loudly. 'I should have taken a photograph,' he calls, as I approach them. 'Your chicken legs,' he says.

'I see you made an effort to dress up,' I say. The jacket he's wearing is waist-length, thick black denim, and a blue shirt open at the chest, which reminds me in a flash of when Shirin was born.

'Gap sale,' he says, pleased with himself. 'And the trousers.'

He opens his jacket to where the vape sits like a pen in the inside pocket. 'Is it allowed?' he asks. He offers it to her. 'Taste it: what flavour do you think that is?'

She sucks. 'Vimto?'

'Blackberry and apple,' he says. 'Not bad, is it?'

The waiters have brought out black stacking chairs and set them out for us in a semi-circle. We sit at one end, Shirin between us.

'What now?' he asks her.

'I've got to finish packing,' she says. 'I have to be out of my room by six.'

'They don't waste their time,' he says.

'Do you have any friends?' she asks.

'Plenty of friends. I'm next to the YMCA. You have a friend in Jesus, they tell me.'

'How is the new flat?' I ask.

'They've shut down the Chinese under me.'

'Why?'

'The council discovered the partition wall they took out was holding up the whole building. And there were rats. The smell from the drains used to rise up the stairs—'

'It sounds disgusting.'

'It is disgusting. But convenient.'

'Shirin says you're opposite a registry office? Is that convenient?'

'Cows to the slaughter.' He chuckles. 'I see them from my window trooping in.'

His train is at three and he's determined to walk the twenty minutes to the station. We take him to the gates of the college, where he pulls out his wallet. 'Might as well give you my English money,' he says. In the flap of the wallet is a photograph of Shirin in the blue cardigan I knitted when she was a year old.

'Thanks,' she says, pocketing the two notes. 'Well,' she asks us, 'was that weird, seeing one another again?'

Before I can answer, he fixes my eyes with his. 'It was fine,' he says. 'Me and your mother, we have a deep connect.'

Whether he's being ironic or not, it's a shock, a kind of freefall, to find it is no longer true. The electricity is off; there is no traction. His eyes are the same brown pools, but where once I'd have gladly thrown myself in, I keep a distance, losing the urge to know what, all those years, has remained opaque to me and unknowable.

The rucksack is strapped to his back and he's found an umbrella to use as a walking stick. Dick Wittington, Dick Van Dyke, he cuts a sad figure as he shuffles away. We watch him as far as the crossing, then do him the favour of not looking, turning to make our way back to your room.

It's been a long day, a steep climb, five floors up, and you are much fitter than me. At the top I am dizzy, and for a moment it looks as if the sea has broken in, a junk of clothes and boxes strewn across the floor. I make for the bed to join you there, you with your legs drawn up, and we sit together far longer than we should, letting it sink in.

Gratitude and acknowledgements are due:

To Jessica Feaver, Esther Feaver and Nell Leyshon; to Sarah Castleton, James Gurbutt and Olivia Hutchings; to Tamsin Shelton; to Peter Straus; to the TS Eliot Estate; to Clare Reihill and Dana Hawkes; to Carol Hughes; to Melissa Brooks, Daisy Hay, Sam North, Lisa Rowe and Will McCarthy; to Hawthornden Castle for a fellowship in 2017; to Karen Stevens and Jonathan Taylor for commissioning a story from me, 'I know where I'm going,' for *High Spirits* (Valley Press, 2018), the seed of this novel; to Arts Council England for generous support in 2019 towards its completion.